FIC
JAY

#13

BLUE ISLAND PUBLIC LIBRARY

3 1237 00332 0786

FEB 2 8 2014

INEVITABLE
ACT I

DATE DUE

APR 2 2 2014	JUN 0 2 2015	
FEB 2 0 2018		

PRINTED IN U.S.A.

**BLUE ISLAND
PUBLIC LIBRARY**

Delphine Publications focuses on bringing a reality check to the genre urban literature. All stories are a work of fiction from the authors and are not meant to depict, portray, or represent any particular person.

Names, characters, places, and incidents are either the product of the author's imagination or are used fictitiously, and any resemblances to an actual person living or dead are entirely coincidental.

Inevitable © 2013 Johnie Jay

All rights reserved. No part of this publication may be reproduced, stored in or introduced into a retrieval system, or transmitted, in any form, or by any means (electronic, mechanical, photocopying, recording, or otherwise), without the prior written permission of both the copyright owner and the above publisher of this book.

ISBN 13 - 978-0991022816

Published by Delphine Publications
www.DelphinePublications.com

Edited by: Tee Marshall
Interior Layout: A Reader's Perspective
Cover Layout: Ts Pub Creative

ACKNOWLEDGMENTS

I think it's unfair that positivity and positive people always get the credit for everything. I wanted to make sure that I gave negativity a special shout out in the acknowledgments of my first novel (In my next novel I'll be sure to pay homage to positivity). Of course in an ideal world we would want everyone to cheer us on and believe in us but in reality, even those closest to you sometimes will give you what you think an outsider should and the so called outsiders will end up being your biggest supporters. Many people will never accomplish their dreams because they aren't strong enough to feed off the negative and use it for fuel to push through. I made sure I kept that thought close to me while finishing Inevitable. Even if people are against you even if the people that are close to you don't support you and want you to fail, failure is still your choice. I will not give them the satisfaction.

Dedication

This novel is dedicated to true love and the evidence that it can and does exist. This novel is dedicated to the marriage of my parents.

INEVITABLE
ACT I

ANGEL

YOU can have all the success in the world, but if you don't have anyone to share it with, it ain't worth squat!

I really believe that God has created someone for everyone, a soul mate if you will. One person that is tailor made, designed and created just for you; a person that will push you to your limits, instead of pushing you over the edge. A lot of marriages and relationships today either fail or struggle simply because we don't ask God to send us our soul mate and if we do ask, sometimes we are too impatient to wait on that special person.

We pick partners based on their looks, status and, "I'll bet that he'll make some pretty kids." We pick our partners on their net worth instead of their self-worth and refuse to focus on whether or not they are going to make you happy for the rest of your life.

I wonder how many people can truly say that they are with their soul mate. Better yet, how many could even say that they are with someone who they are compatible with? I feel sorry for the women out there who haven't found that special guy, because all women deserve to be happy and in love.

Soul mate! My soul mate, he is just...he just...got it! I don't really know how to describe it. It's like when he walks in the room, everything goes in slow motion around him. He demands attention from everyone, even the guys. They either admire or secretly hate on him.

Yep, he just got it, and that's not even describing his physique. When you do get to that body of his, *whew...good Lord*, I really have to cross my legs to stop them from frantically bouncing up and down. Or, I simply do what I'm doing now while jogging on this treadmill, always stay aware of my nipple status because looking at him always seems to make at least one of them stand at attention.

He sort of reminds you of Will Smith, not that he resembles him, but he's handsome in a non-standard, non-traditional kind of way. Things that would normally be considered flaws actually make him look better and add to his character, like cracks on a marble sculpture.

There is a scar right above his left eye that splits his eyebrow in half. Instead of subtracting from the pleasantness of his face, it gently guides you directly to his eyes.

Those big, bright, soul-searching eyes that will always give you a glimpse of how he looked as a child are the same ones that would charm the bra and panties off any woman.

I even love the way that he walks. I would bet all that I own that he is great in bed. *Look at the bulge in his shorts.* Damn, almost slobbered on myself. I wonder how it looks. Definitely looks like he's packing.

I quickly glanced to my left and right as if the ladies on the treadmills could hear my thoughts. If they could, they would probably think that I was crazy. I can hear them now, "Are you celibate or something?" I would tell them that I never said that he was my man. In fact, we have never met. Yeah, they would really think that I was crazy then.

I wouldn't blame them though, because sometimes I think I am, especially knowing that this guy and I haven't even said one word to each other. Yet and still, I believe that he is meant to be in my life.

I know it is not infatuation and it's not just lust either. It's more like every time I see this guy, something deep down in my soul tells me that this is your man, this is your future. It's actually a little scary because a while back I prayed and asked God to send me someone after my ex and I broke up. Ever since then, it seems like this man keeps popping up in my life.

"Oowee girl, look at those arms! He can bench press me any day," the lady on the treadmill closest to me said while staring across the gym.

"Girl, you ain't never lied," the woman on the other side of her replied, "I'll do some squats alright, squat this big ass over his face and down on them juicy lips of his." The three women broke out laughing.

"Sheri, you are a mess," the third piece of the trio added, "but that *does* sound kind of good." She continued breathing like she was going to fall out even though she was walking at what appeared to be the lowest possible speed on the treadmill.

If I didn't know any better I would say that those three heifers were talking about my future husband. I glanced over and followed their gaze directly towards the area where he was working out.

What they need to do is concentrate more on burning those big bellies off and less time salivating over...over...this is so ridiculous, he has me over here about to go Bruce Lee on these broads and I don't even know his damn name. This is how it has been ever since his soul introduced itself to mine. Our eyes locked and we looked at each other with such a familiarity that we had to have been lovers from another lifetime.

My brain tried to search the meaning of stranger, but my heart…my heart found the definition of love. A love never felt or witnessed. How can I even be thinking love at this moment in my life?

I remember it like it was yesterday, the first time that I actually saw my Future…

"Get it together, Angel. You are so over him. It is time to move on," I said to myself while putting on my M.A.C. lip gloss as I gazed in the mirror. *Now, what you are going to do is go out with your girls, who you've been neglecting while being with that no good, asshole of an ex-boyfriend, Damien. Tonight, you are going to drink, dance and have a good time.* "Nope, not tonight, I'm not going to think about him."

I slammed the lip gloss down on the counter, frustrated with myself that I would even let thoughts of him invade my mind. I don't think I'm mad at the fact that he cheated. I think it's more that I allowed him to do so.

I knew what he was doing every time he went to pick up his son from his baby momma's house. He just happened to fall asleep over there every time and come home smelling like Irish Spring soap. Men are so stupid, they don't even think that we would notice or smell a totally different soap than what we use at our place. I took all the lies and all of the bullshit just because

I wanted us to work so badly. I didn't want to be alone. I wanted to prove to myself that I could actually be in a good relationship for once. I am really tired of breaking up and finding someone new. They say that black women don't hold their asses down. *Puhh!* Even when they cheat, we hold them down. Even when they don't have a job and never have any money, we hold them down. I am so tired of being the good person in the relationship. Tonight is a new start, just my girls and I.

Speaking of which, "Where the hell is Tierra?" I looked at the clock and saw that it was almost 10:00P.M. When it came time for her to drive, she would have you waiting all day and night. When it was your turn…she would call you every minute on the hour trying to hurry you up. As a matter of fact, let me call and give her a taste of her own medicine. As soon as she picked up the phone, I dove into her. "Tierra, damn chick, where are you?"

"Hey Angel," she answered a little too nicely, "I was just about to call you."

"Girl, please! Stop lying, where are you? I'm ready to go and get my boogie on." I did a swerve in the mirror to check out how I was going to be looking while dancing in the club tonight.

"Don't be acting like you're all excited about going out now. When you were with *Deadbeat*, we couldn't even get your ass to come out for an ice cream cone. Now look at you, Ms. Party Animal!" Tierra had no sympathy for my recent breakup, especially when she always tried to get me to leave him.

"Key words, *was* with." I said putting my hand on my hip and rolling my eyes as if I was 10 years old. "Now I'm, *not* with, so hurry your ass up or I'm leaving here *with*…out y'all."

"Girl, open the door, we're in front," she said laughing before disconnecting our call.

She was right about one thing though, when Damien and I were together I didn't want to go out anywhere, unless it was with him.

Okay, one last look in the mirror. My new haircut was looking good, the twins are sitting upright and the ass…*damn, thanks Mom!* Let me go and open this door before this girl end up short-circuiting my doorbell.

"Well hello there." I answered the door matching her previous overly nice tone.

"Don't *hello* me you were practically cursing me out over the phone. You ready?"

"Yep, let me grab my purse." I peeped out of my door and looked at Tierra's silver Ford Flex. "Is that Brianna out there?"

"Mmm hmm, you know she broke up with her girlfriend this week too. Maybe y'all can compare notes," she snickered.

"Ha, very funny. I thought one of your girls from your job was going. And the last time I spoke to Bri she was taking the breakup pretty hard, didn't think she would even want to go out."

"Well, technically she didn't want to. I kind of sort of went over and forced the situation. Plus, it will be more fun with the three of us instead of bringing outsiders."

"Outsiders?" I grabbed my purse off the couch and we headed to her car. "You're talking like we're the mob or something." I saw Brianna with the visor down checking her lipstick in the mirror. "I still don't see how she does it. Trading in dick for coochie?" I felt my face frowning at the thought.

"Shhhhh! Would you stop talking so loud? She didn't trade it in, I think she enjoys dick more than the both of us. She just so happens to enjoy coochie more than the both of us also."

"You are too funny. I don't even have to ask if you've been drinking already."

"Oh you already know, now hurry up and get in!" she directed while getting in the driver's side, "you know we have to get to the club before 11 so we can get in for free."

I hopped in the back seat. "Hey Bri!"

"You look good girl. I love the haircut," Brianna said as she turned around and looked me over.

"Thank you, I forgot that you haven't seen me since I whacked it all off." I ran my hands through my newly cropped hair. Even though Brianna was my girl, whenever she complimented me I couldn't help but wonder if she was really trying to tell me something.

One thing that I can say about Brianna is that if I were a man or bisexual I would definitely go for her. She was absolutely beautiful. I'm talking body, face, good hair and red-boned. It's too bad that tonight she's the second best looking chick in this car, thanks to me.

"So how are you making it so far?" Brianna asked, looking over her left shoulder back at me.

"As good as I can be. It'll take a while, but I'll get over it. What about you and your significant other, anything new?"

"Naw, it was a long time coming. She was so jealous and insecure. I mean, every time I stepped out of the house she thought that I was going to cheat. Or when men would look at me and say something, her entire mood would go south. She would stop talking to me as if it was my fault. Over the past year, she gained almost 50 pounds. I just couldn't baby her anymore. I got tired of feeling guilty for something that I wasn't even doing. So, unfortunately I had to bounce."

We lost track of time as we reminisced about our past relationships. Whether straight, bi, or gay, I guess everybody still had the same problems.

Tierra did her usual pre-club ritual, tried to set up some after hour dick for later on. She hung up the phone with a huge smile on her face, so I'm guessing her mission was successful. She slid the phone back into her purse. "Enough of this ex-talk ladies, it's time to get our minds right for those good looking guys standing over there in line," she said as she pointed out of her window. She then turned her attention to the passenger side. "Oh yeah, there's some cute chicks over there too for you Bri." We all laughed.

"Shut up Tierra. Shit, the way these women are acting nowadays, I might have to make a trip down Dick and Balls Boulevard."

Tierra kept looking around like she was lost. "What's the matter, you can't find a parking spot?" I asked, trying to spot one for her.

"Shit, I'm looking for Dick and Balls Boulevard, that's where I want to park. Where is it Brianna?" Tierra asked, hanging onto the steering wheel. Tierra kept our abs and oblique muscles tight and in shape by making us laugh non-stop every time we went out.

I think tonight is going to be a good night. Tierra's right, there are a lot of cute guys in line. What she needs to do is hurry up and park. I'm in serious need of a drink. That glass of wine I had before leaving barely gave me a buzz.

I let out a long sigh as Brianna and Tierra continued talking from the front seat. *The first night of my new life.* Even though I had been officially broken up for a couple of weeks now, this felt like the first night of my freedom.

And a perfect night it was. The sky was clear, there was a warm breeze and a beautiful full moon to top it all off. I continued looking at the guys in line and decided that I might flirt a little tonight, but that's it. I didn't need any more complications right now. The more I think about it, men suck! They really do. So why is it that I can't take my eyes off of that one?

Maybe he's not really a guy. He can't be because a mere mortal couldn't stop me from breathing like he has. No human could make my heart feel like it was trying to rip through my chest to run over to him. Obviously, he is some type of charmer or magician that possesses mystical powers. Maybe that explains why everyone else in line has faded to black.

What the hell is wrong with me? I can't move or take my eyes off of him. The first night of my new improved future and I now have my eyes fixed on someone who for some reason is making me feel like he's going to be a major part of it. Damn!

"So what do you think?" The woman on the nearest treadmill asked bringing me back into the present.

"Excuse me? Think about what?" I answered, trying not to wrinkle my face. These heifers just didn't know when to quit. Can't say I blame them. There is no telling the last time any of them had a man, let alone some dick.

"About the guy over there doing curls," she continued, "with the body of a Greek god. My girls and I were over here debating on whether it was just for show or can he really work it in the bedroom."

I looked around the gym pretending not to see who it was

that they were drooling over. "I'm sorry, what guy are you talking about?" I asked, unenthusiastically.

"Are you serious?" she screamed out, making her girls laugh. "You mean to tell me that you haven't even seen him yet? Girl, I've just about figured out his workout schedule and I'm here damn near every day he is."

"Shit, I can't tell," I whispered to myself.

"What was that?"

"Huh, oh nothing." Guess I didn't whisper low enough.

"If I keep coming like this, I'll have a cute little body like yours," she said while looking me up and down.

I couldn't help but smile on that one. *Hope she's not holding her breath for that to happen.* I twisted my head over to my soon-to-be-man. "Are you talking about the guy over there? He's alright, I guess."

"Alright? Alright?" one of her girls jumped in to back her up. "Baby, you've been on that treadmill too long, I think it's starting to affect your eyesight."

"I mean, I see him, but in today's times, odds are that a guy that looks that good has at least three kids with a crazy baby momma, is married, or he has a boyfriend. So why even bother?" Maybe with a little of my convincing, they would calm down a little but the way all three of them continued to stare, I doubt that's going to happen.

"Well, first of all, I'm not trying to marry the guy. I just need him to help me out with an orgasm. So who cares about a baby momma, kids, or a wife?"

"Not me!" the biggest of the three chimed in.

She continued to answer my question all while huffing along on the treadmill. "He can stay with the missus, that's even better. And as long as he's fucking me just as good as he's fucking his boyfriend, then who cares?"

Wow! These women are pathetic, look at them, high-fiving over that stupid ass comment. Over a man that will never be theirs because whether he knows it or not he is already mine. I just hope that neither one of those hypothetical scenarios I gave them are true. *Oh God please, especially not the gay one.*

The woman with the biggest mouth of the three pressed the stop button on her treadmill and hopped off. "Trish, watch him for me, I'm about to walk over there to that water fountain next to him and give him a close up view of what we all know is a black man's kryptonite, a big, juicy, plump ass. Let me know how hard he stares at it girl."

"Oh you know I got you, just make sure you arch that back while you're drinking." They started laughing like a pack of hyenas.

I really didn't know that women were this desperate for dick. I can't wait to see the look of disgust that he's going to give her. I knew men loved big booties, but I at least thought that they had to be good-looking ones. I mean there is such a thing of a booty that's too big, right?

She continued her stroll towards the water fountain, booty bouncing and jiggling behind her. This is going to be so funny...is he...is he turning his head? I know he is not staring at her booty. I know he is not *still* staring at her booty. *Asshole! Am I going to have to go over there and snatch his eyes out?* The more I witnessed what was happening, the higher I felt my blood pressure rising.

She started walking back to the treadmills wearing a smile as bright as the sun. Made me want to punch her right in the face, him too. Why did he even give her hope, give her the confidence to come throw that shit up in my face? *Ugghhhhhh!*

"Well baby," she said, looking at me while putting her hands on her wide hips, "I didn't catch ya name, but the way that cutie pie was staring at my ass, I think we can eliminate that gay scenario of yours." She slapped fives with her girls.

"Girl, you should've seen him when you started to walk back over here. He was basically drooling on himself," her plump partner said while laughing.

"Oh I saw him, I was thinking about stopping mid stride and doing the Beyoncé booty shake for his sexy ass."

That's all I can take. I'm out of here. I think I'm getting sick. I can't believe he even looked at her.

"That bitch is probably gay herself," I heard one of the ladies say as I walked away.

Just keep walking Angel, I said to myself as I ran my towel over my face and grabbed my bag, *they are not even worth it*. My eyes briefly met his in the mirror on my way out of the door, "But you *better be,*" I whispered to myself as I released my stare. *You, just better be!*

FUTURE

DAMN my arms are killing me! If it weren't for all the people at the gym today, I think I would be screaming right now. I played off the pain as I bobbed my head to Jay Z's "Money Ain't a Thang" banging through my headphones.

I looked in the mirror and immediately noticed a big difference in my body ever since I've changed my workout regimen to five days a week instead of three. Judging by the reaction of women lately, they have too. So, no matter how bad it burns I keep going.

It's amazing just thinking about how I looked five years ago. I was so skinny and frail. I took a lot of heat from the females back then. That's what really started me to working out. The frustration of being looked over was overwhelming. I was a nice, pretty decent looking guy, but for some reason they didn't seem to like that because they always took advantage of it. Women want a nice guy, they say, until they actually get one, and then they don't appreciate him. Instead, they stick with the guy who treats them like he doesn't care.

So I said, 'Okay if that's what you want, that's what I'll give you.' I mixed the two. I'll give them the good guy because I genuinely was, that's how my parents raised me. Being a gentleman was instilled in me from both of my parents, especially my dad, from an early age. So, yeah I'll open doors, pull out chairs and be a good listener. Hell, I'll even give back massages and rub their feet while they complain about the hard day they had at work, all in the name of pussy.

With all of the good, I gave them just as much bad. I can't even count the number of females that I've had sex with and never called again. Or, how many that I've told I would never give my heart to because I'll never let another woman hurt me again. Instead of that turning them away, it presented them with a challenge and all men know how much women love challenges.

That combo of good and bad, nice boy features, bad boy body, tattoos and attitude seemed to have them throwing their panties at me. The type of women that I couldn't get to look at me five years ago, now I can and do get quite often with minimum or no effort at all.

Speaking of ass, I looked over to the water fountain beside me. Look at this woman arching her butt out so that I can look at it. So damn obvious.

This gym is setup perfectly. There are two water fountains one in the front and the rear, and every day I make sure I strategically place myself near one of them. That way I can check out the goods, and they can too. On top of that, there are mirrors everywhere that allows me to enjoy their long trip back to the treadmills and stair steppers.

It's funny watching women sometimes though, like right now, the huge booty that was just at the water fountain is back at the treadmills giving her girls high fives as they stare over here at me.

It looks like they might have offended cutie pie running on the treadmill next to them. I wonder what they said to make her abruptly stop her workout.

My eyes focused in on the mirror, catching the reflection of the briskly walking beauty as she neared. Mmm, so far so good, body is tight, long, lean, nice haircut, familiar haircut. Shit, almost too familiar of a haircut. I felt my eyes widen as she came closer and more into focus.

"Naw couldn't be," I whispered to myself. It can't be…is it? It is… it's Her! "Damn it. You are not getting away from me. Not this time," I said to myself as I racked my weights, grabbed my bag and raced for the door after her.

Can't believe I'm chasing after this chick. All the work that I put into making women finally take notice and chase me and here I am going backwards. I couldn't let another opportunity present itself with this woman popping up in my life and me not doing anything about it.

With any other woman, I would be planning on getting what I wanted and be out. Make them think I'm all in to get the hit. This one, shit, I don't know. With this one, I feel a little strange. Feel embarrassed to be a dog. She makes me feel and that's something I haven't done in a long time. I don't want to have feelings at all right now, but somehow seeing this woman makes me think otherwise.

What's really weird is the fact that we've never met or spoke, but I know that we are supposed to. Sounds crazy, but there has to be a reason why this woman keeps popping up in my life. She actually has a brotha contemplating what it would be like to settle down for a change.

I stood outside the door of the gym and surveyed the parking lot. Instead of sweating her, the little devil on my shoulder was telling me to get back inside to see what was up with "Thickness" with the big ass. The hold this mystery woman had on me was overwhelming. She drowns out the thoughts that I have about other women whenever she is near. I remember when I first saw her it like it was yesterday.

One month prior...

It was just another Saturday night, which meant my boy and I going to the club to get our party on and getting on females. It seemed to always be the same predictable outcome; me spitting game to some poor unsuspecting female to set something up for either that night or later on that week.

These women out here that have read Steve Harvey's book and think that a 90-day rule will help them sort out the real from the fake are highly mistaken. Most men are dealing with more than one woman anyway, so while one woman is making him wait, another woman is feeding his appetite.

That's what I would do, take their sex timetable and see how far and quick I could bring it down to mine. If I thought it would be easy and quick, there was no need for me to pull out all the romantic and secret tricks. It was really a game to me and to most men.

Playing women wouldn't work if I didn't know them as well as I did. I studied them as a lion did his prey. It started when

I was a teenager. I would pay attention to conversations that women would have and watch their reactions to what guys said and did. When I listened to the men they were totally off track about what they said about a woman's needs and wants. Most men thought that they were running things in the relationship when in reality, the women were just allowing them to believe that they were.

I remember my mother having a lot of books about women and subscriptions to all the women's magazines from *Essence* to *Cosmopolitan*. I remember the shock I had when I first started flipping through them. I never would have imagined the ammunition that they would give me. That was one of my secrets that I still don't let people know to this day.

I know most guys would probably say, "Fuck that, I'm not reading a lady's magazine. That's gay shit." That is perfectly fine with me. That's what I'm counting on, as a matter of fact, I would tell them not to.

But I hope they don't get mad at me for saying the shit that their girl wanted to hear that night she went out when she was pissed off at their ass. I hope that they don't get mad when I comfort her, bring her back to my place, and caress all of those sensual spots that allow her to let her guard down. And please don't get mad at me when I'm fucking the shit out of her, giving her blended orgasms all night, but they probably don't even know what that is, let alone how to give their ladies one. Naw, don't get mad at me, instead I would tell them to get mad at *Cosmo*, because that's where I learned it from.

I would rather that they keep reading the *King*, *XXL*, and *Blackmen* all, which have probably one or two articles about women and what they want written by a man. I mean, I read those magazines as well, faithfully, but just not to get tips about how to satisfy women.

Sometimes men can be too manly. There is nothing wrong with knowing the latest trends in purses or the hottest high-heels or jeans for women. Women love men who can appreciate the things that they wear. I mean, if she spends two to three hundred on a pair of heels and another two to three on a pair of jeans to look good when she goes out and nobody knew that it was expensive or that it was the latest trend then what would be the point of her wearing it?

What women love more than us being up on their fashion is us being up on ours. I don't care how good a guy thinks he looks; if his wardrobe is busted, he's going to have a hard time finding a woman. I mean, you can get chicken heads with no problem, but to get that dime, your gear has to be right. I'm not talking about loud ass colored hoodies and fitted caps. If a man is 25 or older and going out to a club where the women are looking nice and dressing up, what would make him think that the women would want him if he's not at least putting forth the same effort with his wardrobe? Like for instance the guy that we're standing behind right now, I thought as I shook my head in sorrow.

My boy, Caesar and I were next in line to enter the Elysium Lounge, the only place to be on a Friday night. The women were definitely out tonight. Out to get into the club and their body parts were all out, everywhere.

Looks like another easy night. I've already locked eyes with five females that the bouncer let past us to get in the club. The key is not to seem too desperate or too overly excited. Dudes that go overboard, "Damn you're fine, ouuuweee, look at that ass," being all loud and obnoxious have already lost the power battle. She has the upper hand from the beginning and knows it.

Women like intrigue, suspense, a little mystery. So I give them just enough. I lock eyes, let them know I'm interested, see if the look is reciprocated, and flash my award winning smile. Upon entering the club is when I would carefully choose which prey I would eat and devour, literally.

My boy Caesar was my protégé, living proof that all of my studying and research is true to form. He too was a, loud obnoxious tip-your-hand and show-your-cards, kind of brother until I took him under my wings and schooled him. Now every time he goes out without me, he comes back saying that he can't believe how easy it is being a player. Almost brings a tear to my eye when I think about how far he's come under my tutelage. I patted him on the shoulder while displaying a proud smile.

"What's up?" he asked, looking back.

I sighed, "Oh nothing, just thinking that's all."

"I hope you're thinking about these females. It's going to be crazy in there tonight. It's nothing but ladies coming up in here." He crept a little closer and dropped his voice, "If I didn't know any better I would say that we were at a lesbian convention."

"You're right," I said while looking at the fat ass of one of the ladies in line, "it's like a buffet, so many to choose from. I am so glad that I'm a guy, women have such slim pickings that it's almost sad."

Caesar looked back at me with a confused look. "No it's not sad, it's better for us. We don't care about them or their feelings, we just pretend too, remember? You're not going soft on me are you?"

He was right, but tonight I felt a little different for some reason. Might be the full moon but it felt like someone was watching me. I'm not going to look around and see who it is but it felt like one of these females had their radar locked in on me for real. Tonight's new mission is to find out which one. First, let me address Caesar's statement. "Going soft, who me? The Kid?" I chuckled, "Going soft is something I wouldn't know much about. I'm sure we can find a couple of my female sponsors in here that would attest to that."

Caesar laughed at my little comeback while still looking at more beautiful prospects go into the club. "Tonight, Future, might just be the night that the pupil gets one up on the teacher."

I replied confidently, "Come now lad, let's not get carried away. Do not fool yourself with such wishful thinking. We both know that is not possible."

Before we stepped in the club, I felt the intense stare on me again. I smiled and thought, can't wait to meet you either sweetie.

When we stepped in, we went straight to the bar. I waved one of the bartenders over. Even though the bar was super crowded, she came right away. I ordered myself the usual, Hennessey and Coke, and then ordered my boy his Ciroc and cranberry. Getting the bartender's attention and my drinks so promptly caused the ladies to throw me interested looks while guys threw me shade. It was all because I was a very good tipper and even better flirt. I always complimented my favorite tall, voluptuous, blond bartender Tammie. After handing Caesar his drink, we kicked back and took in the scenery.

The DJ was in his old school rap session and had just dropped Biggie's "One More Chance." The entire place went bananas and flocked to the dance floor.

"Future, I know you're heading to the floor. Biggie? That's your shit!"

"You go on ahead," I screamed over the music, "I'll catch up with you in a few."

"Alright, I'll try to save you a few females."

I sat my drink down at the bar and laughed at my boy. He really loved to dance. "Yeah you do that."

Caesar walked through the busy crowd toward the dance floor bobbing his head. When I turned for my drink who did I see staring at me, from the same spot where I met her two weeks ago? "Ms. Red Dress."

Names were something that I was really bad at. I didn't want to ask for their name every time I saw them, so I called women by something that related to the first time we met until I got their names down pat. Most of the time they thought that I was calling them by their own personal pet name, so it worked out in my favor.

Ms. Red Dress was a stunner, and she was wearing an even shorter and more stunning red dress than the last time I saw her. I'm talking about this thing came right below the booty cheek. I didn't press her too hard two weeks ago; it was too expected. I chatted with her a little while, let her know how sexy she was a couple of times, and bought her a drink.

After that, I pretty much avoided her for the rest of the night. She was looking confused when I told her that I would try to find her later on that night. From the looks of things my little tactic worked. Now it was time to seal this little deal.

On the way over to her, I saw all the guys at the bar gawking and making comments. Few even had the courage to step to her. Obviously, they didn't say the right thing.

"Hey, I hope I haven't kept you waiting too long," I said with a playful grin.

"And who says I was waiting for you?" she said returning the smile.

"Well, nobody said that, and excuse me for assuming, but looking around at my competition and seeing you standing here all alone—"

She cut me off mid-sentence, "Well Future," I smiled at the fact that she remembered my name, "you and I both know what happens when you assume."

"You make an ass out of you and me," we both said in unison. "I know, I know, and I definitely don't want to do that," I said as I eyed her down. You definitely have enough ass as it is.

She ran her tongue softly over her lips. "I have to be honest with you though, I was really hoping to see you in here tonight. I mean, who do you think I'm wearing this short ass dress for? I said to myself 'who knows he might just ask for your number this time'."

I couldn't help but to smile at that one. "That was funny, and about not asking for it the last time, I—"

"Baby it doesn't even matter," she said interrupting, "the important thing is that we're here now. So what are we going to do with the opportunity?" She sipped on her light green martini, which was garnished with a cherry, and undressed me with her eyes.

There's nothing like a woman who doesn't beat around the bush. I took a sip of my almost gone drink and quickly tried to think of a good comeback, but it was too late, she was now inching her way closer to me and coming in for the kill.

"I love a man who knows how to dress, Future. It's good

when you guys give us girls something nice to look at." She moved even closer, took the cherry from her martini, and held it slightly above her mouth. I watched the liquor hypnotically drip from the cherry onto her lips and trace every crease and crevice of her two luscious, Angelina Jolie look-a-like lips.

She then exposed one of the most tantalizing tongues that I have ever seen. It was so juicy, so pink, and kissed slightly with brown freckles. Mmmm, reminds me of a ripe strawberry. She flicked it out making sure that I got a good glance at the length, rolled up and pulled in the cherry that was dangling in front of her. All of this probably took no more than five seconds but I swear it seemed like an eternity and I enjoyed every moment.

"I'm a sucker for satin ties," she said while looking at mine and placing her hand on the lapel of my vest.

I tried my best to keep Buddy from springing to attention. I had to stay cool, had to keep calm. I took another sip of my drink and cleared my throat. "Ties huh," I said smirking, "and why is that?" That was all that I could think of saying at the moment. She was taking me there fast. I didn't even know where there was but she obviously did and knew the shortest route.

She took another step, shrinking our personal space to virtually nothing, and wrapped her hand around my tie and pulled it out from up under my vest. Her left cheek was now touching my left cheek and her warm breath on my ear sent chills down my spine.

She enlightened me of her little fetish. "I love the way they feel on my skin especially around my wrists while I'm tied to the bedpost."

Yep, that did it. I was now there. The control was gone and Buddy was taking on a mind of his own. When she moved away, I was definitely going to have to use my hands to cover my bulge.

Ms. Red Dress backed up to the spot where she began her teasing and caught a glimpse of my excitement before I could conceal it with my hands. Her eyebrows rose along with the corners of her mouth.

I looked her directly in her eyes, "So, I take it you're coming over tonight."

"From the looks of things," she said, looking down towards Buddy then back up at me, "I may be cumming, over and over and over again. Call me as soon as you leave baby. Don't have me waiting too long. I've wanted your sexy ass for two weeks now."

Damn she's direct. "I definitely won't make you wait. If there weren't so many people in here I would bend you over this bar and take you right here and now."

"Mmm," she licked those luscious lips of hers while raking a strand of hair out of her face. "Now you're talking my language. You know," Ms. Red Dress let out a small chuckle, "I never heard you say my name. You don't remember it do you?"

Shit, me and my bad memory. "I have to be honest with you, I'm horrible with names. I apologize, but it did slip my mind."

She looked at me and smiled. "It's Kandi, with a K. You can practice saying it later on tonight"

"Kandi? How fitting. I'm sure you'll live up to that name.

"You better watch out though, you know sugar is addictive."

"Kandi, that's one cavity I definitely wouldn't mind having."

"Give me your phone," she directed. I could tell that the nasty talk was turning her on more. I watched as she programmed her name and number. "As soon as you leave!" she demanded, looking directly into my eyes. She handed me my phone and seductively walked away leaving her aroma behind as a reminder of her presence.

I had to take a couple of seconds to get myself together. I was used to being the aggressor when it came to beautiful women like Ms. Red Dress...I mean Kandi. She knocked me off balance for a second but I'm good now. I quickly glanced at my immediate surroundings to make sure our little pre-sexual tennis match went unnoticed.

Everyone seemed to be carrying on like normal. This woman did everything short of undressing me and she did it undetected. Like a damn sex ninja or something. Unfortunately, I didn't know much about martial arts so I'll give her this battle. When I get her to my place, on my turf, in my bedroom, I will get my revenge. I will win the war.

I went back to the bar to replace my empty glass with my usual. Where is she? I asked myself looking for my girl. There she is. My favorite bartender finally stood up from getting more wine glasses from under the bar. It really works in your favor to be cool with the bartender. Your drinks tend to be a little bit stronger. I got her attention and winked at her while pointing to my empty glass. She picked up on the signal and began mixing my drink.

She wasn't what I would normally go for, blonde, white, but she was really cute with a nice ass body. She also had the one thing that most white women had over black women, breasts. The kind that when you take off her bra they will drop down just enough for you to lift them back up with your hands and place them in your mouth.

Black women have ass, white girls have chest. It's been this way since the beginning of time. Until recently, somewhere, somehow, white girls broke that secret genetic code for onion booties and narrowed that gap.

My blonde bartender returned with my drink. I paid for it and gave her a more than generous tip.

"You know I really appreciate the tips you give. Your next drink is on me," she said while wiping the bar down in front of me.

"Are you sure? You don't have to do that. I'm just showing my appreciation for how great you make my drinks."

"Well, I want to show my appreciation by buying you a drink and I'm not taking no for an answer."

I smiled and took a sip of my refreshed drink. This time it was extra potent. It took everything in me not to make the "Damn, this is strong" face. "Okay you win," I said, suppressing the grunt that wanted to escape.

She smiled and stacked up a couple of clean glasses. "You know, I've been making your drinks for a little while now and I never caught your name." She leaned on the bar a little, giving me a better view of those voluptuous twins that were wrapped snuggly in a baby tee with the club's name on the front.

"I'm sorry, where are my manners. I'm Future."

"Future, are you serious? That's your real name or your club name?" She giggled causing her chest to bounce up and down.

"Club name? No, that is my real name. What, you don't like it or something?"

"Actually, I love it. It's so different, kinda powerful."

"Powerful huh?" That brought a smile to my face. "Never heard it put that way before. You know, you don't look like a Tammie, more like a Brittany."

She laughed and ran her fingers through her golden locks. "So you're trying to call me crazy now?" she asked laughing. "Actually, this is my friends name tag. My name is actually Present."

I stood there for a few seconds staring at her while she stared back at me. "Tell me you're lying."

"Yes, I'm lying. Present and Future, we would be soul mates for real."

"Now that would've been something." We smiled for a few, discreetly checking each other out before she went back to her job of bartending. I had never had sex with a white woman. I've received head twice but never intercourse. As I watched Tammie walk towards me, it made me anxious to experience my first. I took another sip of my drink.

"So, Future, when is it going to be my turn to wrinkle your tie?"

I started coughing. Her comment caught me off guard. "Excuse me?"

She smiled. "You heard exactly what I said. When am I going to get a chance to wrinkle your tie?"

"Um...wow...you saw that huh? Whenever you want, just let me know."

Tammie looked me up and down and asked my age. I informed her that I was 27 and she responded by saying, "That's good, so you are old enough to know when a woman is asking you a serious question." She stared at me with her piercing blue eyes.

I smiled and asked, "And how old are you?"

"Twenty-five," she answered.

"So you're old enough to know when a man is giving you an equally serious answer. Like I said, whenever you want."

She smiled back and took two business cards from her pocket. One she handed to me and she flipped the other one over and asked for my number. "I can't wait Future," she said after jotting my number down. I became a little jealous of the card after she tucked it away in her breast.

"Me neither." She turned away and returned to work, transforming from naughty to nice right before my eyes. I read her business card before placing it in my back pocket. Personal massage therapist huh? Must be her side job. Yeah, she will definitely come in handy. I turned and headed for the dance floor. Time to get my dance on.

I didn't take more than two steps before I was graced with the presence of another beautiful woman. Damn, at this pace I'm not going to get to party. She looks too good to pass up though. I'll just make this quick and say the first thing that comes to me. She can either take it or leave it.

I squeezed up in the empty space beside her and noticed the frustrated look on her face. Let's see if I can make her smile.

"I'm sorry," I said after grazing her arm.

She still sported an attitude on her face. "You're good," she answered not paying me too much attention.

"I don't mean to bother you, but can I ask you a question?"

"Sure, why not." I can tell by her frustration that she was tired of the lines and the lies. She's probably been hit on ever since she got here.

"How do I look?" I asked brushing imaginary lint from my clothes.

"Excuse me?" Her look of aggravation was replaced by a look of shock and amazement. I started to see the corners of her mouth slightly turn upwards and her eyebrows rise.

"Do you think I look good? I mean, be honest." She tried to read my face for any signs of humor and I made sure that there wasn't any.

"What...what kind of question is that? You can't be that arrogant...can you?"

"Arrogant?" I asked in mocked disbelief. "You know what, I'm sorry maybe that question came off the wrong way. I wasn't asking because I'm conceited, I was asking because I saw a young lady on the other side of the bar that I wanted to introduce myself to. I figured before I go over, I would ask the first woman I saw, how she thought I looked. I just wanted a female's perspective, you feel me?"

She looked at me a little softer now. "For some strange and crazy reason it kind of sounds better now." She let out a little giggle, "I can't believe, I just—"

"Believe what?" I asked, still playing innocent.

The once fierce lioness had now let down her guard and had turned into a pussycat. She busted out in laughter, exposing all of her pearly whites, and making her long, curly spirals bounce around. She had the kind of hair that looked like it smelled good. That Herbal Essence shit.

"I was just going to say it's kind of weird when a guy, instead of trying to get with me, uses me to...get with another woman. Guess there's a first time for everything huh?"

"Wait a minute, you thought I..." I let out a short chuckle, "you must have thought that I was coming over here to hit on you."

"I'm ashamed to say it, but yeah I did, you got me." She hung her head down in embarrassment.

I figured that since I had her, there was no reason to let up. "This is funny. No wonder you were looking all frustrated when I stepped beside you."

I saw a little frustration sweep back into her gorgeous, light-skinned face. "Naw, the reason for that is the amount of time it takes to get a drink in this place. It is entirely too crowded. Think I've been here for about 15 minutes now."

"Really? What are you drinking?"

"I was going to get my girl and I Cosmos, but I'm going to tell her that we might not be drinking tonight." She folded her arms in defeat.

Superman to the rescue. I took a sip of my Hennessey and Coke. I caught Tammie's attention and told her to give me two Cosmopolitans. I had no doubt in my mind that she wouldn't get jealous or catch an attitude. Even after seeing me ravished by Kandi, Tammie still flirted.

"Two Cosmos." Tammie said in her usual chipper voice as she placed the drinks in front of me and my soon to be new friend.

"Thanks, how much do I owe?"

"They're on the house, sweetie," she said, as she winked and walked away. Damn this worked out better than I thought.

Shirley Temple looked at me shocked with her mouth wide open. "Are you serious, you get a drink in 10 seconds while I don't even get looked at for 10 minutes? On top of that, you don't pay? It must be nice to be you."

"Well you know, what can I say?" I responded in my ghetto J.J. Evans voice while rubbing my goatee.

She started laughing. "Yeah you're racking up cool points for real."

"For what?" I asked putting on a fake confused face, "I told you that I'm not trying to get with you. You're not even my type."

I think that might have deflated her a little bit. She immediately started looking around the bar as if to find someone.

"What's wrong, you see your man or something?"

She shook her head, "Naw, I'm just looking for this Superwoman of yours that you want to make such a good first impression on. I mean since I'm not your type, I'm just dying to see who is!"

"Well why didn't you say so? I would love to show you. But I have to go spit this game before she disappears." I looked around to find a good target. Bullseye, there she is. I looked at Shirley Temple and nodded my head to get her to look across the bar and to the left.

She looked over, but still I saw her eyes wandering about. Obviously, she still didn't see my dream girl. "Where, which one is she?" she asked looking puzzled.

"Right there," I said, actually pointing in the direction this time.

"Where? It looks like you're pointing to the woman in pink." She looked back at me and her eyebrows rose along with her voice. "I just know that you are not pointing to the woman in pink."

We both focused our eyes on who had to be the most unattractive woman in the club. I mean it's one thing to be big. Lord knows I know some big, sexy, attractive women. To be big, dark, and not have your hair done when you come to the club is an entirely different thing.

To top it off she wore a hot pink dress. No, make that a super tight, hot pink dress that squeezed every single lump, bump, and ditch. Oh yeah, can't leave out the white patent leather heels with the matching belt that wrapped around her wide mid-section. Her girls need to be ashamed for letting her come out of the house like that. But then again they didn't look that much better.

Shirley Temple was now staring a hole into the side of my face as I kept looking straight ahead licking my lips at the woman who reminded me of a big ass sloppy slice of strawberry shortcake. I tried to hold my composure, but her intense stare caused me to do otherwise.

I turned my face right into her confused, contorted, and disgusted look. It was too much to bear. My laughter escaped me at full force. She did the same, even louder than me. We both laughed so hard that we had tears in our eyes.

"So that's what you meant when you said I wasn't your type," she managed to say in between laughing. "In type you meant, human?"

"Nope, humans never did it for me. I'm a Klingon kind of guy," I said starting to calm a little. "Incredibly beautiful and absolutely gorgeous women always turned me off," I said, smiling staring directly at her now.

Her laughter transformed into a smile and her cheeks were now the color of a sun-kissed rose. "Awww, you wouldn't be referring to me would you?"

"Woman you need to stop. You know you are beautiful. I'm sure at least 20 guys have told you that tonight alone. So I couldn't come with that, I'm a little different, had to be original."

"First of all, yes, I have had about 20 guys step to me, but it wasn't to say that I was beautiful. It was to say, 'Damn girl,' or my personal favorite, 'Oooweee look at that ass.' So if you want to count all of them, then yeah I'm killing em' tonight. I have to admit your line was a little original."

"Thank you kindly ma'am," I said in a southern drawl. I loved it when guys made it so easy for me. Don't even know how to switch their game up. They came at a gorgeous woman the same way they came at a chicken head. "So, Ms. Shirley Temple, what cho name is?" I asked, trying to keep the mood upbeat.

"Aye yo son, I beez Brianna. Who you and what side you claiming?" she shot back.

"Whoa, whoa, now you're scaring me. You are a little too comfortable sounding hood. I started shaking my head from side to side. "I knew you were a hoodrat." I snapped my fingers for emphasis.

She busted out laughing again. I had her eating out of my hand now. "Whatever, crazy. So what is your name?"

"Future." I loved saying my name and seeing how women reacted.

"Future? Okay good one, so what is your real name?" She twisted her lips up to the side.

"Real talk, my real name is Future, as in yours."

"Good one. I see you're just original all the way around huh? Future, I'm Brianna." A few seconds passed and she started looking around frantically.

"What's wrong?"

"Boy, you've made me forget all about my girl and her drink! Knowing her though she's probably still on the dance floor."

Her statement made me think of Caesar. "She's a party animal, huh?" I asked.

"Actually quite the opposite," she kept looking out towards the dance floor, "by the way I think she would be your type."

"Is that so?" I didn't know exactly how to take that. Was she throwing me to her girl because she wasn't interested?

"Yeah, you're definitely her type," she said looking me over and smiling.

"But not yours?"

"Didn't say that, just said you were hers." I don't know why but at that moment me having a threesome with Brianna and her unidentified friend popped up in my head. "The entire time she was with her man, she never really went out," she continued. "This is sort of our 'Hell yeah we're single' party. We're with another one of our girls but we probably won't see her until it's time to leave. That's why I didn't have to worry about her drink."

"Mmm hmm, now back to the 'Hell yeah we're single party.' Was that we're as in, you're single too?" I asked for confirmation.

"Yep! I'm single too."

"Your man must be retarded or something to let you go."

She grabbed both the Cosmos from the bar and took a sip out of one. She then looked at me like she was struggling to make her next statement. "And who said I was with a man? Come help me look for my girl," she said quickly, leaving no room for questioning.

I decided not to press her on her statement but the way he instantly pressed up against my zipper, Buddy definitely wanted me to. "Okay let's see here, I'm looking for the woman you're trying to throw me off on right?" I asked sarcastically. As I stood behind her, I got the chance to see what she was working with and now I see why the guys were making some of those comments. Baby had ass for days, I'm talking big fat juicy ass. She could've easily been in any rapper's music video.

"I was just letting you know that there is at least one other woman in here that would find you very handsome," she paused, "other than me."

She made me smile a little on that one. "Okay, what is this friend of yours wearing?"

"Capris, a red sleeveless top, and oh yeah a new, short, cute haircut."

"Sounds cute."

"Cute doesn't do her justice, she's very pretty."

"Face too?" I asked of her friend who was starting to sound more intriguing by the second.

"Especially her face," she replied.

We walked toward the dance floor. The DJ was on fire. People have been dancing from the time we got in. Brianna led the way the entire time. Probably loved to be on top, I thought as the scene played out in my head. You can learn a lot from a woman just by watching her everyday actions. By watching Brianna walk, I could tell that her ass would look great with my face all up in it.

"I think I see her." Brianna raised up on her tippy toes a couple of times. "Damn, she's still dancing with the same guy."

We walked a little closer and she told me to wait so that she could hand off her girl's drink and come back. She obviously wanted to tell her girl something that she didn't want me to hear, so I nodded okay and looked at my Breitling to check the time. Baby girl was almost nearing her time limit. No matter how pretty a woman was, I wasn't going to spend all my time with her, not at a club. You never know, there could be a woman here that was prettier.

I saw Brianna split the crowd, doing a balancing act with a full Cosmo in one hand and a half-empty one in the other. She stopped in the center of the dance floor. Her back was turned and she momentarily blocked my view of her friend.

She handed over the drink and I stood anxious to see if her description really matched her friend. I bet she's going to be the least attractive one of the group.

I maneuvered myself a little to the left and was blocked by the guy that Brianna's girl was dancing with. On further examination, that guy turned out to be Caesar. I have to make a mental note to work with him on that. I'm always telling this dude to work the room. Guess he hasn't mastered that part of the game yet.

I was starting to get a little frustrated. Thoughts crossed my mind about just going over and introducing myself but I didn't want to seem too pressed. Caesar and Brianna were performing like a tag team, the way they unknowingly shielded her from me.

All of a sudden, I felt my palms get a little sweaty and that hasn't happened since high school. I started to feel like I was on a blind date and was just about to find out for the first time how my date looked.

Then it happened. The moon, planets, and stars were all aligned. Felt like I was supposed to be at this exact spot, this exact moment. Caesar walked away while Brianna pointed towards me, said a couple more words, smiled and started on her return.

At that point, everything moved in slow motion. My eyelids blinked and I saw the haircut first. Not boy cut short but Halle Berry in Boomerang, sexy short.

Blink.

Then finally, what I was waiting for, her face.

Blink.

Damn! This girl was…let's see what word I could use. It

wasn't gorgeous or what some guys would call beautiful. Probably wouldn't stand out over her girl by most guys' standards but by mine she would and did.

Blink.

She was pretty. Not the downgraded pretty that we use today. I'm talking old school pretty. The pretty that accounted for everything, every feature and not just tits and ass. She had the evaluated look, like when you're with your boys and you had a picture of her and broke down everything, she could hang with the best of them.

I don't know how long I actually stared at her but it seemed like forever. My eyes noticed every detail. She didn't have too much of one thing, but the right portion of everything. She was proportionately perfect.

Her skin was dark, rich, even toned and flawless. I'm sure her complexion got her teased a lot when she was younger, now it makes her look like Isis or Nefertiti. The little light-skinned girls who once teased her are now the ones with acne and blemishes. They wouldn't be caught dead going to the grocery store let alone the club without any makeup on. Surface beauty. I hate that shit. Can't even dance up close with them or get a hug or you'll have makeup all over your clothes not to mention your sheets and pillowcases.

Not this woman. I could flip her on her side or even if she buried her face in the pillow, she wouldn't leave a trace. Even her height was perfect. There would be no bending down or slouching to get a kiss. Naw, just bend your neck, she looks up, and mwahh! Yeah, I could definitely do some things with her.

It started to feel like I was gawking. Better take a sip of my drink. I don't want her to think I'm staring at her. Shit! Think she saw me the entire time. Fuck! Okay just turn your head Future. You know what fuck it, she's staring at me, and I'm going to stare back.

This was really weird. This woman has me feeling as if I was naked, almost like she was looking through me, into my soul. It felt like she knew me, the real me. The me before I turned into…this. Who is she and why can't I move?

What's taking Brianna so long to get over here? Why is everything still moving in slow motion?

Okay take another sip, I told myself and as soon as I swallowed… "Future." I heard my name being called out loud as if it wasn't the first time they tried to get my attention. "Fuuuuture!"

"Yeah, um hey." I said wondering how long Brianna had been standing beside me.

"Um, are you okay? Who are you staring at?"

"Huh, oh nobody. I just thought I saw someone that I knew that's all," I spoke to Brianna but still looked for my Nubian queen who had disappeared into the crowd.

"I don't want to keep you from partying. I have to get back to my girls, but I want to thank you again for the drinks. Not a lot of men do stuff like that anymore, especially for two women. So again, thanks."

"Hey, no problem it was my pleasure. Maybe I'll see you and your friend later on and we can have another drink," I said trying to get a closer look at her girl.

"Only if I'm buying, maybe then I can introduce you to her," she winked and smiled.

"That's definitely cool with me. I'm getting offered a drink and a woman. That's a win-win. Don't be trying to slip me any date rape drugs either. I don't want y'all taking advantage of me and trying to get in my pants," I threw in for good measure.

"If I wanted to get in your pants Future, I wouldn't have to do all that. I'll just tell you," she said briefly looking me over. "I'll look for you later." With that, she walked away.

I walked around the club for a few and saw a couple of women that were worthwhile but not good enough for me to go out of my way for. I decided to look for my boy to see how his game was going and to get the inside scoop on the woman he was dancing with.

I made my way to the back of the club and stopped short of the bar. I saw Caesar laughing and socializing with Brianna and her girl. Normally, this would be an ideal situation. I would go in and play wingman to Caesar or vice versa. Tonight, I don't think it's going to happen. For some reason, I was feeling too timid to meet the Hershey colored woman right now. Just looking at her gave me a strange feeling. And me getting any feeling from a woman other than sexual was strange in itself.

Yeah, this is some weird shit!

NEVER BE THE SAME

I have to admit, being out for a change did feel good and to top it off this club was all the way live. There is nothing worse than dressing up and going out to party and then everyone stands on the wall all night. There was none of that here. It seemed like everyone was on the dance floor. Even though I'm not supposed to have men on my mind there are some good looking ones here.

Unfortunately, the ratio for good looking and bad was 5 to 1 in favor of the bad. Men do some of the weirdest things sometimes. Like for instance the guy that's standing in front of me, I don't know how he even got in the club. This place is supposed to be grown and sexy and this dude has on white Air Force Ones, a pair of jeans that are way too big, and a white tee. I can't believe that grown men actually come out to a nightclub like that. To make matters worse, he's not the only one. Brianna pointed the first one out as soon as we came in and we all just shook our heads.

"Angel, seriously, what the fuck is up with the long white dress this dude is wearing?" Tierra said pointing to what had to be at least a 4X white tee.

I laughed at Tierra and shook my head. "He's keeping it gangsta. Why spend all that extra money and effort—"

"When they can still get females, I know I know," she said finishing my sentence. "But this is one bitch they better not come up to with that shit on. Especially after I squeezed in these too tight jeans, these uncomfortable ass heels, and almost too small bra to make my tits sit up right. And on top of all that I had to sit my ass at the hairdresser all day long to look good for these guys and they come up in this bitch with a fucking white ass tee on!" One thing about Tierra, she always spoke her mind. Exactly what she thought was exactly how it was going to come out.

"Dang girl, chill out, breathe! It's going to be okay," I said rubbing on her shoulder.

Tierra exhaled loudly, "Yeah, yeah, I'm okay."

"Good, but I do have one question for you."

"What is it girl?" she asked with her eyes closed trying to calm down.

I looked at her and scratched my temple. "Um, yeah, so if you don't like these non-effort making, non-dressing guys so much, then why did you take a drink from one?"

Tierra took another sip from a drink that she said was purchased by a guy that had on some busted up shoes and a sports coat that was three sizes too big. "Well, Ms. Smart Ass, that guy did put forth a little effort to look decent, he just did a horrible job at doing so," we both busted out laughing, "plus it is a drink. I pretty much don't turn them down…from anybody. I faked like I was interested in what he was saying for about two minutes, got my drink, and came back over here." She swung her head to the left and then to the right. "Where is Brianna?"

"Well, when you did your normal calculated disappearing act, we knew we wouldn't have to worry about you scoring a drink, so I sent her for ours."

"I mean, I was going to get y'all one too but—"

"Please, save it." I said knowing my girl all too well. All of a sudden, Tierra turned her back to me like she was hiding her face. "What the hell?" I looked around to see if the cops were coming or something. "Girl, what's the matter with you?"

"Shhhh, level five clinger."

"What?"

"Stalker!" she whispered. "The guy who bought my drink," she nodded her head, "six o'clock!" I looked around but didn't see anyone who fit the description.

"No, not your six o'clock, mine." I looked behind her and saw a guy that looked like he was drowning in his sports coat with a goofy look on his face. He was staring a hole in Tierra's back. After a couple of seconds, he decided to come over and speak. I tried my best to hold in my laugh.

"Hey baby, you enjoying that drink I bought you? I've been looking all over for you, had me all worried and shit."

Tierra turned around and looked at this dude as if he were crazy. It was funny how a man will buy a drink for a woman and really think that she's obligated to stay with him the entire night. He was questioning her as if he was really her man. She lied to him and said that she had to go to the ladies' room, gave me the wink to let me know that she would be back when he was gone, and disappeared.

Tierra never stayed in one spot for too long. We always had to look for her at the end of the night. So now, I am standing by myself, bobbing my head to the music. I was getting many stares but no one has said anything to me yet. I think I might be getting a little disappointed. I looked around to see if I could spot Brianna. She should've been back by now, I thought to myself, tapping my finger on my thigh.

The DJ had been doing a Biggie Smalls session for a while, but all of a sudden, he dropped Jay Z's "I Just Wanna Love U" and everyone that had been standing around, including me, went to the dance floor. This was my song and I was determined to dance with somebody while it was on. It was time that I put this booty magnet to use. I made sure I switched my booty more than usual as I stepped to the floor.

Seconds later, I felt a gentle tug on my left wrist. "You mind if I dance with you?"

I looked over my left shoulder to put a face with the voice. Hmmm decent, not bad at all. "Sure!"

He led me to the least crowded spot on the dance floor. Everyone was so hyped on this song that the DJ must've felt the energy because he did a little scratch and started the song over from the beginning.

My back was to the person I was dancing with and I decided to turn to face him. He was somewhat cute. Dressed pretty good, nice line up, a little shorter than I like my men though. My heels brought me very close to his height. Actually, he looked more to be Brianna's type. All in all he was good for dancing. It was always better when you danced with a guy who was at least attractive.

He kept looking at me and smiling. He had a nice warm, friendly smile. Made you feel comfortable, I figured I would start a little conversation. "What are you smiling at so hard?"

He nodded his head towards me, "You. I like that do of yours, getting your Halle on huh?"

It felt good hearing that compliment coming from a guy after cutting all my hair off. It was reassuring. "I bet you tell all the shorthaired women that," I teased.

"Yeah, right. You and I both know that many women have the wrong shaped face and head for the hairstyles that they wear. But yours," he paused looking me over again, "perfect."

I ran my hand over my ear touching my hair with a few of my fingers. "Thanks!" He didn't look like the type to have game but he was starting to make me blush a little. Okay new guy, you've earned it, I'm going to give you a little back, let you bump up against this onion for a while.

It was funny watching how men reacted to ass especially on the dance floor. Some just stared, some acted like they were afraid of it and made sure that their crotches didn't touch it at all, probably because they knew that they would get a hard on. Then there were the fellas who didn't give a damn, all up on the ass as if they were really up in it. I wondered which one he would be.

I was feeling a little frisky tonight and unlike Jamie Foxx, I couldn't blame it on the alcohol because I only had one glass of wine before I left the house. It might have something to do with me not getting any loving for the last three months. As of late, I've been relying on my favorite chocolate covered eight-inch dildo, Mr. Dependable.

Even before my boyfriend and I called it quits, the loving had become nonexistent. It wasn't because he didn't try to get any, I mean he did damn near every night, but every time he tried, I turned my back to him and said I was too tired. After a while, he didn't even put up a fight about it, probably because he knew I was fed up with the bullshit and lies.

All of a sudden, I felt a poke at my shoulder and turned around. "Brianna, where are the drinks?" I asked trying to hide my disappointment.

"Girl, the bar is crazy," Brianna responded. She acknowledged my dance partner by smiling and a brief wave. "I didn't even get looked at. I'm about try my luck at the bar over there. Be back in a few." Before she left, she gave me wink letting me know that I made a decent choice for my dance partner.

I turned back around and smiled. Free, free to do whatever I wanted to do, I thought to myself. Right now, I wanted to get a little freaky on the dance floor. If I'm feeling like this now, how am I going to be after a couple of drinks? That is, if I ever get a drink.

The new guy and I danced for about three more songs and Brianna still wasn't back with my drink. Tierra also was nowhere in sight. I'll give them both a couple more minutes before I go looking for them.

My dance partner for the moment has impressed me, I must say. At first, I thought he would be a little stiff, but he wasn't at all. Every time I swayed, he swayed. When I swerved, he caught it and swerved back. He told me his name was Caesar and I told him it sounded New York-ish. He laughed and told me that his parents were from New Jersey. All in all, he seemed pretty cool. He even offered to buy me a drink since Brianna was taking so long. I laughed and automatically thought about the situation with Tierra.

"Now, if I accept your offer, does that mean that we have to get married?" I teased.

He looked at me with questionable eyes. "Are you serious? Don't tell me I look like one of those guys. I would never expect anything out of you for just buying you a drink. Car…house…you might have to come up out them draws, but a drink, never."

I smiled. Felt good to smile. "In that case, I accept." We were just about to walk off when I saw Brianna, finally splitting through the crowded dance floor towards us with two drinks in her hand. "Wait a minute," I said touching Caesar's shoulder, "there's my girl." Brianna's lustrous spiral curls bounced with every step she took as if she was in a commercial. She could easily be a model in my opinion and judging from all the attention she's getting from the guys they agreed.

She had the look that made men and women alike take notice. I wonder what kind of lover she is. Was she soft and gentle, matching the way she looked or was that just a cover up for her down and dirty side? She would tell Tierra and I stories about what men and women would do to her but never too much about how she got down. Hmmm, I wonder.

Brianna stepped to me rolling her eyes, "I know, I know but it wasn't my fault though," she said before I even had the chance to get out a word.

"Whaaa, I didn't even say anything."

"Yeah, but you were thinking it, can tell by that intense stare that you were giving me on my way over."

Damn was I that obvious, I thought to myself. "I was just concerned that's all," I said trying to sound convincing, "this is a big place after all, I can see how you could get lost for 20 to 30 minutes to go get a drink."

Brianna laughed, "Whatever, anyways here's your drink."

"It better be good for how long it took you to get it." I raised the glass to my lips and took a nice size gulp. The liquor in the Cosmo almost brought tears to my eyes. "Damn Bri, I see you made sure it was strong enough so you wouldn't have to go back anytime soon." We both sipped on our drinks. This time I took much smaller sips while Brianna asked the whereabouts of our third compadre. While I tried to explain the stalker story, she kept turning her head as if she was looking for someone.

"What, do you see her or something?" I asked turning my head also.

"Oh naw, I just met this guy who actually bought us these drinks and I didn't really thank him."

I took another sip from my drink and said, "Well, go thank him then just in case he wants to by us another one or something."

"Um actually, I told him that we would buy him his next drink." Brianna put her head down like a child waiting to get scolded by her parents.

"We?"

"Me, we, same thing."

"Wow, must be some guy if we're offering him a drink."

"Actually he is, but I think he's more of your type than mine."

"Whatever," I said laughing, "don't be trying to act like you trying to pass him over to me now."

"No for real," she said smiling, "I already told him I think you two would look cute together."

"You did what?" I asked raising my voice.

Brianna ignored me and stood on her tippy toes as she looked over my shoulder. "And who was the cutie pie all up on your booty for like two hours?"

"Two hours? You swear it was for that long. I think he's your type though, I kind of told him that too," I said laughing at us having the same thing on our minds.

"You did what?"

"Oh don't even trip, you did the same thing." I almost forgot that I had Caesar behind waiting to buy me a drink. When I turned around, he was giving a couple of guys the universal pound and a half arm hug. It appeared that he knew them from somewhere. I waited for him to finish and introduced him to Brianna.

I tried my best to hold in my laughter. He tried his best to look serious, but you could tell that he thought she was beautiful. Watching them shake hands made me look at them both at the same time. They actually did look good together. Brianna loved nice guys, and it seemed that he was. I liked nice guys too but they had to have a little bad boy in them, a little edge. Tierra, well she just loved straight up thugs.

Brianna told me that she would be right back and pointed in the direction in which she was headed. I told her to meet me at the bar in the back. She turned around and began to walk away. At the same time another guy came up to Caesar and made some kind of comment about my booty that I don't think I was supposed to hear, but did, which was cool with me because everything and everybody faded into non-existence shortly after.

When I saw who Brianna was walking towards my body froze up like I was bitten by a paralyzing, poisonous snake.

It was Him!

THE MAGICIAN!

I knew he was powerful and dangerous, but now he has worked his spell on my girl. Had her over here looking like she was possessed or something. If he has that type of effect on someone who is bi, just think what he'll do to a woman who was 100 percent into men.

Look at him standing so tall shoulders so broad, so confident. He has to be at least six foot three. Geez, he is so brown. Kind of reminded me of a fudgesicle. Naw, that goes down too cold when you swallow it. He would definitely be warm, pleasantly burning my throat. He's definitely Kahlua. Three parts Kahlua, one part Amaretto, so sweet, so good, and one part Bailey's, rich and smooth.

I would drink every drop of him. I wanted him in my mouth so bad. I wanted him on my tongue. I took a nice sized sip of my drink, held it in my mouth and moved it around savoring the taste, while imagining it to be him.

I felt a little ashamed of myself for feeling this way toward a man that I didn't even know, but it felt good. Felt real good. I wonder if he is an athlete. He can't be single.

After Caesar finished up with his boys he informed me that he was about to get himself a drink. He invited me to join him and being that I didn't have anything else to do at the moment but stare at this sexy ass man, I accepted. I had to do something to break me out of this trance.

"Are you okay?" Caesar asked.

"Yeah why do you ask?" I knew that I must have had a puzzled look on my face.

"Just asking. It looked like you were blushing a minute ago. I didn't know I would have that effect on you this soon."

"Oh you wish," I said smiling.

While leading me to the bar he tried to tell me something about his friend but I couldn't hear him over all the noise in the club.

"What did you say?"

He slowed down his pace and leaned in a little closer to my ear. "I was just saying that my boy that I came with tonight would love your friend."

"Oh, your friend would huh?" I asked with a smirk. "And how do you know that? You don't even know what kind of personality she has or nothing about her. Does this friend of yours just go off of looks?"

"Exactly," he said with a grin.

"Don't be trying to put it all on your boy. I saw you drooling when she came over."

He chuckled, "Girl, what are you talking about? I wasn't looking that hard, besides I was standing next to you so my eyes were preoccupied before she arrived."

"Key word, before, and when she arrived, your eyes became occupied with my girl, you know you was looking at her donk."

We both laughed. "She does have a big one though," he said looking like he was drifting off.

I wanted to let him know that I didn't mind him being into my girl, partly because I wasn't into him and partly because I had my eyes already set on someone.

"Brianna is one gorgeous woman. If you didn't look at her I would have to wonder."

"Gorgeous huh, you say it almost like you're not."

"That's because I'm not. Now by no means do I think I'm an ugly duckling, but in the looks department she's on a higher plain than most women."

"Usually when two women go out, one of them tends to be a bit…you know how it goes."

I looked at him and put my hands on my hips. "Well, maybe that's how it usually goes but both of my girls are tight. So sorry we can't fit into your little theory." I gave him the now take that look and smiled.

"Well, excuse me. So you're telling me that there are three of you here and neither one of you looks like Godzilla? Sorry, I just can't believe that," Caesar said waiving his hands in disbelief.

"I'll let you judge for yourself. Here comes my other girl now." Tierra walked past Caesar to my other side. I looked at him to get his reaction. He gave me the two thumbs up. I mouthed, "I told you so." The moment I turned to speak to Tierra, I saw Brianna making her way towards us. Caesar didn't see her because he was too busy trying not to stare at Tierra's almost fully exposed breasts.

The bar was packed but when he turned to the bartender to order his drink, he got her attention rather fast. When he turned around his eyes widened as he gawked at me, Brianna and then Tierra. He tried to hold his composure but with the three of us standing together, he wasn't doing such a good job.

The bartender brought him his drink and after paying, he stepped over closer to us. I introduced him to Tierra and she made a noise to signify to us that she thought he was cute. He shook her hand and looked like he was trying not to let his eyes drop down to her chest level.

Caesar cleared his throat to excuse himself. "Ladies, Angel, it was nice meeting you but I have to let you breathe a little now. Think I'm getting a little tired of all these guys giving me these salty looks because I'm standing with the three sexiest women in the club." We all smiled at his compliment. "If y'all see me later though don't be acting like y'all don't know a brother."

I took another sip of my Cosmo that was now near empty and put my ghetto sassy attitude back on. "I know you ain't trying to call us stuck up; are you Caesar?"

"Stuck up? Naw, I was thinking more on the lines of conceited."

We all shared a laugh as he turned and walked away becoming submerged in the sea of partygoers. I stood for a second anticipating what my girls were going to say about me giving a guy the time of day. They both had their eyes locked in on me.

"What? Spit it out. Say whatever it is you two heifers have to say."

Of course, the outspoken Tierra came at me first. "Look at you Angel, pimpin' these dudes up in here." She turned to Brianna who was grinning like the Cheshire Cat. "I'm telling you girl, I came from the ladies room and saw the two of them all up in each other's face like they were about to kiss or something."

I knew she was about to come with an exaggeration but not like that. "Tierra, why are you lying? You know that I was not—"

"Don't be trying to front while Brianna is here, you know that you're busted." Tierra started laughing uncontrollably. Something tells me that Tierra has had more drinks than Brianna and I.

"I don't think she's trying to front for me," Brianna interjected.

"Thanks girl, at least one of my friends is in their right mind."

Just when I thought Brianna was on my team, she shot back with, "When I was bringing her drink to her I saw ole' boy humping and grinding all up on her ass."

My mouth almost fell to the floor in shock. Both of my girls had sold me out. "I really can't believe y'all. Lord knows y'all are lying."

"She is moving fast. Trying to hurry up and get some replacement dick, huh?" Tierra asked laughing.

"That was just a guy," I tried to explain, "nothing more, nothing less, not even my type really. I tried to push him off on Brianna."

"So you mean to tell me you didn't even get the digits?" I see Tierra wasn't going to leave it alone, probably trying to make sure I didn't like him so she could push up.

"No Tee, I didn't. I don't think I'm even ready to start talking to guys yet."

Brianna was bouncing her big booty to the beat and causing all kinds of ruckus behind her from onlooking horny males. "You know they say the best way to get over that old love is to find a new one. Damn, I need another drink."

"Yeah that's what they say, but we know that all guys are the same. They might seem good at first, but in the end they are all full of shit," I responded.

The crowd at the bar that we were standing by had thinned out a little and Brianna took advantage and ordered three more Cosmopolitans. "Well guys may all be the same, but I think I may have met one tonight that might be actually worth taking a chance on." Tierra and I looked at each other then back at Brianna as she continued talking. She handed us our drinks, "I'm just keeping it real y'all, just his voice had the kitty percolating like a coffee maker." We all busted out laughing but mine stopped short when I realized whom she might have been talking about. There were other men here too so maybe it could've been someone else but a little inquisition on my behalf wouldn't hurt.

"So what are you trying to say Bri? Are you selling us out now? I thought we were supposed to be the Breakup Clique, remember, fuck guys?" I tried to sound as playful as possible. "Must be some guy for you to say he might be worth breaking the pact for."

"Damn he must be," Tierra said snapping her neck back. "Look at her all blushing and shit. If I didn't know any better I would say that you were over there having an orgasm."

"Whatever, I'm not having an orgasm, well not right now anyways. Angel I know I told you that he was more of your type, which I really think he is, but tonight while I'm in the tub with my massaging shower head it's going to be a totally different story." She high fived Tierra then held up her hand for me to do the same. Instead of giving her five, I wanted to slap her in her pretty ass face. I settled on going with my better judgment, smiled and played along.

"I'm telling y'all I have this guy's picture imbedded in my brain and tonight along with my pink rabbit I'm bringing him along for one hell of a threesome." We all cracked up. I had to laugh at that one.

I figured since we were all buzzing this was the perfect time for a question. "So if this guy was all that, what made him not your type?"

"Well to be honest, he didn't seem to be too pressed. I mean we had good convo, laughed a little bit and even though I don't expect every guy to ask for my number he didn't even hint to me that he wanted to ask. Just told me that maybe we'll see each other later on. There was something about him, like as soon as I saw him that made me say, 'This guy has Angel written all over him.' I know that sounds kind of crazy but by him not pressing or pursuing me, being all confident and a little cocky makes his sexy ass even sexier."

I couldn't believe hearing my girl talk about this guy was frustrating me like it was, but I was ready to change the subject and change it quick. "So anyways y'all, enough about that, we are supposed to be partying and we're up here talking about men, what's up with that?"

"Yeah, you're right," Tierra said throwing back the rest of her drink, "let's go hit the dance floor."

"Wait a minute! I think my glass has a hole in it. Where the hell is the rest of my drink?" Brianna asked laughing.

We all sat our glasses down and started on our journey towards the dance floor. On our way, we did our usual swaying and bobbing our heads to the music while checking out guys that were checking us out. But I did something extra. I used the hell out of my peripheral vision to make sure I didn't run into the mystery man, or if we did I had to make sure I had enough time to get my composure, because Lord knows how I would act if I saw him up close and personal with Brianna.

I felt the beginnings of a smile invade my face and wanted to tell someone about my little secret and how I was feeling but I knew my girls would tease the hell out of me. Maybe another time.

"What are you smiling at girl? Who do you see, fill me in," Tierra asked.

"Nothing, it's nothing for real, I'm just in a good mood that's all." I couldn't believe I was acting all giddy over this guy. He really had me behaving way out of character.

We reached the dance floor and went straight to the center. Now that there was only an hour left to party it seemed like everyone was trying to get their party on. People had taken their recommended doses of liquid courage so now even the shiest patrons were brave enough to dance.

All of the women assumed their positions, backs arched and asses melodically swerving on the guy's crotch and in return the guys were jack-hammering their pelvises into the cracks before them.

I'm not really a liquor girl. I usually do a couple glasses of wine, but after having two extra strong Cosmos I was starting to get a little hot and bothered. I noticed every move, grind and sway. The men began whispering in women ears, probably trying to make their last appeal to continue their sinful acts immediately after the club. I saw women tilting their necks back and closing their eyes, reaching back grabbing thighs, pulling partners closer into them until they meshed, becoming one.

The more I witnessed the more I wanted to be jackhammered.

I wanted to be someone's concrete and have him break me wide open by driving himself into my cracks and crevices. I was feeling so warm inside.

First, a guy came up behind Tierra and then another came up behind Brianna. The four of them danced to the mid tempo song. Then I felt someone behind me. First, I noticed his shoes, hmmmm very nice. I didn't have the courage to turn around. I was facing my girls and had my back to my new dance partner. They looked at me then up at him and smiled. Then they smiled harder. Okay, smiling is good, I thought not wanting to smile back, but that's not telling me what I wanted to know.

He smelled so good, so clean. The mystery dancer then reached his arms out and enveloped me, making my insides melt. I mean I just became lost, closed my eyes and took a trip.

I guess it's been longer than I thought since I'd actually been embraced by a man. I felt his hard chiseled chest on my shoulder blades. I felt his firm sculpted thighs when I let my arms drop and tapped my fingers on them to the beat. His thighs were like granite. He obliviously had a knockout body.

I pictured us dancing in the same position, but naked. Feeling his rod nestled in the small of my back. My firm nipples were swollen and tingling from his hands caressing them. I felt my breath getting heavy. Mmm, feels so good.

He scrunched down, I spread eagle. I want to make it as easy as possible for him to slide into me, into a spot that hasn't been penetrated by a man in oh so long. The anticipation is driving me crazy. My pussy is so wet, so hot. I feel the heat, feel it all between my legs, felt it on my palms and fingertips as I cupped my kitty.

I felt his thickness slide down the crack of my ass and curve up towards my sweet spot. I arched my back, getting ready to accept him, naw fuck that, I'm beyond ready. I feel him getting closer, feel it touching, sliding, feel it throbbing—

"Alright people, last call for alcohol," the DJ announced over the speakers. The once dim dusky lighting that had set the raunchy mood was now bright and revealing. It seemed like the ugly people began to scatter like roaches, scared to show how they really looked, who they really were. The light always seemed to show the truth.

I couldn't remember anything I was doing while dancing. Lord, please tell me I wasn't really touching myself. I looked at my girls to read their faces but they weren't even paying me any attention. They had their eyes fixed on him. I figured he was cute but their mouths were gaping as if he were a superstar. I had to turn around now and at least thank—

"Thank you for the dance love."

Guess he beat me to it. I turned around and saw his rather large outstretched hand and then the ridiculously diamond flooded Franck Muller watch that was attached to his wrist. I saw a couple of rappers sporting one similar to it in a couple of videos.

"Oh, you're welcome," I said as I tilted my neck upward to look at his face. Wow! It…It was him, well not Him, but the guy that's on all the commercials and billboards around the city. It was Juwaun, Juwaun Jones, star wide receiver of the Detroit Lions. Even though he was quite handsome, I still was a little disappointed that it wasn't who I wished it to be.

He held my hand longer than needed and stared at me. "You know it's not polite to stare," I said gently slipping my hand from his grip.

"I wasn't staring, I was admiring. I know this may sound like a line or something but you are absolutely beautiful!"

"Yeah, you're right, does kind of sound like a line." I continued to look up at the receiver who had to be all of six foot seven as he smiled back down at me.

"Well, I don't know what else to say because that's the word that truly fits." His face all of a sudden started to look a little concerned. "Um, is that your girl over there choking?"

"Choking...what?" I turned around and saw my girl clearing her throat so hard that she was bending over looking like she was hacking up a lung. Tierra was so over the top.

"So, do you mind telling me your name?"

"Only if you allow me to introduce you to my friends."

"Sounds like a deal, but do you want to know mine?" he asked smiling.

"I think everybody in here knows who you are." I started to notice the pointing and whispering from the attention that Juwaun was drawing. I ran my finger through my hair still not used to it being so short, still a little insecure about it. "I'm Angel." I extended my hand again.

"Indeed you are." He looked me over and looked to be struggling with his next choice of words. "I'm Juwaun, and it's my pleasure making your acquaintance. Now let's go give your girl CPR." I had to laugh at that.

"Tierra, Brianna, I want you to meet Juwaun Jones."

"Heeyyyyy," they both chimed in unison as if they were singing a duet.

"Oh my God, Juwaun! I watch all of your games. You are hands down the best quarterback in the entire league!"

Juwaun chuckled at Tierra. "Is that so?"

"Tierra dear," I gently rubbed her shoulder, "um, he is not a quarterback he's a receiver." She looked like she had just swallowed a foot.

"Tierra is it? Don't even sweat it. All of the different positions in football can get a little confusing."

"Oh I'm not confused on positions, I know exactly the ones I like," Tierra responded seductively.

I gave her the look that told her that she had better behave. "Brianna, are you okay?" I asked looking at her just standing and staring.

"Yeah, I'm okay I just didn't want to interrupt that's all."

"Are you serious," I responded, "you're getting shy on me now? Juwaun, you have to excuse my girls, this is obviously the first time that they have met anyone famous."

Juwaun smiled wide. "I like y'all. Especially you Angel, so look," he pulled out a business card and handed it to me, "I'm having a little after party or whatnot at my spot. You beautiful ladies should come through. I would love having you as my guests."

"After party or whatnot huh?" I raised my eyebrow, "What does that mean, like a freak party or something? Groupies stopping by, stripping and frolicking around?"

He busted out laughing, "Frolicking, wow, sounds like a word that my mother would use. No, Angel there will be no frolicking at my place. No strippers or groupies for that matter. I do have many friends, male and female and a big enough place to fit them all in. I only hang around good people because that's what I am, good people."

He sounded convincing. I looked at his business card. "Sounds like fun, Juwaun but it's getting a little late for my girls

JOHNIE JAY

and I. I think we're going to have to take you up on your offer at another time."

"Okay, I think I can take rejection. Just do me a favor, give me a call whenever you get bored or better yet call me whenever you make it home tonight so I can know that you made it in safely."

"I might be able to do that," I answered with a slight smile.

"Mmm hmm, you are not going to call are you?"

"I might, I'm not making any promises though."

"Okay then, I'll take might. You ladies have a good night."

"You too," we all said on one accord, waited until he was out of sight and then…

"Oh my God girl! I couldn't breathe, I thought I was going to faint," Brianna started first.

"Damn it! I made myself look like a damn fool. Quarterback? Damn, that may have ruined my chances of him hooking me up with one of his superstar friends." Tierra was really looking stressed out as she looked into the unforeseen future. "And don't think that you are not going to call him Angel, because you are! Even if I have to tie you down, take your damn fingers and dial him for you, you are going to call."

"Girl, you are a mess and I don't know for sure if I'm going to call him or not. I just don't want to look like a groupie. It's too expected. It's not like women are going to turn him down. I'm supposed to call him just because he's Juwaun Jones?"

"Uh, hell yeah bitch!" Tierra said raising her voice. "And not just because he's Juwaun Jones, but because he's *the* Juwaun Jones." And he's handsome, he's rich, he's tall, probably has a big—"

"Okay dang, I get it. You sound like his damn publicist or something. At least I can count on my girl," I said looking over at Brianna who was looking up in the air and whistling some made up tune.

"Whaaa, oh, were you talking to me?"

I shook my head, "Where's the love?"

Brianna put her arm around me. "You know I got your back, whatever decision you make. It's just men like that don't come around too often and I think it may be a little unfair categorizing him just because he's an athlete. Who knows, he might just be a standup guy who just happens to be a millionaire. Shit girl, you deserve it. We all do. We all are some good ass women."

"Awww, you're going to make me cry Bri," I said feeling sentimental.

Tierra chimed in, "Y'all are the best friends a girl could ever have." We did a group hug and finally decided to make our way out of the club to avoid the traffic. They both told me on the way to the door how envious the other females were looking when Juwaun was up on me. Of course, Tierra reassured me that she would have busted a bitch in the back of the head with a beer bottle if they would've tried to step. She is so hood, but I love her and Brianna.

I have to admit, Juwaun did get my heart pumping with his sexy ass voice, 'Thanks for the dance love.' That made the tiny hairs on my arms stand up and applaud.

Well mystery man, I'll try my best to hold out for you. There is no doubt in my mind that we will see each other again. They say good things come to those who wait, but sexy ass Juwaun might have a sister jumping offside for a five-yard penalty.

THEY'RE ALL THE SAME

AFTER seeing Caesar, Brianna, and her friend at the bar, I decided to go and drain the weasel. Hennessey and Coke was going straight through me now and I had a nice buzz. I had decided that as soon as I finished, I was going over to invade the little discussion group. I can't believe I was second guessing myself. Yeah, I'm going over.

After using it, I came back upstairs and headed to the bar where I previously saw my boy. I stopped short when I heard someone calling my name.

"Yo Future, wait up. Damn, you must have been busy with the ladies. This is the first time I've seen you since coming in."

I could tell he was in a real good mood. "Yeah, I can't complain. What about you? You're looking a little geeked up yourself."

"Man, my night has been crazy, and for the most part I've only been chilling with one chick."

"One? One chick? And that's how you think you're going to surpass the teacher?" I asked while laughing.

"Yeah, yeah, I know how it sounds, but baby girl was tight."

"Was she Beyoncé? Because that is the only woman that'll have me chilling with her all night."

"Naw she wasn't Beyoncé but she was straight. Now her girl on the other hand," Caesar threw his head back and closed his eyes to add some flavor, "wheweee! Now she was the closest you can get to Beyoncé without being her. I'm talking ass for days. Future, this woman was hands down the tightest up in here."

He was obviously talking about Brianna, he loved him some light-skinned women. Unfortunately, she was of no concern to me. If I wanted her, I could have wrapped here up no problem. My concern was Dark Chocolate.

"So you mean to tell me that you didn't pull a number?"

"Why you say that? I didn't tell you that I didn't."

"Come on Cease, I know you. If you would've pulled her number, that would've been one of the first things out of your mouth."

Caesar smiled because he knew I had him pegged. "Anyway, I didn't pull her number. I could have, but when Beyoncé showed up, she changed all plans. I didn't want to make it seem like I was all up on her girl, so that later on I could try to get her number."

"So let me get this straight," I said stroking my goatee, "you gave up on an almost for sure thing with the chick you were chilling with all fucking night for a desperate attempt at her friend who you only seen for a couple of minutes?"

"Yep, you got it," he replied with a wide grin.

"Quick question, how many times did Beyoncé see you with her girl?"

He thought for a few seconds and held up two fingers. "Tres."

I laughed at his poor attempt at Spanish, "It's dos, do-do bird, two is dos, three is tres."

"Whatever, you know what I meant."

"Playboy, you might as well throw that hand in because it's dead," I said shaking my head.

Caesar looked at me confused. I didn't know if he was that clueless or whether to blame it on the liquor. "Why do you think that?"

"Let's just say that Beyoncé saw y'all on the dance floor, and then later on she saw y'all together again somewhere else. She is at least thinking that her girl likes you enough to continue with you off of the dance floor."

"But Future it wasn't like that. She just happened to be the first chick I met and danced with tonight. Afterwards I invited her to the bar for a drink. Now don't get me wrong she was hot, but when I saw her girl it was a wrap for her. Hell, I was hoping to see your ass so I could've passed her off to you. She's way more your type than she is mine anyway."

It was reassuring to hear that he wasn't really pressed over Dark Chocolate. I didn't want any unnecessary rifts between my boy and me. "Yeah I hear you, but do Beyoncé know that? Which don't even matter Cease, because if they are any kind of friends, they will not get with someone that their girl may or may not like. I hope that you were not drooling over Beyoncé when she came over because if you did you probably messed up your chances with both."

Caesar hung his head toward the floor while smiling.

"Oh shit, tell me I don't know my boy, tell me I don't," I said laughing.

Caesar continued to smile, "Man, you know yellow women are my weakness. It ain't fair man, they ambushed me. Set me up, I tell ya. To make matters worse, there was a third one. All of them looked good. That should've told me right there that they were evil."

I looked at my watch, "I'm out of here in a few man, think I'm going to make one more round, see who's up in this piece."

"Alright, I'll hookup with you in a few. I see a little honey I met from the last time that we were here. Gonna see if she wants a little company after the club."

"Go handle your business. Oh and speaking of the last time that we were here. Guess who I was kicking it with earlier?" He looked at me as if he had no clue. "Red Dress."

The look on his face made it seem that he was more excited about her than I was. "You're talking about Sexy Red Riding Hood?"

"Yep, that's her. You should've seen her tonight. Ass was damn near hanging out." I stretched and yawned as if it was no big deal. "She's coming over as soon as we leave. This is exactly how I told you it was going to play out two weeks ago. All because I was patient and didn't press her the first time. This time though, she damn near molested me at the bar."

"You know I hate you, right?" Caesar stated with a smile.

"You know Caesar, if I wasn't me; I think I would hate me too." We walked in separate directions, Caesar towards his hopeful, and me towards, the unknown. I walked past the bar towards the dance floor and stopped when I saw Her.

Not Ms. Red Dress and not Brianna. I saw the one that just by looking in her direction made me feel as if she was essential to me. I really didn't like the fact that from the first time I saw her up until now I couldn't get her off of my mind.

I finished what was left of my drink and set it down on an empty table beside me. I brought my focus back to what appeared to be my new addiction, for the time being, and all I noticed were those legs. Those long shapely legs that seemed to go on forever. Killer calves that showed from up under her capri pants, and they weren't from the heels she was wearing. Naw, these calves were all hers. Whether she worked for them or they were genetically wrapped as a gift, she definitely earned them. Then her hips and thighs, although covered in what looked to be stretch capris, there was no hiding them.

Every time she would sway to the left and the right I could see her quads tighten and contract. I imagined myself lying on top of her and her wrapping her limbs around my waist and squeezing me like a python, hugging, pulling me in deeper and deeper.

My eyes then raced north, to that part of her body that brought life to my crotch area earlier. Mmmm, that juicy ass booty. To my dismay, some guy was obstructing my view. Who in the hell is this all up on her? Better yet, why do I even care? I mean she is nobody to me. I don't even know why I'm watching her frisky ass grind all up on…is that… naw can't be. Damn, that is Juwaun fucking Jones from the Detroit Lions. Damn, maybe she's his girl.

I doubt it. She's probably just a gold digger all up on his shit. I should have known. Bitches are funny and they are all the same. As soon as you give them a little credit, they'll let you down every time. They think a nigga with money is going to save their ass. Yeah right, he is just dangling his golden carrot in front of their face, making them hop along like a bunny rabbit. Then before you know it...cut...slice, their fucking foot is dangling on his key chain. That's what their gullible asses get.

As the DJ announced last call for alcohol everyone began to make their last efforts to close whatever deals they were working on, but I stayed put. I looked at her continuing to make a fool out of herself, holding his hand getting dreamy eyed and shit. Just because he plays professional football. I guess regular dudes are not good enough for her. Women are something else. Guess my boy made the right decision on that one after all.

I felt myself beginning to get frustrated over a woman that I have never met and decided to make a beeline for the exit. While maneuvering through the people that had the same idea as me I looked to see if I could spot Caesar.

"What up, I was just looking for you, ready to go?" he asked.

"Yep, you?" I quickly responded still feeling as if I was wearing the remnants of an attitude.

"Yeah, I'm really ready now that I hooked up my private after party."

"Oh baby girl took the bait huh?" I asked smiling.

"Hook, line, and sinker. She told me that she was hungry so I figured I would swing by her place and feed her this dick." We gave each other a pound. I have to admit my boy was really becoming a player. He's coming along very well.

We exited the club, handed our tickets to the valet and chilled. We loved this part of the night because this is when we got a chance to floss our rides. Living in Detroit and hanging out downtown it was all about your ride.

I loved working for Ford. Some people look down on the autoworkers or think of us as uneducated grease monkeys. They can call me what they want, but for damn near 30 dollars an hour you can't call me broke. In Michigan, where our economy was almost dead, the urban community only had three real moneymakers. They were the people who worked for the big three automotive companies, Ford, GM, or Chrysler; those who were in medical field, and the ones involved in some kind of street narcotics. It was sad but true.

I made a very comfortable living. I had a nice income from the investment properties my family owned and my job just put the icing on the cake. I owned a nice loft downtown, had fly gear, jewelry, and money to spend. But the most important reason, I'm realizing right now, is that it allowed me to be able to afford my favorite girl, Sally. Here she comes around the corner now, turning heads.

My new Mustang Shelby convertible. Damn! She's a showstopper. There were only 500 of these cars assembled and I was lucky enough to have one. I had a lot of custom work done to her so nobody had anything that looked like it. I stuck my chest out like a proud boyfriend of a stallion.

Caesar, who worked at the plant with me, smiled as he saw his brand new Platinum edition F-150 pulling up behind Sally. He had put a lot of money into his truck as well. I'm talking 30-inch rims, crazy sound system, the works.

"Well, my little student," I said as I flipped out my phone, "I had fun, but right now, as you know, I have a little business to handle."

"I feel you dawg, I gotta go serve up this late night snack. Oh shit!" Caesar pointed to the other side of the street. "Future there she is! Beyoncé!"

"Who?" Here I am breaking my neck thinking my future baby momma, Beyoncé Knowles was leaving the club in a Bentley or something and this fool was talking about light-skinned and her girls. I'm a little mad at myself that I even looked.

I kept pressing the down arrow on my phone now reaching the J's in my contacts. Jasmine…Jaleesa…July, then, finally the K's. There she is, Kandi. Just thinking about what was about to go down made me smile.

I looked at Caesar and smiled, "You know my dad always taught me that a bird in the hand is worth more than 10 in the bush."

I handed the valet my ticket along with a 10-dollar bill and told my boy before he hopped in his truck, "Aye, I might have to borrow the truck tomorrow to go to Art Van. After tonight I might have to go pick up a new head board." Caesar busted out laughing and hopped in his truck.

When I closed the door, I switched the CD changer to number three, *Doggystyle*, and found the appropriate track for tonight, "Bitches Ain't Shit." I turned the volume up on my newly installed Bose surround sound system. I revved up the engine and looked around as if I was checking for pedestrians, when in reality I was checking to see who was checking me out.

I hit the convertible button and Sally took off her top, causing people to take notice. I revved up the engine again, looked in my rearview and saw the knock off Beyoncé and her friends look my way. With that, I burned rubber and pulled out. Time to get my fuck on!

CALGON TAKE ME AWAY

AFTER my girls and I left the club, we walked toward Tierra's car. Now I wish we had parked in valet because my feet were killing me. Guess I wasn't used to dancing as much as I did tonight. Probably had something to do with the fact that this was my first time out partying this year.

And to think I didn't even want to go out at first. After a few persuasive comments from Tierra, I agreed to come and actually really enjoyed myself. The only thing that I don't like about going to a club is leaving. That's when guys were in full hunting mode, trying to spit their game, lies, and manipulation on any woman who they thought might be overly intoxicated. I mean guys will grab your hand, clothes, thigh, or ass to try to talk to you. I guess they're just doing what women allow them to do.

Then you have the guys that want to show off what they are driving, rolling their windows down yelling at you, "Aye yo ma, come here." Yeah right, I can't believe women would actually go out into the street and up to their cars. If you want to talk to me, you better get your lazy ass out of that car and come up to me!

What was even worse was when guys just wanted to show off by acting crazy. Like the fool we just saw in a Mustang, revving his engine all loud and burning rubber. I have to admit his car was hot. After a couple of inconspicuous head turns, I was a little disappointed that I didn't see my mystery man after the club.

Even though I had fun tonight, I had to get used to coming home to an empty apartment. Finally, I can relax, I thought as I turned on the hot water in the tub and added bath salts and triple the recommended amount of bubble bath. I loved suds.

It felt good to pull off my smoke-filled clothes. I was only wearing my lace bra and boy cut panties as I walked through my apartment and checked the front door to make sure that it was locked. I then went to the hallway pantry and removed four scented candles, two apple spice and two cherry blossom, to place in the bathroom while I bathed.

I smiled as my nipples hardened, just thinking about Mr. Mystery's lips. I lit the wick to match the fire that was now burning inside of me. I shook my head as I noticed myself hastily doing everything so that I could hop in the tub.

Damn it! I forgot my wine. I briskly walked back to the kitchen to get the half glass of Moscato that I had taken a couple of sips out of earlier before leaving for the club. I also grabbed my purse and noticed the business card almost falling out of the small front pocket.

I debated on whether to take Juwaun up on that call. "What the hell." I placed the purse on my bed, grabbed my phone, and entered the numbers. After turning the water off, I sat on the edge of the tub and contemplated if I should really go through with it. Okay, here goes nothing. I pressed dial.

RING. Should I hang up?

RING. Okay that's two. I looked at the bathroom clock as it read 2:53, and then after the third ring...

"Hello?"

"Um hey, um may I speak to Juwaun?" I asked timidly.

"This is he. May I ask who I'm speaking with?" Juwaun asked in a proper and polite voice.

I sipped on my Moscato and savored its sweet flavor. "You tell me. Oh and I'll give you a hint, I'm one of the women that you met tonight and gave your number to." This ought to be good hearing him ramble through names.

"Wow! Okay, being that I don't normally give my number out and I only saw one woman tonight who I wanted to give it to," he paused for a second, "I'm going to have to say this is Nicole."

Oh no he didn't. I felt my heart drop into my stomach. I can't believe this son of a—

"I'm just playing Angel, I know it's you." He began laughing at his corny joke.

"Mmm hmmm, don't try to change your answer now. You almost got the dial tone."

"You know I was just playing. I'm really glad you called. I was sitting up here waiting for you too."

I smiled. "Were you now? Well, I didn't want to interrupt your after party. I was just calling to let you know that I made it in safely."

"You've just made my night Angel." I heard the voices in his background become faint. He was either removing himself from the after party or they were moving away from him. "And for the record, I'm not busy and you're not interrupting anything. I'll put them all on the back burner for you."

"Awww, that's so sweet. Unfortunately, I'm about to be a little busy. I'm about to soak in the tub before I hit the sack." I knew saying that to a man would automatically pop a picture into his head.

"Bath huh? All by yourself? Now that's no fun. You sure you don't need company?"

"Yes, I'm sure," I said seductively, "and I never told you that I was bathing alone."

He laughed, "Well, I figured if you had a guy there then you wouldn't be calling me this late, especially while you are about to get in the tub."

I made a low moan, "Guess you've never considered the fact that my bathing partner could be a woman… talk to you later Juwaun." While he was stuttering and trying to get in another word I hung up, leaving him wanting more. Sorry Juwaun, but actually I'm not bathing alone. Tonight I'm going to be with my future man.

I sat the phone on the sink and unhooked my bra. I inched my boy shorts down my thighs and to my ankles. I glanced at my manicured landing strip and ran my thumb down it resting it on my love button. The juices inside me began to stir. I stepped into my steamy oasis. It was so hot, just the way I like it.

I laughed at the memory of when my ex-boyfriend, Damien, used to take baths with me and would have to cup his balls because of the water temperature. After squatting down in the relaxing bubbles, I grabbed the glass of wine that sat on the edge of the tub. Ahhh, felt so good. I felt the tiny bubbles bursting on my skin. Chills ran up my neck. The more wine I drank, the more addictive it became.

Flashbacks of the mystery guy staring at me popped up in my head. I wish He were here with me right now, drinking, so I could steal the sweetness off of his palate with my mouth. As I closed my eyes and sank further into the bubbles, I realized what the lady in the Calgon commercial must have felt like.

He looked so intense sitting in the tub in front of me with his legs on the outside of mine. He looked as if lathering his hands with the bar of soap was his profession. The suds dripped down his forearms and plopped into the water as he placed the soap back into its holder.

"Come here baby," he said to me while beckoning with his head for me to scoot closer between his legs. I grabbed my glass of wine again. This sip was so much better than the last. I was caught off guard by the sudden cool, slippery grasping of my breast. Oh my. Although his hands were large and strong, it barely felt like he was applying pressure. Then he sternly grabbed them and kneaded them with his palms.

Yeah! He definitely had to be a professional breast masseur. There was no other explanation for this guy squeezing my twins so good that it gave my asshole contractions. Mmm. I want to feel him there, too. Maybe with his finger, possibly with his dick, but definitely with his tongue.

He went from massaging both breasts to concentrating on my left one, the fuller and more sensitive of the two. "How does that feel baby?" His baritone voice bounced off of the bathroom walls in acoustic surround sound.

"Mmmmm, it feels so good baby, don't stop, please don't stop," I replied.

My pussy was now the Euphrates, the Tigris, the Nile and all the other rivers that I was too horny to remember. I was leaking with no end in sight. I smelled my nectar as it swirled and mixed with the aromas of the candles and the bath salts. I was now drunk off ecstasy.

His thick dick peeked out of the water and suds. It looked so tasty. I cupped it with both of my feet and gently stroked it up and down, feeling his pulse.

"Angel, just being around you always makes my dick so hard."

I giggled and replied, "I see, and just to warn you, you better stop talking in that deep, seductive ass voice or we're going to be bathing in my juices instead of this water." He told me that he liked the sound of that. He's so freaky.

After rinsing my breasts squeaky clean, he began massaging them again, this time with his tongue. Those full lips wrapped around me like a newborn baby. My nipples were so hard, so sensitive. I loved the way he flicked his tongue.

Tonight, my nipples and my clit were related. They were sisters, identical twins, feeling the exact pleasure that the other was feeling. Although he was licking my nipples, it felt like he was licking my clit. My hips had a mind of their own and began shaking and going into short spasms. I felt my orgasm building up fast as if it was a snowball rolling down a snowy mountain. Mmmmmmm. Almost there. Feels so good right before I cum. My breaths were getting short, body started to pop and tick like a break dancer.

I grabbed the back of his neck, "Ooouuu, don't stop, suck'em harder baby, harder, harder. Oh yeah! Here it comes." My volcano had taken all that it could. It was time to let go of all of this hot steamy lava. I started to buck like a bull, "Baby… ba…beeee…I'm…I'm cuummmminnn, ouuu God, I'm cu… sooooo harrrddd!"

My body felt so good, so relaxed, and so limp. Felt like a noodle. I looked at him. He smiled. I blushed, embarrassed by how his face was now covered with water that I splattered on him during my eruption. This guy accomplished more with his mouth on two breasts than most guys could do with a hard dick in a wet pussy. Fucking amazing! I thought as I looked toward the ceiling.

"I love you, Angel."

"I love you too, baby."

And with that, I woke up. I looked around the bathroom. "Damn, where is he?" I asked myself. Where did he go? How long was I in here? The bubbles were gone and so was my wine. I smelled my scent and my pussy was still pulsating. It was time to get out.

I put on my terrycloth bathrobe and walked to my room. After rubbing myself down with cocoa butter, I snuggled under my comforter and shivered at the thought of his mouth on me. If I was a smoker, I would've blazed one up right now.

I smiled thinking about what Brianna told me earlier about the mental threesome she was going to have tonight with my man. I wonder if she's going to replace that little pink rabbit with me in her fantasy. I wonder how a threesome with her in real life would be. I felt my kitty pucker at the thought.

What would Tierra say if she knew that I was thinking like this? Hell, Tierra's freaky ass probably thought about it before too. The only way that Brianna was going to have him was in her dreams, so I hope she enjoys. I hope he does her just as well as he did me tonight. That bastard has sucked me to sleep! This was definitely a first. For some reason, I knew that with him there would be many more firsts to come.

A LITTLE PIECE OF KANDI

"COOL...okay baby, just give me a call when you're on Jefferson...uuhhuuh, can't wait to taste, I mean see you either." Yeah this is going to be fun. I have to make sure everything is perfect. I surveyed my entire loft.

"Damn, my shit is tight!" I've been living in Riverfront Lofts now for about eight months. Before that, I was on the waiting list to get in for a year and a half, and it was well worth it. I mean, females see my place and the panties just fall off.

Another thing that I like about this place is that a lot of movers and shakers live here. On any given day, you could see anyone from high-powered attorneys to Detroit Lions and Tigers players.

"Hmmmmmmm," I let out a loud sigh. This is the life. No woman, no kids, a spectacular view of Canada on one side of my place, and an extravagant outlook of the Detroit skyline on the other. What more could a man want, well besides a piece of Kandi?

I walked around, lit a couple of candles, and then selected a seduction playlist on my entertainment system. My eyes focused in on the bed, which was set up on a platform like a throne. It was my favorite item in the loft.

I took sex seriously. My bed was my boxing ring and there, I was the heavy weight champion. I have defended my title too many times to count without any losses to date. Tonight, I had a worthy opponent. She'll probably hit me with some devastating low blows and in return, I'll stick her below the belt with some stiff jabs of my own.

I did a couple sets of pushups to get the arms and chest pumped. Then I put on my favorite cologne, Ralph Lauren Polo Black. "Down boy, down," I said while rubbing my crotch. "She'll be here soon, be patient." A few minutes later, the call that I was waiting for finally came through. "Hey beautiful!"

"I didn't make you wait too long, did I?"

"Of course not. Where are you?"

"I'm on Jefferson now. What street am I going to again?"

"Joseph Campeau, when you get there, turn right and take that all the way to the last street in front of the river and make a left. You'll see the Riverfront Lofts."

"Riverfront Lofts huh?" she asked sounding impressed, "I see Mr. Future is a baller."

"Who me? Naw," I tried to put on my modest voice, "I'm just a small fry trying to make it."

"Mmm hmmm."

"What are you driving, baby, so I can tell security to let you into the underground garage?"

"Range Rover," she replied.

"Range Rover huh? I see Ms. Kandi is a baller, what color?"

"Red," she responded.

"But of course. Okay, I'll tell him you'll be here for me.

Come up to the 14th floor, my address is 14B."

"Okay, see you in a few."

I have to make sure that I come correct. She just might be worthy enough to earn a spot on my roster.

I surveyed the loft again, called Leroy downstairs at the gate, and waited for the buzzer. It came about five minutes later. It was showtime!

I walked to the door, checked with Buddy, his imprint was showing through my jogging shorts just enough to let me know he was there. I opened the door and smiled. There she was at my spot, Kandi, Ms. Red Dress in the flesh. I looked her over, gave her a hug, and let her in.

"Kandi, wow, you are gorgeous!"

"Why, thank you," she said staring at my crotch with a smile, "you don't look bad yourself. Don't know which I like better, you dressed," as she ran her hand over my chest and down to my abs, "or undressed."

I couldn't take my eyes off of her legs, so luscious. She had on a short trench with big red buttons and had her hair twisted up with one of those long Chinese hairpins. And to top it all off she wore those sexy ass red heels that I saw her in earlier.

"Where are my manners, let me take your jacket."

She untied her trench slowly and unbuttoned it even slower. It felt as if she was unwrapping a gift for me. After she took the trench off, I definitely felt like it was my birthday.

She was wearing only a low cut bra and matching cheeky thong set. Of course, they were red as well. Her body was flawless. Flat stomach, small waist, nice thick legs, and a juicy ass. "Mmmm, mmmm, mmmm," were the only words that escaped my mouth as I took her coat and laid it on the couch.

Buddy was at full attention.

"Mmmm, I like those shorts, Future. Come over here to me baby."

I cannot lie; not knowing what she was capable of made me feel a little timid. I walked closer to her, poking straight out while admiring her pose. She definitely knew what she was doing. I wasn't fucking with some girl. This was indeed a woman.

She grabbed Buddy through my shorts and used him as a handle bar to steer me in closer. "What a thick dick you have," she said stroking me through my shorts.

"The better to fuck you with, my dear," I replied. That set her off. She devoured my mouth and held my tongue hostage. She tasted so sweet, like butterscotch. She aggressively pulled me toward the bed.

One thing was for sure. Kandi was definitely proud of her body. I have had women who seemed to be very confident while they were clothed but as soon as their clothes dropped to the floor, they would dive for the covers or want all of the lights off. Some of the tightest women seemed to have the lowest self-esteem, but not her, she wanted me to see her, and I liked that.

"Baby you've had me horny from the first time I saw you tonight at the club." She raised her knee and propped her foot on my bed. "Feel my pussy baby, feel how wet you've made me."

I was still standing behind her so I reached my hand up under her raised leg and put my fingers inside her thong. "Damn Kandi, you weren't lying about being horny huh?" Her pussy was literally dripping. My fingers were quickly saturated with her juices. "I want you baby, want to drink every last drop of you," I whispered in her ear from behind. She had my dick throbbing and I couldn't wait to get inside of her.

"Future, I have to tell... you something." She maneuvered my fingers, taking control of how she wanted me to stroke her. "How wet you feel me now," she let out a slow moan, "is nothing baby. I... mmmmm, I get embarrassingly wet. Are you okay with that?"

"What, are you kidding? Am I okay with that?" I asked, surprised at the question. "Kandi, I don't know who you are used to fucking with, but right now," I gave her two quick pecks on her neck, "you're fucking with a freak. So of course I'm okay with that."

"Okay Daddy, I warned you. Mmmmm, keep your fingers in me. Mmmmm, yeah like that." I loved a talker.

"You like that baby?" I asked, not believing how incredibly wet she was getting. Her juices were now dripping down the palm of my hand.

"Mmmm, I love it. Finger me harder Future. Ooouuu yeah, put another finger in me."

"You are so wet, damn!" I accompanied my ring and middle fingers with my index.

"Harder Future, harder!" Kandi demanded.

I was really turned on now. Her juices were now running towards my wrist. I started to remove my fingers, but it seemed as though her moist, fleshy cave didn't want to release them.

The more I inched them out the tighter her pussy muscles clinched. It reminded me of when I was a kid and we used to play with this device made out of paper called the Chinese finger cuffs. It was easy as hell to slide your finger in, but removing them was an entirely different story.

I was brought out of my recollection by her beckoning moans. I ran my tongue under her shoulder blade. My tongue spiraled up towards her neck leaving a trail of saliva that sparkled from the candles that I had previously lit.

"Ooouuu right there! That's the spot. Stay there Future." Kandi's body swerved as if she was a snake.

I removed my fingers all the way from her now throbbing pussy and smiled as it made a small popping noise. I used one of my saturated fingers to replace my tongue and traced over the spots that I had just licked. It was only right for me to add her flavor and her spices. I couldn't wait to suck the moistness off.

My finger and mouth traded places again and I fed my other two fingers to her. I figured there was no need to be stingy. Since she made the delectable treat, I had to share it with her. The noises she made let me know that she was one cook who enjoyed her own cooking. She licked and sucked every drop, turning me on even more. I moved my tongue down her spine towards her thong.

"Bend over, Kandi," I said low and demanding, "let me see that ass." When she complied, I had no choice but to take a couple of steps back and be her one-man audience. Shit! I really felt like applauding. Her booty was incredible. She moved it slowly like a snake charmer and had my King Cobra at full attention. I saw her plump rump from the back and was obedient when it told me to come and get it. Yep! It was dinner time, and I was going to put my entire face in the plate.

I knelt down behind her and moved my face a couple of inches towards her. Her scent was strong and sweet. I inhaled and held her in my lungs.

Her juices were smeared between her thighs and ass. When I grabbed her cheeks and spread them apart, I saw the eye of the storm, the center and source of this flood.

"Your pussy is so fucking pretty, woman," I whispered.

"Taste me baby. Taste this pretty pink pussy," Kandi said now arching her back more.

I dove in face first into the cream pie. I savored her taste as I tongued, flicked, and sucked her. I made slurping noises as I put both of my lips around her juicy clit. I grabbed her thighs and pulled her closer to me. My nose slightly rubbed up against her slit. I couldn't get enough of her honey. I still needed more. Removing my face from her pussy, I looked at her puckering asshole. I gave it a quick lick.

"You want me there baby?" I asked as I teased her second hole with my tongue. "Hmm, do you want me to suck that ass like I did your pussy?"

"Please baby, stop teasing. Put your mouth on it. Suck my ass. Please suck it!" Her voice had turned into a slow and soft whine as she begged me to lick her ass. I had her now. I sucked then licked, then licked then sucked. She was mine for the moment. Tonight this pussy and ass belonged to me.

"Whose shit is this Kandi, huh? Tell me, whose ass is it?" I asked, in between slurps.

"It's yours Future, I'm all yours. Your tongue feels so fucking good." Kandi was winding her ass all in my face, speeding up her intensity and cluing me that she was getting closer to blast off.

"Future!"

"Yes baby?" I responded, still slurping away.

"You remember when I said that I get really wet?"

"Mmmm hmmmm, I see. Tastes so good."

"Well it," she continued trying to talk in between her moans and groans, "it gets worse when I cum."

"No baby, better. You getting wet is not bad at all." I removed my face for a moment so I wouldn't sound too muffled. "I love it. No matter how wet you get, so keep it coming. Don't worry, no matter how wet you get, I'm not going to cum fast if that's what you're worried about. It just ain't happening. You are going to be totally satisfied when I'm done with you."

"I don't want to hold back any more. I want to let loose for you."

"That's what I'm talking about Kandi, be my freak, be… my," I didn't even finish my statement. I went right back to dining, doing figure eights, swirls, and circles. My tongue was figure skating in the pussy and she loved every minute.

"Ooouuu, Fu…baby I'm cumming, I'm…cu…minnnnngg, ohhshiiiit!"

I really went into semi-shock when I felt my face being sprayed by her pussy. At first I thought she R. Kelly-ed me! But after no piss smell and seeing it gush out more, I realized that Ms. Kandi was like the women in some of the pornos that I own. Kandi was indeed a squirter and my first one at that. Damn, I used to jack off to shit like this now it's right here in my face, literally! I was hooked. As a matter of fact, I'll take another order of that. Give me all you've got.

"Kandi?"

"I'm sorry, I tried to tell you," she said now, stiff as a board.

"Tell me, what the fuck do I have to do to make you do that again?"

We both laughed and she loosened back up. "I see that I'm dealing with a freak. I think I'm going to have to keep you around for a while." I chuckled because her statement was something that I would say. Shit, actually I was thinking the same about her.

I stood up and we were now facing each other. She licked her juices from around my mouth like a kitty cat. Then she placed her thumbs in the elastic waistband of my shorts and pulled them all the way down. While taking a seat on the bed, she held my dick as if she was examining and admiring it at the same time.

"I must say, Future," she said as she stared at Buddy, "this is the first time that I can truly say that I'm looking at a pretty ass dick." I laughed out loud, not because of what she said, but because I got that comment or something similar a lot. "I mean, it's so smooth," she continued, "and even toned and so…so thick, damn! It's…perfect." She wrapped her small hands around my girth struggling to get her fingers to reach around it. "So…so thick." She seemed to put emphasis on her k's, making the back of her tongue pop off of the roof of her mouth. "And the head looks like one of those giant blow pops." I laughed and smiled at Buddy, women loved him, and they always complimented. "Your length, the girth…geeez! I don't think I've ever seen a dick that makes me crave to suck it like yours do."

Kandi was now making my other head feel big. She moved her face closer to my dick then closer and closer and just when I thought she would take it in her mouth; she went on the side of it and looked towards the floor. What the hell is she doing?

She kept a tight grip on Buddy as she came back up with her

thong in her other hand. She released me and said, "I promise this won't hurt, you'll like it."

At this point I probably would've done just about anything that she wanted me to do. Teach me, Mami. She stretched the thong around Buddy and tied a loose knot, pushing it all the way back to the base.

"Does that hurt?" she asked. "It's not too tight is it?"

"Naw it's cool. Now what is this supposed—"

"Shhhh," she whispered, placing her index finger on my lips to quiet me.

Okay, maybe she had a dick decorating fetish. But after a few seconds, I realized that Kandi wasn't an arts and crafts teacher at all. Instead, she proved more to be an architect. She had just created a sexy lace cock ring that made my dick head bigger than I have ever seen it. Buddy was pulsating so hard it looked as if it was a puppet on a string. I'd never felt Buddy this hard before, ever.

She sat back and smiled, obviously proud of her invention and its accomplishments. "Now, my turn to eat," she said, licking her lips. The way she handled my dick with her mouth was nothing short of astonishing. She had me backing away from her in retreat only to have her grab my ass and pull me right back.

She did everything that I liked, deep throated, used lots of spit and slob and she made slurps and gagging noises. Yeah, she was a pro.

She had my toes and fingers clenched and made tears form in the corner of my eyes by flicking her tongue on a spot under my head. She slowly pulled her mouth away from me, inch by inch leaving her DNA behind. Damn my head was huge. I have to try this trick with my other chicks, I thought, making a mental note to myself.

"And don't be using my trick on your other little hoes either," she said seeming to read my mind. "Now come on baby. Put it in me. Fill me up with that big, fat dick." I started to untie the thong when she said, "Don't you dare. You're not about to rob me of that." Guess I was still in the learning phase.

She crawled up on the bed close to my headboard, bent over, and arched her ass perfectly in the air. I hated when you had to tell a chick, "Bend down a little more," or, "Baby, arch your back more." I looked at that pretty pussy of hers and noticed that it was leaking again. I could only imagine what it felt like inside of her.

She turned her face toward my closet. "Future," she called me as I looked at her face lying sideways on my pillow.

"Yeah baby, what is it?"

"Are those ties that I see in your closet?"

I remembered the fetish that she told me about at the club earlier and instantly became more excited. "Those would be ties."

"Satin?" she asked with excitement in her voice.

"Yep, satin," I said, with a proud grin.

"Bring mama two of them." I jumped out of the bed, excited for my next lesson with Kandi. If I had known that my Kenneth Cole ties would be used for sex games, I probably wouldn't have complained about the price. Shit, probably would have bought more.

She propped herself up on her knees and instructed me to secure a tie around each of her wrists. I was eagerly awaiting her next instructions. Here I am thinking that I was the man and Kandi kept coming up with shit that made me feel like an amateur.

She had me tie the loop ends to the adjacent bedposts. Her arms weren't long enough to reach and grab the posts, so she wrapped some of the slack in her hand and held on for leverage.

She looked so intense and horny. I could really tell that she loved this kinky shit. "I have just one more request baby," she said looking back at me with a serious gaze.

"Anything for you. What is it?"

"Fuck the shit out of me...now!"

I opened my nightstand drawer ripped open the gold foiled condom, slid it on, and mounted up. My dick head was kissing her lips causing her to squirm with anticipation. When I entered her, I entered bliss, euphoria, ecstasy. Her pussy was so tight. Every time I stroked out her pussy gripped me, when I pushed in she opened up.

Her pussy juices had now changed from that clear sweet nectar, to tart thick cream. Mmmmm, that's that shit you had to go deep inside to get and I loved searching for it. I tried to reach her stomach.

"Fuck me, oh shit, fuck me!" she cried out. And I did. I mean, I was pounding the fuck out of her pussy. Wrapping my arms under her, squeezing her supple breasts, running my fingers through her hair, licking her ear, kissing the sides of her face, all while I pounded.

"Don't you...dare... stop fucking me! Don't...stop, fuck me harder!" Kandi demanded.

I looked at my ties, stretched to capacity and made a mental note to write the company a letter complimenting them on the durability of their fabric.

"Here it comes, baby, right there, keep...it right, therrrre, ooouuu!" Her kitty spewed again, this time more than the first. I looked at the evidence of her being a squirter on my thighs, stomach, and dick. She had made a huge ass puddle on my sheets. I stopped stroking and kept still, I wanted to feel each contraction.

She took a couple of deep breaths to recoup and asked me to untie her. "Lie down, Future," she demanded as she caught her breath. I did and she climbed on top, squatting down on me, slowly, making sure that I felt all of her and that she felt all of me.

She leaned forward and kissed me passionately. I closed my eyes and savored her tongue. When I opened them I squinted to make sure what I was seeing was true.

Is this a fucking trick? It was...Her. The girl from the club, and she had switched places with Kandi. She had her hand on my chest as she rode me steadily. Then cupped her bouncing titties, looked me in the eyes and said, "Future, I love you."

"What did you say?" I asked blinking hard. Now Kandi had taken her original spot. I think I'm going crazy. I thought that maybe she spiked my drink, but ruled that out because I haven't had anything since the club. Maybe it's something in that pussy juice that I was drinking so much of earlier.

"I said, I love the way your dick fills me up," she answered. I held on to her thighs and she directed me to squeeze her nipples. "Mmmmm, yeah, like that. Squeeze them harder, ooouuu shit, baby I'm...cumming again." And cum she did. Kandi's explosion sent her liquids dripping down my thighs and onto the sheets.

She held on to my chest and leaned her head back, riding out her orgasm. When she sat up, her face wasn't Kandi's. It was the mystery woman from the club again. I was hoping that this moment was real. I wanted this to be her so bad. I saw her face, her complexion, and her sexy ass haircut. She definitely had her hooks in me.

"Future, do you want me?" she asked, running her fingers through her short do.

"Of course I do, I wanted you from the moment that I laid eyes on you," I responded.

She continued to stare at me. "This night is so perfect, we fit so perfect. It's like...like we're made for each other."

"I feel the exact same way," I said closing my eyes, feeling like I was in heaven.

"What was that baby, you feel what?" Kandi looked at me with a bit of concern on her face, which made me realize I had zoned out again. I have to make up something fast.

"Um, I was just saying that I feel...like...I never want this session to end." That got her smiling again and back to riding. After about five more minutes she came, squirted, and fell limp on my chest.

I held her and played in her hair for a few minutes. I thought she was going to at least try to stay for a while or do what most women do that are privileged enough to come over, try to stay the night. But Kandi was nowhere near most women.

"Mmm, you were good baby, makes me want to fuck you all night, but," she said as she dismounted me, "I think I better get going."

"Going?" I asked sitting straight up in the bed, "What's the rush? What about round two?" I looked down at my stiff rod. "What about my nut? I haven't even cum yet," I said pointing down at Buddy who was pointing back up at me.

"Oh, I'm sorry baby. You want me to jack that off for you before I leave?"

What the fuck? Jack me off? I can do that my damn self. After all of the orgasms I just gave you? "Naw, I'm good. I don't want to hold you up." Maybe my sarcasm will make her reconsider leaving.

"Thanks, Future. I knew you would understand," she said as she continued to get dressed. I started to get a little pissed. She was really acting as if I just didn't fuck the shit out of her.

Kandi put on her heels and walked back towards me. She leaned in and gave me a quick peck on the lips. "Thanks for the good time. You were pretty good!" she said as she smacked me on the ass.

Pretty good? Now I'm tripping for real. Maybe I'm reading too much into this, but I swear this chick sounded a lot like me. I can't believe she tapped me on the ass like I'm a little bitch!

"Guess I'll talk to you later," were the last words that I heard from Kandi before I shut the door behind her. I haven't felt like this in a long time. I usually get praised for fucking women better than they have ever been fucked. Kandi was kind of making me feel as if the shit she was saying during sex was just shit that she was saying during sex. Maybe, that's just her defense mechanism. Yeah that's it; she's probably trying to protect herself from falling for me.

My cell phone beeped and vibrated on the kitchen counter letting me know that I had a text message. I smiled as I walked with my chest out. "Must have come to your senses, huh girl?" I said as I pressed enter and saw Kandi's name appear. I grinned to myself and read her text.

Thanx again 4 da orgazmz ba, I'LL CALL U again when I get horny ☺.

There were two things wrong with this text. The first thing was for the most part the entire text was in lower case letters all except for I'LL CALL U, as in "Don't call me for ass, I'll call you when I'm in need of some dick." The second problem is the fucking smiley face at the end. It was almost like she was laughing at me or something and I really don't see shit funny.

I slammed my phone down and walked to the bathroom to start the shower. It's time to get this woman's aura off of me. I was standing in front of the mirror looking at myself. Look at you, she should be thinking about you not the other way around. I don't even know why I'm tripping on her anyway. Even worse than that, I really don't know why this other woman keeps popping up in my head. Especially while I was focused on banging another someone else. And why am I standing in front of this mirror with a hard-on starting to jack off?

"Shit! Fuck you Kandi!"

MR. TELEPHONE MAN

IT's been three days since my girls and I went out on the town and partied it up. It has also been three days since my imaginary session in the tub with a guy that I haven't even officially met yet. My orgasm that night was so good and so strong that not touching myself every time that I bathe or shower is a constant struggle.

I'm not ashamed of the fact that I pleasure myself quite often. No one can satisfy me like me, but I have never thought about fucking or pleasuring myself as much as I have since seeing Him.

I feel so pathetic that I have to resort to masturbating to thoughts of a make-believe knight in shining armor who doesn't know me from doodle squat. I can't believe that I actually thought about my ex, Damien, yesterday. I can't wait until I move out of this apartment. I still have about three more months until I can move into my brand new condo and it can't come soon enough. There are just too many memories locked up in here and most of them are bad.

Like the way I found out that Damien was sleeping with his ex or baby momma or whatever she was. I guess she wanted me to know that his dick still belonged to her so bad that she decided to leave me a note. A note folded up so tiny that only a woman who does laundry and checks even the smallest of pockets would find it.

I shook my head remembering unfolding the note. She wrote, *Hey bitch! While you're washing your so-called man's pants make sure you soak his draws. I know you probably want to get the smell of my pussy off of them. He forgot to wash me off him this time, oops. P.S. sniff and enjoy.*

She was so articulate and well spoken, I wondered if she ever considered becoming an author. I tried everything in my power not to do the scratch and sniff test that she requested but somehow curiosity got the best of me and sure enough, I smelled what remained from hot stinky sex.

We were pretty much over even before that incident but that was the breaking point. I knew that I couldn't live with him and pretend any longer. There wasn't a need to do any more questioning. He had to go. Which brings me to where I am now. Lonely! A book I have read too many times, the story of my life.

Monday's were usually rough for me at work, since it was one of our slow days it gave me too much time to reflect on the past and I definitely didn't want to be there. I also had to get my mind readjusted from the weekend, which also was a hard task for me. Surprisingly, thoughts about Sexy Chocolate from the club guided me to lunchtime with little effort. Hell, it has also raised my horny meter to eight with little effort as well.

While reading my magazine in the lunchroom, a voice from out of nowhere startled me. "Hey Angel! What's up?"

"Nothing much, just sitting here finishing up my lunch." I glanced up at Darnell and went back to reading my article.

"Um, yeah speaking of lunch... I know I was out of line for disrespecting your relationship by continuing to ask you out, but now—"

I cut in, "Darnell."

"I realize that, it's your life and if you—"

"Darnell," I called out his name again but he kept talking.

"...choose to stay with him, then that's your business."

"Dar...nellll!" I called louder this time.

"Yeah, what's up?"

"We broke up," I calmly said and continued reading my Essence magazine and sipping my vitamin water. There was an uncomfortable silence as he stood behind me. I knew he was a little happy because he'd been trying to get at me for a while now.

Darnell was my co-worker. We both work for Charter One Bank, just in different departments.

We met about two years ago in one of the cafeterias in the Charter One Technical Center and have been cool ever since. He asked me out several times, but we never went out together alone. In fact, we only saw each other outside of work when someone at the bank would have a party or a get together. But he let me know from day one that he was digging me. I turned him down and let him know every time that while I'm in a relationship there was no cheating, well, at least on my behalf. I admit that I was wrong for telling him some of my business. It's not good telling people that you're having trouble with your man, especially when it's a guy and he happens to like you. It figures though that when I'm actually looking for male company he would stop offering.

"You...you, y'all broke up? Wow! Um, I'm sorry to hear that."

I snickered, "Boy please! You know that you're not sorry to hear that, so stop playing."

"Yeah, you're right," we both laughed. "So are you okay?"

I continued looking in my magazine, "Mmm hmm, actually I'm doing pretty good." My response was followed by more uncomfortable silence. "So, does the offer still stand?"

"Offer?" Darnell asked, sounding and looking confused.

"Yeah, the lunch offer."

"Oh, yeah, sure, of course it stands." Before Darnell was so confident, but the discovery of the breakup seemed to have thrown him off his game a little. "So what are you reading?" It seemed like he didn't know whether to back off or to pick up where he left off a while ago.

"Essence, it's a good article too." I placed a marker on my page and closed the magazine. "Let me ask you a question. What do you think about consensual, no strings attached sex?"

"Wow, um, I think uh, it's a great thing."

"Do you think that women can actually commit to that?"

Darnell looked at me as if he was choosing his next words carefully. "My personal opinion, I don't think most women can, but if they could, I think it's all good." He flashed a smile.

I looked up at him and smiled back, "That's your kinda woman huh?"

"I didn't say all that."

I twisted my lips to the side, "Mmm hmm, so what's up? When are you going to be ready?"

"For the lunch date or the consensual sex?" he asked playfully.

I went back to looking at the Essence article and replied, "Both."

More uncomfortable silence. "Saturday, is Saturday cool for you?"

"Yep, Saturday's perfect." At first, I was just saying both to play with his mind, but when I noticed that he thought I was serious, I went along with it. I needed dick; he has a dick, that's supply and demand at its finest.

As we continued semi-entertaining each other with a little more small talk, I studied his physique, hands, and feet. They were a nice size I guess. I know that doesn't really matter when it comes to the size of a man's dick, but at least he should have good balance and be able to get a good grip on a sista's ass. I felt my kitty twitch a little at the thought.

His lips were okay. Not as big as I like, but okay. He should definitely be able to kiss the twins decently. He was a little stocky, not fat, not muscular but solid. I discreetly checked out his crotch area to size up the bulge. Looked okay, couldn't really tell but I could see a little something. Overall, I think I could do him.

It was about time for me to get back to work, so I gave Darnell my number and told him if I didn't see him before Friday to call me and let me know what time to be ready Saturday. I also thought about my exit strategy just in case Saturday was a disaster. If push came to shove, this building had four lunchrooms and if I needed to, I could avoid him all together.

The thought of me finally getting some sex made the rest of my day scurry along quite nicely. Lord please let it be worth my while and while you are at it, please let Saturday hurry up and get here. I am so desperate, can't believe I'm asking God for his help in getting some sex. I'm going to hell! At least I'm not going to be horny when I get there.

After work, I called Tierra to see if she was home. She lived in Belleville, which was only 10 minutes from where I worked. I wanted to stop by to fill her in on my upcoming weekend.

"Hello."

"What's up Tierra?" I responded, surprised that she answered on the first ring.

"Nothing much, girl. Just getting off of the phone with this guy I met from the club the other night."

"Oh for real? I didn't see you exchange numbers with any guys."

"Exactly! You know I be in stealth mode girl, I have to keep my options open. If you didn't see me chances are other guys didn't either," Tierra replied.

"You are too much. What are you about to get into? I'm a couple of minutes from your place."

"Come on over, I'm not doing anything, just folding clothes. Hurry up so I can tell you about my new boy toy!" There was always a new boy toy with Tierra.

"Okay, see you in a few," I said before hanging up. I couldn't wait to hear about Tierra's sexcapades, they were always good.

After parking, I went up the stairs of her apartment complex and knocked on the door.

"Tierrrrraaaa!"

"Angellllll!" We always exaggerated our excitement for seeing each other. "I missed you so much, hoe."

"Me too, trick," I replied matching her overzealous tone. We hugged each other and erupted in laughter.

"Come in the living room so I can finish folding these clothes. For the record I'm not a trick. They pay for ass. I get paid. Please don't get it twisted. I'm a hoe, duhhhh!"

"My bad, how could I ever get the two confused? So tell me about this new one."

"Girrrrl, oh my god! He came over Saturday, right," I shook my head at the notion of her bringing someone home after only knowing them for one night. After the mood that I've been in lately I better not speak too fast. "I know, I know, I'm a slut. But I don't see any reason why I can't act on it if I see a guy and I'm physically attracted to him. I mean, it's not like they're gaming me or tricking me into sex. Hell most of the time it's the other way around. I can't help it though, I'm a freak and I love dick. Mmm can't get enough." I gave her a look that told her that she didn't have to explain anything to me. "Damn Angel, shut up so I can finish my story."

"But I didn't—"

"Anyways," she continued not paying attention to my plea, "by far, this was the biggest dick I have ever attempted to fuck. It actually made me gasp and catch my breath when I first saw it."

"Wow!"

"Exactly what I said. I'm talking Lexington Steele big."

"Damn Tee, that's damn near 11 inches." One thing I learned from my ex is the names of all the black porno dudes. He had a collection of flicks that we would watch. I held my hands approximately a foot apart to get a better view. "You took all that?"

"Well, not exactly all of it, but I did my best. And for the record, I think it was closer to 12. I lubed up very well too, but it still felt like he was going to tear me a new pussy at first."

"Ouch," I giggled.

"That's what I said in the beginning, ouch! But in the end, he had me saying ohhhhh ooouuu! It took a while to loosen up but when I did, your girl took that pole like a trooper."

"You go girl," I said giving her five, "you sure your ass hasn't done any porn while you are talking about him?"

"I mean, homemade personal ones, nothing professional," she responded nonchalantly. "You can borrow some if you want."

"You are really something else." Tierra was my best friend no matter what and how she thought. I knew I wasn't as promiscuous as she was, but sometimes I wished I could do things that she did and not worry as much.

One thing that has remained consistent with all of these stories that Brianna and I have heard is that there has never been a bad fuck. Sometimes the guys show their crazy side afterwards and make Tierra wish that she never slept with them but as far as the act, always perfect or better than. Never a small dick, never a skinny one, she always came at least twice, and the guy lasts all night long. Now, I'm not saying that my girl is exaggerating, but damn! At least let a bitch know that you are human. I guess it's no wonder why so many woman have all these unsatisfactory sex stories, it's because Tierra is doing all the good ones.

"How many times did you cum?" I asked.

"Shit, I lost count after four." It figures. Must be nice to be her. She has to be the luckiest woman in the world when it came to choosing sex partners. "He wanted to come back again tonight, but I told him I need a five day coochie break from his Mandingo ass."

"Well I'm glad that one of us is getting some. I need to

call Brianna to see if she hooked up with anyone from this weekend." That statement made me automatically think about if Brianna and Mr. Mystery really did exchange numbers and she just didn't tell me. I felt my face frowning a little and tried to straighten it before Tierra noticed.

"Angel, you okay?"

"Yeah, I'm good."

"You were starting to look a little down over there. Oh, and I talked to Bri, she ain't getting any either. Still making her transition from twat to cock."

"Well, I guess Brianna's about to be by herself because come this weekend I'm going to be in the hoe club, right along with you girl." I raised my hand to give a high five.

"Hoe club?" Tee cracked up laughing. "You are crazy. Are you trying to tell me that you are about to get you some? You," she asked, pointing in my direction, "are about to get some? Are you going back to baby daddy?"

"Hell naw, I'm not that desperate. It's this guy from my job who's been trying to get at me for a while. I basically told him I don't want any strings attached. Just two adults getting together and whatever happens, happens."

Tierra started making sniffling noises, as if she was crying. "Angel, I am so proud of you. You are going to be just like me in no time."

"Please, that's what I'm afraid of. I know one thing, Darnell better come with it because I'm on about a five month drought and I just got off of my period so you know that I'm super horny."

"Dang Angel, don't hurt the poor guy. You have a lot of pent up energy huh?"

"Naw, it's not that bad. I've been cumming, just not with a real dick." That made us both laugh. Tierra told me to make sure that I filled her in on all of the details. She is such a freak. Before I left, she also made sure to ask about our progress with Juwaun Jones. That's my girl.

I called Brianna on my way home to see how her week had been going.

"Hey, mami."

"What up, Bri Bri, I see you lost my phone number huh."

"Absence makes the heart grow fonder, you know that. I wanted to make you miss me more," she said snickering.

"Whatever, tell me anything."

"How was work?" she asked.

"It was cool. You know I just came from over Tierra's."

"Oh Lord, did she tell you about Super Dick?"

"You know she did."

"I think Tierra must get her men from the planet Perfect Penis, because the bitch has never had a bad fuck."

I started laughing loudly, "That is so crazy because when she was telling me the story I was thinking the same exact thing."

"Must be nice," Bri exhaled.

"Must be. Look, I need your advice on something. I'm going to stop by for a few."

"I'll be here," she told me before hanging up.

About 15 minutes later, I pulled up in Brianna's driveway. After stepping in, we did our usual hellos and hugs before I sat on the couch and vented.

"I'm kind of new at this and I feel like a little inexperienced kid. I've never had a one-night stand, but now with no man, I'm horny as fuck and I just want a sex partner ASAP. If it turns into something later, then fine. If it doesn't then that's fine too. But, for now, I just want to fuck. Is that wrong?" I let out a long exhale.

"Wow, what the…wow! Baby, where is all this…what happened since the last time I saw you?" We both laughed.

"I set up a little lunch slash booty call for this weekend. I know, I'm bad…right?" I asked timidly.

"I don't think so at all. Men do it all the time. I don't think you have to be in a relationship to have sex," Brianna softly laughed at me, "you are so eighties girl. Go out and get you some. Just be safe that's all. That's what sex is made for, enjoyment, entertainment—"

"Babies!" I said cutting her off.

She laughed, "I did say be safe. Live a little."

"Yeah, yeah you're right. I'm going to have me some fun for a change."

"So who is the lucky guy? Anyone we know? Is it the guy from the club?"

"Guy from the club? Naw girl, he wanted to do you more than he wanted to do me."

"Don't tell me it's Juwaun," she said smiling as bright as the sun. My girls were more excited about the football star than I was.

"No, not Juwaun! It's a guy from work."

"Oh okay, well good luck with that."

"Thanks I guess," I replied. "So how you holding up with your ex-relationship situation?"

"Guess I'm okay. She keeps calling trying to get me back." Brianna walked in her kitchen and opened the fridge. "You want a glass of wine?"

"What do you have?"

"Girl, please!" she yelled sounding muffled from having her head in the refrigerator door. "I'm a wine-o; the question is what don't I have."

"I see you're like me. Just give me a half glass of whatever you are having."

"Toasted Head, it is. You know Angel, I think I can say that I'm truly done with her. I can't deal with the stress anymore."

Brianna handed me my half-filled glass of wine. "Damn Bri, when I ask for a half glass I really mean three-fourths, duh." I took a sip of the champagne colored wine. "Mmmm, this is good. So, you never get the sexual itch?"

"Ughhh," she said sitting next to me on the couch, "that sounds so nasty, sexual itch?"

"You know what I mean, urges?"

"Of course, I do. As you know Angel, you never want sex more than when you're single. You realize how good that shit is when you're not getting it any more. I'm going to have to do something quick because this is one bitch who loves getting her clit sucked. Dildos and bullets can't do that. There is nothing like a set of lips and a tongue."

"Wow!" I said in between sips.

"Well it's true," she said sipping her drink. "Don't try to act like you never thought about sucking a clit," she joked. Well, I think she was joking.

"Ughhh! You are so nasty. I have never thought about that. I'm strictly dickly baby." I thought of a dream that I had awhile back where another female was performing oral sex on me. I do remember vividly that I enjoyed it because when I awoke, I was soaked between the legs.

"Well you are missing out because I get both, but right now

I think I need a guy. Should've hooked up with cutie from the club," she said barely loud enough for me to hear.

Now I was alert and curious. What didn't she tell me about him? "What guy?" I asked trying to sound as dumbfounded as possible.

"You know that one handsome piece of man that bought us the drinks. Damn what was his name again? It was something funny, strange. I was a little tore up that night because I was supposed to masturbate with him on my mind but instead sleep took over."

"I wish I had seen him," I said.

"I thought you…you know what, maybe you didn't. I think I told you something like, I thought you two would make a good couple when I brought your drink. But he didn't come with me he had stayed off to the side."

I looked towards the ceiling as if in deep thought. "I don't remember, but why did you say we would make a good match and not you two?"

"Even though he's yummy looking, he also had that little bit of edge, not a thug but a little bit of a bad boy. I like that too, but when I first saw him and we started talking, I automatically thought about you."

"Look at you," I said smiling, "acting like you know me."

"It's true. I know both of my girls all too well. So when are we going out again? I had so much fun Friday."

"Me too, I forgot what hanging out with my girls was like."

"So what do you have up for the rest of the day?" Brianna asked, taking our empty glasses to the kitchen.

"Oh nothing much, going home to relax awhile before going to the gym."

"That's where I need to be headed. You see how big my booty is getting. I can barely fit in any of my jeans. It's like everything I eat travels a direct pipeline to my booty cheeks," she giggled while running her hands across her ass.

"You are crazy, and ever since I've known you, you've had ass. I don't see guys complaining. They're drawn to it like ants to sugar."

Brianna sighed, "Yeah, they are aren't they. But, now it's getting wider than I would like and a little soft. Not like yours. Yours sit up so perfect, so plump and firm." I don't know if it was just me or the fact that I know my friend is bisexual, but every time she would give me a compliment, she would go into such detail like she really was studying me. It made me a little uncomfortable during the early stages of our relationship, but now I try not to think anything of it. Now I take her compliments as just that, compliments. "I'll trade my ass for yours any day," she continued.

I tried to downplay my best asset. "Well you let me know when you want to make that swap because guys don't flock to my ass like they do to yours."

"They do, you were just too wrapped up to notice." I thought about how deep I was into my ex, and even if guys would've noticed me or my ass Brianna was right, I probably wouldn't have noticed. "Well if you get a chance, call me later," she said following me to the door. We said our goodbyes, hugged and I headed home.

While driving, I rambled through my memory of all my exes. When I was 16, my first boyfriend cheated on me with my best friend because I wouldn't have sex with him and she would and did. The boyfriend I had in my senior year of high school broke up with me because I didn't have sex with him on prom night. Quan, the boyfriend I had when I first attended college was the first one to break the cheating trend, with a woman that is. Yep, he left the door to his apartment unlocked one day and I walked in on him giving a guy head better than I ever have. That brings me to Damien, who took my virginity at the tender age of 22. Along with my virginity, he took my heart and threw it down the drain. I really thought that I was in love with him and after dating for a short time, I had made up in my mind that he wasn't going to be another guy who would cheat on me for not having sex. But I guess that didn't matter, because even though we had sex often, it never stopped him from cheating.

Maybe it was my fault. Maybe they just didn't like me. Whatever the case, I'm definitely not ready for another emotional roller coaster. From now on, no emotions were going to be involved. No more pushover. When I get horny, I'm going to get my thirst quenched and that's it! No guy is worth my tears. Thoughts of the one guy who might have been my last hope crept in. Nope, I thought to myself, not even you.

I sat back and tried to relax as I cruised down Wayne Road towards home. I turned the volume up on the radio when I realized Michael Baisden's radio show, *Love, Lust. and Lies*, was on. I was flipping through the radio one day about two months ago, trying to find something interesting when I stumbled onto this show. I've been hooked ever since. He was your typical egotistical man, but I still loved his show. The conversation topics always ended up in a battle of the sexes.

"Hey, what up family, this is Michael Baisden. Mr. Baisden if you're nasty. If you are just tuning in, today we are asking the question, are there any good men left? Where are the good men ladies? Do you have one? Do you know one? And hell do you even want one? Fellas, if you are one, hit me up."

I laughed at the topic and said, "Hell naw there ain't none," at the top of my lungs.

"Hello, Tomeka from Baltimore how is everythang?"

"Everythang is everythang, Mike," the caller shouted out Michael's trademark response for the show.

"And what do you have to say on the topic?"

"I have to say hell nawwwwww there is not a such thing as a good man! They are all liars, cheaters, and dogs!"

"Wait a minute Tomeka," Michael cut in, "you mean to tell me that you are just going to generalize all men like that?"

"Hell yeah, I am. If the shoe fits then wear it."

"You tell him girl," I shouted from inside my car.

"I mean, at first I used to think it was just the brothers, until I dated a white guy and he did the same thing. All men are dogs and I say they need to be neutered!" Tomeka shouted.

"Cut it off!" I yelled out again. "Snip, snip!" I laughed at myself as I made my two fingers into a pair of scissors.

"Oh hell naw," Michael exaggerated his displeasure, "so now you playing dirty? Okay I see now that you want to hit below the belt."

"Whatever," Tomeka was getting extra ghetto now, "y'all play dirty all the time. I don't see what's so hard about keeping your peckers in your pants. Just keep it zipped up."

"Girl, you have my phone lines buzzing! You hold on right there. Let me get my next caller and see if they agree with you. Wait a minute, is this true? Baby Boy from Detroit, is this you man?"

"The one and only," the next caller answered. Wonder who he was. He sounded sexy as hell.

"Where have you been, playboy?"

"Well you know Mike, I been a little busy. Being a player is hard work. You know a brother had to tend to his flock." Mike and Baby Boy continued to talk like they were the best of friends. They even hinted to the fact that he was a regular caller. I never remember hearing him calling in. I'm sure I would've remembered that voice.

"You're my boy, you know that. Every time the women gang up on me, I can always count on you to help a brother out."

"That's what I'm here for Mike. You know I have to comment on your last caller right?"

"Get her Baby Boy, get her!" Michael egged on.

"You should've asked how much she weighed or how she looked. I bet you any amount of money that she's as big as a house." I was starting not to like this guy now.

"Ohhh nooooo," Michael started laughing hysterically, "you're not going to play the fat card are you?"

"I'm playing the entire damn deck Mike."

"You know you are about to get in trouble right? I'm telling you man, every light on my board is lit up right now. Wait a minute, my producer Juan D. just said we still have Tomeka on the line. Ouuuuweee you are in trouble!" This was better than a thriller movie. Michael was a master instigator. He knew exactly how to keep the drama going.

"Tomeka, are you there?" Michael asked.

"Yeah I'm here. Where is he?" Tomeka sounded like she was in attack mode.

Baby Boy answered cool, calm, and collected, "Here I am, baby."

"I'm just wondering is this just an act or are you really this ignorant?"

Baby Boy laughed at Tomeka's comment, "So I'm ignorant because I'm telling the truth, huh? Well, seeing that my boy Mike is scared—"

"Hey hey, I'm never scurd," Mike interjected.

They both laughed. The male caller continued, "Since he is scurd I'll ask. How big... I mean, what size are you, Tomeka?"

"Oh, I'm not embarrassed of my size baby! I am a sexy 26."

"No sweetheart maybe you misunderstood my question. I didn't ask for your age, I asked for your size."

"I heard you," the plus sized caller answered, "and I said that I am a size 26."

"Oh snap!" Mike and Baby Boy yelled out in unison.

"No, no, no Tomeka, why didn't you lie?" I said hanging on to my steering wheel. She had just given them a case full of ammo to use to hunt her down. Out of my peripheral vision, I felt someone watching me and looked to my left. My friendly neighboring driver and his passenger were looking at me like I was crazy because of the tirades they had just witnessed. I shot them back a "what the hell are you looking at" look. They got the picture.

"Didn't I tell you? Didn't I tell you?" Baby Boy repeated. Now it was only the two men. They ended up disconnecting Tomeka for all of her verbal explicitness. "I knew it, women be talking all that smack man while they sit their fat behinds up eating a Big Mac. Black women are the most obese women on the planet. And that's not me saying that, it's a fact. They wonder why we cheat on them. They wonder why we go to other races. Women need to do their part before they complain about us."

"Oooweeee, Baby Boy you are acting up today man. You are killing these women out here."

"They don't want none Mike, they can't handle me." Michael told Baby Boy to stay on the line with him while he went to commercial and gave out the number to the station.

These other women probably can't handle you but I can. I picked up my phone and began dialing. *And I'm looking forward to it.*

Surprisingly on the first ring I was connected. "Michael Baisden Show, may I help you?"

SUPER HEAD

"I'M telling you Mike, they can't handle ya boy!"
"You be having these women so riled up man!" Michael Baisden told me in between commercial breaks. "If you keep getting me all of these calls, I might have to make you part of my show."

I walked around my living room liking the sound of that. "Hey watch what you say now, I might hold you to that."

"I'm not playing Baby Boy, hey look we go back on air in 30 seconds, are you ready?"

"Come on now, you know I'm ready," I said smiling.

"Cool, keep doing exactly what you're doing." Mike was obviously hyped off the buzz that I always created when I called in. "Okay, here we go. Hey family we're back and our topic, if you are just tuning in, is where are all of the good men? Our last caller, Tomeka, bless her heart, was going off on us saying that there is no such thing as a good man and that we are all dogs. But my dawg, Baby Boy came to the rescue and said that women need to start taking care of their men and themselves and maybe guys wouldn't cheat."

"That's right Mike, I said it, I think a lot of sistas out here are lazy and do not, I repeat, do not want to take the time out to go to the gym and work it out! Mind you, these are the same women out here giving a lot of demands. I'm sure all women know by now that men are physical and very visual. If you are not giving me anything good physically to look at then, what do you expect me to do?"

"So you're saying that women need to start looking the part?" Michael asked.

"You damn right! And I really don't blame them solely for being lazy. I have to give some of the blame to the clothing lines that are making some of these jeans," I said.

"Okay Baby Boy, you have to explain this one to me. Why the clothing lines?" Mike asked trying to get me to bring it home.

"Well, what I mean is that they are now making jeans so good that it's turning women into fool's gold. I'm coming up behind her like damn! I'm saying the ass is banging, hips and thighs are tight, have you all in, right?"

"So what's wrong with that Baby Boy, that's a good thing right?" Mike asked, starting to see where I was going with it. He started cracking up.

"What's wrong with it is, when those jeans come down and the magic girdles come off, the fat spills out. I'm talking dents and dimples everywhere. Asses looking like a big ass golf ball."

"Oh no you didn't say golf ball. Baby Boy, you didn't go there."

"You in the club looking one way, but when I get you home and naked you're bigger and shaped totally different. Man, it's a damn shame. I mean, you almost respect a woman who is out of shape if she's at least letting you see exactly what she looks like." I was in a groove now and having fun.

"Man, you are fooling. Baby Boy, my lines are lit up like a Christmas tree. I have to take another caller. You know it's going to be a woman right?"

"I'll take all of them on. Put them all on at the same time if you have to. I don't care."

"Just one at a time man. Let's see, Halo, how is everything?"

"Everything is everything Michael. By the way I love your show."

"Don't be trying to kiss up, but I do like that name you are using and get this, Baby Boy, she's from your neck of the woods, Detroit."

"Is that so Halo?" I asked, my curiosity now rising. "How are you today?"

"I'm actually doing good, just listening to you and Michael act a fool."

"Damn Halo, you sound so… sexy," I said wanting to hear more of her voice.

"Thanks, Baby Boy. I really appreciate it. And Mike?"

"Yes, Halo?"

"I wanted to say I do agree with Baby Boy, to a degree."

Michael raised his voice in disbelief, "What, a woman agreeing with Baby Boy? This might be a first. I have to go and check the records."

The woman with the sexy voice and heavenly name continued, "Yeah, I know the women are going to kill me for this, but I do think we as women tend to get a little lackadaisical with our appearance and our physique. It should be the same if you're single and trying to get a man and if you have one and want to keep him. Men are simple, and as Baby Boy said, they are physical and visual. I don't think there's anything wrong with hitting the gym or the treadmill to tighten up our bodies."

"Wow!" Mike and I said at the same time.

"What planet are you from? You have to be a robot or something." I was very intrigued by this mystery woman.

"Y'all are crazy," she said laughing.

"Halo, so this is your normal voice, or are you just trying to seduce me?"

"This is really me," she answered, seemingly with a smile on her face.

"Well, I want to personally thank you for coming to my side to school these other women out here." I walked over to my picture window and looked at the beautiful view of the city.

"Don't thank me yet Baby Boy. I agree with some of the things that you are saying but definitely not all. Even though we as women should do our part and hold up our end of the bargain, that is still not going to keep that man at home and from on top of another woman. I don't think we could ever accomplish that no matter what we do. I do believe we probably can drastically cut the probability down though. Ultimately, a man not cheating is totally up to him. Unfortunately, most guys can't handle that challenge.

"Halo baby, that was deep," Michael said obviously impressed, "what are you, some kind of relationship expert or something?" We both laughed.

"You're silly," she answered. "Not at all, I'm just a woman scorned who learned a lot through living."

Okay now it was my turn. "That was beautiful Halo. I applaud you for that speech, but let me make sure I get this right. You are saying that no matter how good a woman looks, she can't keep a man from cheating, right?"

"That's exactly what I'm saying," she replied.

"I think I can go with you on that to a certain extent but when I think about Beyoncé and if she was my woman, there is no way in hell I can picture myself stepping out on her."

"Amen to that brother. Amen!" Mike agreed.

"That's because men are shallow," Halo stated.

"Uh oh, watch out now," Mike said feeling the temperature rising and trying to raise it a little higher.

"It's the truth. Your thinking is very shallow because we all know that pretty women are cheated on all the time. Let's take Halle Berry for example. She's considered to be one of the most beautiful women on the planet. Now you probably will not cheat on her because you might not be on the level that she is, and by level, I mean super megastar. When you level the playing field and have a superstar boyfriend or husband like she has had, who sees women as beautiful or better every single day, they ended up treating her the same way you regular men treat your regular women, like crap."

Just as much as I loved a beautiful woman, I loved a woman that could mentally stimulate me. Haven't encountered one of those in quite some time, and frankly she was turning me on.

"And if I may continue Baby Boy, I'm going to go out on a limb and say that even if you hooked up with Beyoncé, after a while you would find something that you don't like that will probably give you an excuse to cheat. 'Aw man, this chick can't cook, I'ma bout to cheat on her ass.'" Halo kept going on in her imitation male voice. "'Damn B, I can't get any tonight? I'm about to cheat.' And if she gets pregnant and gains 20 to 30 pounds, 'Aw hell to the naw, this chick got her fat butt all up in my face, I'm out.' That's why we don't think there are any good men out here. Y'all will leave a woman for the next new thing smoking while we stick with y'all through thick and thin." Everything she was saying is right on the money. *Say something for the men, anything.*

I was stunned. This woman was saying things to me as if she really knew me. She talked like a woman who was hurt by someone like me. "So Halo, that's if you don't mind, you should paint a picture and give us some insight to your physical makeup."

"I'm five foot eight, about 150 pounds, dark brown. I guess you can say athletic build."

"Face?" I asked.

She laughed, "Yes, I have one." Mike laughed at that.

"Cute?" I continued.

"I think so. I would say very cute," she replied.

While I was on a roll, "Pretty good so far. Booty?"

"Apple bottom," she replied confidently.

"Mmm, do you have a man?"

"Nope, all of them cheated on me."

"Damn shame! Okay, last question. Go out with me."

She laughed, "That didn't sound like a question to me, sounds like you're demanding me."

She was teasing me, playing with me. Something I wasn't used to. "Okay then, will you go out with me?"

"I'm sorry, Baby Boy, but you couldn't handle a woman like me. I happen to be a woman who looks good, loves good, and cooks good, but unfortunately I have a brain and listening to your conversation today, I can tell that isn't something that you look for in a woman."

There was silence for about five seconds and then, "Wow, I say, wow! Baby Boy, she got you man. I mean I'll be the first to say that today we lost. The women sent this… this battle-bot to represent them and they destroyed us."

The victorious champion chuckled, "You guys are too crazy."

"Well that's our show family. It was fun. Halo, welcome to the family and whenever you want to call in and make us look bad, you do so," Michael said.

"Well, you guys do a good job of that yourselves but I might just do that. Baby Boy, it was nice unofficially meeting you. Oh and just to let you know, even though you are the enemy," she said snickering, "I think you have a sexy voice as well."

"Why thank you, and it was nice meeting you too. I will debate with you anytime. Don't forget we live in the same city so who knows, fate might just have it that we meet one day."

"Oh Lord," Halo said dramatically, "I'll make sure I'm wearing a pair of those fool's gold jeans." We all laughed.

"And on that note, I'm Michael Baisden and I'm out."

Two seconds later, I checked to see if I was still connected to the show's phone line. "Baby Boy, are you there?" Mike asked.

"Yeah I'm here, what about her? I asked, hoping to get to say a few more words.

"Naw man she hung up."

"You have to hook that up Mike."

"You serious?" Mike asked, shocked. "How she went off on you, I thought you would never want to hear from her again."

"Are you crazy? Man, I've been looking for a nice challenge and I think I finally found it," I answered.

"Well, I want her too, for the show that is. You two going

back and forth like that was crazy. My assistant just handed me a copy of the ratings for today's show and they are through the roof. Unfortunately, she hung up before we could get any information or even a call back number. Only thing we have is that crazy user name of Halo."

"Shit!" I startled myself at the passion I had about meeting this woman.

"Look man," Mike said humorously, "I'll keep my ear out, and if you meet her in the D you do the same. I'm looking forward to y'all's next battle."

"Will do Mike."

"Okay Baby Boy, holla at you later," Michael said before hanging up.

I paced around my living room with extra energy. I was hyped. I was angry that I let her beat me in a discussion. I was excited to be interested. Shit, I was hard! I laughed as I looked down at Buddy. I don't know what's wrong with me lately. First, it was the mystery woman from the club, now the mystery caller today on the radio. I have to release.

I went down to the underground garage and hopped in Sally. When I pulled up to Jefferson, I noticed that it was a calm evening compared to the weekend where traffic would barely move. I enjoyed the roar of my engine as it echoed through the barely occupied streets and off the tightly packed buildings.

As I monitored my speed limit, I noticed that Buddy was still a little excited from the drama that went down over the radio. "Gotta get rid of this hard on," I said to myself as I adjusted my leg. Buddy and I are not jacking off any more. Naw fuck that! I'm still pissed at Kandi's ass over that one. Even though I really didn't feel like fucking, some bomb ass head would be perfect right now. And any time I thought of bomb head, I immediately thought of Ricka, my little Eastside freak.

I usually didn't fuck with Eastside chicks. They were a little too loud and ghetto for me. They always seemed to have a fake ponytail, too much weave, too many kids, or too many tattoos. But, with all that, Ricka was a master at fellatio. And the best part of all was that she was cheap. She loved Burger King and beer. And even though I would never take her out or back to my place, she was definitely good enough to go to her place, get a room, or in this case, get head in my whip.

I flipped through my phone's contacts and dialed her up. She answered on the first ring. My kind of girl. "Baaabeeee!" she called in her sad, whiney voice.

"What up mami?" I said trying to suppress my laughter.

"I missed you so much. Why haven't you called me?"

Oh boy, here we go with this shit again. "Baby you know I'm busy and don't want to call you if I don't have the proper time to talk to you on the phone," I said smiling.

"But Future, I don't care about proper time. I've told you that. I just wanna hear your voice. Just call me to say hi, I don't care, but just call."

I sighed, "You're right, I've got to do better, and I'm sorry baby. How could I have been so stupid? I really don't deserve you, you know that?"

"Don't beat yourself up. It's okay. I mean it's not like it's because of other women. I know I'm your bitch." Women are crazy. We really don't have to make excuses for why we do or don't do things, because if they like you, they'll make the excuses for you. "So, how is Buddy?" she asked, snickering.

"You know I miss him too, right?"

"He definitely misses you." I let out a forceful sigh, "I would come see you for a while but I don't have that much time. I have to go in to work early tomorrow."

"Hush crazy. You know you can come over anytime. I just told you anytime I get to spend with my Booboo is good with me."

"Are you sure?" I asked, trying not to sound too excited.

"Of course I am," she answered cheerfully.

"Cool, throw something on, not too much though. I want you to go for a ride with me."

"Yes! I just love your car. Are you gonna let the top down?" she asked with her voice raised an octave higher.

"Only if you take yours off."

"Oh, you ain't saying shit! You know how ya bitch get down, daddy."

"Yes I do, baby. I'll see you in about 10 minutes," I said turning onto the freeway.

"Oh and Future?"

"Yeah."

"Can you stop by Burger King on your way?"

I smiled. That's my girl.

After reaching her apartment, I watched as her petite ass scarfed down the Burger King like it was her first meal in days. Then she washed it down with a Corona that I stopped and picked up at the liquor store on the way.

Every now and then, it was nice being around a real ghetto girl after being with so many sophisticated ones. You didn't have to roll out the red carpet and you didn't have to try too hard to impress them. Ricka was 23 and full of life. I loved her energy. After she finished eating and let out a couple of loud belches, we hopped in the Stang and headed to the expressway. While on the way to her place, I was listening to Sade's *Love Deluxe* but Ricka's young ass wasn't trying to hear that at all.

"Baby, you have to put on some Gucci. You're not supposed to be playing slow romantic shit in a sports car anyways." I smiled at her youthfulness even though sometimes she made me feel way older than the four years we were apart.

I figured that we would chill on Belle Isle for a while. We drove around for a few and I found a nice secluded parking spot that had a great view of the Detroit River and Canada.

"Hmmmmmmmm, this is so romantic," Ricka said sipping on her second 22-ounce Corona. I had just cracked one open and joined her. "The water looks so pretty. Ouuu look! I want to ride on one of those." She pointed to one of the eight passenger boats cruising by.

"One of my partners owns one. I'll see if I can get it one weekend." I took a couple of big gulps of my brew.

"Could you daddy? That's why I love you. You're always taking care of your baby. I can't wait to tell Treshanequa and Alize, they are going to be so jealous. While I'm on the boat, I can tan nude on the deck and sip on Piña Coladas. You are the bomb, you know that?" She leaned across the car and planted a kiss on my cheek.

"I try to be," I said leaning my chair all the way back and closing my eyes. As the music played from my speakers, I drifted away and imagined me on my friend's boat, stretched out basking in the sun. As I looked over to my right, where Ricka should've been, I saw Her, staring intensely at me.

"I love looking at your face," she said studying me.

"Is that so?" I replied.

"Yeah, I like your features, love your lips," she whispered in a low voice as she ran her index finger softly across my mouth. Her touch was driving me crazy. I felt electric currents coming from her fingers. "I can't decide which one I love better though," she said repositioning herself so that she was now kissing on my chest, "your juicy lips or this juicy dick." The warmth from her hand wrapped around me and shielded Buddy from the river's cool breeze.

"Mmmmm, no need to make one of them jealous baby, they can both be your favorites."

"I like the sound of that," she replied. She was so seductive. She maneuvered herself like a snake. No sudden moves, no jerks and nothing mechanical. Just slow, smooth, slithery movements.

She took me in her mouth. With no hands, she took all of me. Her mouth stayed wide open allowing her saliva to drip down and puddle on my balls. Her lips glistened with spit as she removed my head from her mouth. She then straddled me, crawled up towards my face with her mouth slightly open and slob dripping on my stomach, chest, and her chin. She kidnapped my tongue and sucked it with the same intensity that she sucked my dick, leaving it just as sloppy.

She must have taken that jealous statement to heart because for the next 10 minutes she gave my lips, tongue, and dick equal attention.

She and I were dangerous together. If a helicopter flew over us and had a radar, the entire screen would show up fire engine red. No greens, yellows, or blues, just red.

"Let me taste it Future. Please baby, cum in my mouth."

I felt the tingle in my loins that made me tighten my legs

and ass. My body tensed as I felt the sensation nearing to the top of my shaft.

"Give it up baby," she whined. She was deep-throating me and making gagging noises. "Down my throat. Give it to me!"

The talking mixed with the noises and the slobbering was too much. I couldn't keep it down any longer. I grabbed her head, locked my fingers in her short-cropped hair. Her short, wait... what the fuck? This feels like a damn ponytail. I opened my eyes. "Shit!"

"What's wrong daddy?" Ricka asked holding Buddy in one hand while taking a breather from sucking.

"Nothing baby, nothing at all. Keep sucking, keep fucking sucking," I said as I grabbed her by that fake-ass Eastside ponytail and gently pushed her head back into my lap.

I had totally forgotten all about Ricka. I had really zoned out. No matter though, my nut was here now. But, I can't get Her face to pop back in my head. Fuck!

After finishing our little session, I drove Ricka back home and tried to relax. I'm kind of pissed that this other woman keeps invading my space when it's convenient for her. And, I'm kind of pissed that she is not here with me for real. I kissed Ricka goodnight and headed back home.

I retrieved my phone out of the glove compartment, switched it off of silent, and checked my missed calls. There were five, one from Caesar, one from my mother, and three previous sexual encounters. But, no Kandi, no Michael Baisden, and no Her. For some reason the drive home tonight seemed long as hell. Well, at least Buddy is satisfied but for the first time in a while, I wondered... Was I?

HOW DOES IT FEEL?

I can't believe how fast this week has flown by. I guess the anticipation of getting some had something to do with that. I have to admit I'm getting a little nervous now. I have one day to get myself in check. Even though I haven't experienced multiple sex partners, the three years that my ex and I were together we had a very active sex life. In the beginning, it was every day, sometimes twice a day. Once I got a taste of sex, I was hooked.

When I became accustomed to it, I wanted more. Damien was a nice size and could move well, but he was a two-minute brother. To a beginner that's cool, but after getting that first year under my belt I needed him to step it up. I had to calm him down, jack him off almost to the point of ejaculation, stop, then repeat. We had to really work on his mental. I truly believe that a guy who cums quick is selfish and weak-minded. He cares more about his nut than me getting mine. Every guy should take time to give and enjoy giving a woman an orgasm because he's going to get his regardless.

Speaking of my ex, I can't believe that fool had the nerve to call me today asking, "Do you miss me baby?"

"Are you crazy? Why would I miss you?" I replied. Ughhhhh! Of course I miss you. Damn it and I really didn't want to. Even though we didn't talk much towards the end, I missed just having him here. I missed not being alone. I definitely missed the sex. I don't think he's the best. And he doesn't have the biggest dick in the world, but he was good for me and my hefty sexual appetite. I had to get his taste out of my mouth.

I just hope all of the information that I've been hearing from my female friends and co-workers isn't true. It seems like there's a cum-quick epidemic going around. I mean five minutes and out. Women aren't even mad at it anymore. It's almost like they expect it. "Girl, let him get that first one out, then you just get him back up." For what? So he can give me another lousy 10 minutes?

Maybe I'm just spoiled now, but I just can't see myself settling. If I'm super horny, you're telling me that most guys don't even like to eat out...strike one. Then before I get anywhere near an orgasm they're going to nut...strike two. Then, to top that off I'm supposed to suppress my hormones and suck them up, which depending on how well I know them probably won't happen, so they can cum before getting me close to orgasm again...strike three. I don't think so.

"Darnell, please prove them wrong. Don't disappoint me, please?" I said to myself. Now I was a little worried that he wouldn't be up to par. I hadn't seen him since we made the date, which was a good thing. I probably would've been a little uncomfortable. He did call me earlier to confirm and to test me to see if the consensual sex thing was still on the menu along with lunch. I joked and said, "I thought that I was the only thing on the menu, I forgot all about lunch." We both shared a laugh on that one.

I believe that I'm all set though. I bought a new bra and panty set and tonight when I bathe I'm going to give Kitty a fresh trim. The last couple of days at the gym this week I've been jogging an extra 10 minutes to get my stamina up. The last thing I want to happen is to have Darnell end up outdoing me.

I usually try to call my parents about three times a week to check on them. Today, on my way home, my mother beat me to the punch. No more than a minute after I hung up with my folks, my phone rang again. I looked at the display. Two four eight area code, who do I know in that area? My mind started racing as I pushed the answer button on my Bluetooth earpiece.

"Hello?"

"Hello, beautiful," the deep-voiced stranger replied.

"Beautiful? Wow, you know me well enough to call me beautiful and I don't even recognize your phone number."

"Don't know who I am, huh? I think my feelings are hurt," he replied in a weak attempt to convince me. "I'll make it easy on you, I'm the guy you felt worthy enough to call last weekend to inform that you had made it in safely after leaving the club."

That clue immediately shed light on the situation. It was Juwaun. Have to remember to lock this number in my phone. I figured this would be a good time to pay him back for the time he acted like he didn't know me.

"Jason?" I replied. "Hey sweetie, is this a new number?"

"No, and this isn't Jason," he said a little deflated.

"Tommy?"

"No."

"Bobby?" I said throwing out another name while trying to hold in my laugh.

"Nope, not Bobby either." Juwaun was beginning to sound a little frustrated now. "Look I'll just tell you before you run down the list of all your ex-boyfriends."

I cut him short, "Juwaun, I know it's you."

"Whewwww!" Juwaun blew out air, "I was about to say girl, don't know how many more names I could be called."

I laughed out loud. "So, what do I owe this honor?" I asked.

"What, me calling?"

"Yes, you calling."

"I think it's more of an honor for me. I mean, we never established if we would have an open end phone relationship so I didn't exactly know if calling you was against the rules."

Even though Juwaun seemed like a genuinely nice guy, I couldn't afford to let my guard down too easy. "I guess it's okay. I don't want to be a distraction and have you fumbling the ball and all. It's not like y'all can afford to give up any yardage," I said smiling.

"I don't have to worry about that right now. We're in the off season."

I was kind of a rookie when it came to football knowledge. I only knew the basics. "Yeah, I knew that. I was only testing you."

"Mmm hmm, anyways," he laughed, "let me get down to why I called so that I won't hold you up." I really didn't want Juwaun to rush off of the phone. I was just beginning to enjoy his conversation and voice. "I really want to see you again. We could go to breakfast, lunch, or dinner. If you didn't want to eat, we could just go to get coffee or just go for a ride. Really doesn't matter to me what we do as long as I can be near you again."

I smiled a wide grin at his eagerness to see me. I was starting to get a little excited thinking about a star athlete really being on me like this. Since he brought up going for a ride, I had a good excuse to be nosy and find out what the ballers really drove.

"So Mr. Lions' player, if you were to come pick me up, what kind of vehicle should I look out the window for?"

I heard him let out a little chuckle. "Guess that depends on how you're feeling that day. If you wanted to feel the wind in your hair, I'll come through in the drop top Jag. If you didn't want to feel all of the customary potholes in Detroit, I'll come scoop you up in the Range Rover." His macho man attitude was switching into full gear now. "If you want to be all up on me, feel up on my chest and whatnot…" We both laughed at that one. "…then I'll come get you on my Harley. But, if you just want to spend some quiet time alone, just you and I, I'll have the chauffer drive us around in the Maybach."

Dang, guess he really was a baller. Plus, I loved Range Rovers. I've never rode in one, but whenever I drive by one, I instantly get post orgasmic chills. Play calm girl. Be cool. "Nice assortment of toys you have, but have you thought about the fact that someone might see you and I out and might take pictures or spread the word to your um, fans?"

"Fans huh? Funny, and no I haven't thought about that because I don't care who sees me with you. If they did it'll be a good thing for me to be seen hanging with someone as beautiful as you."

"Awwww." I was really blushing now. "That's so sweet." I tried to stop myself from smiling so hard but couldn't.

"It's so true!" There was a brief silence like he was trying to get his next group of words together, trying to figure out was it safe to keep going down the flattery will get you everywhere road or the less is more path. "So how are we going to do this? I think you can tell that I'm going to keep bothering you. I see it like this, either I can keep calling and begging to take you out or you can just make it easy on yourself and tell me when I can come pick you up."

I was very flattered. It didn't seem like he was going to give up. "Um, I'm a little booked this weekend so how about I call you next week so we can set something up?"

There was another brief moment of silence over the phone. "And you're not just saying that to get me off of the phone?"

I laughed. "No, why would I do that? I'm not that mean."

"If you say so," he joked, "maybe it's just me. Maybe you just don't like me."

I really didn't want Juwaun to get that impression of me. I think it was more of the fact that I didn't want to set myself up for disaster dealing with a nice, handsome, very famous athlete. I think I actually could've handled it if it seemed that he wanted to have a nice romantic evening topped off with mind-blowing sex. But I'm getting the notion from Juwaun that he actually wanted more.

"It's not that at all. I just have never had anyone famous taking an interest in me."

"But it's nothing really different. I think of myself as a normal human," he explained.

"Human yes, but a lot more famous, and sought after by every female in the city."

"Wow! I'm flattered but I don't think that every woman wants me like how you're saying."

I wondered if he's really that clueless. "Are you being serious right now?"

He laughed. "Yes, yes I am."

"Okay Juwaun, do you know how many women watch your games?"

"Umm no, but why don't you play my publicist and inform me," he answered.

"A lot!" I said. "And do you know why?"

"Um, I'm going to have to go with no on this one too. I'm sure it's not because of the winning record we have," he said, sarcastically referencing the record amount of losses that the Lions accumulate each and every year.

"No, it's because of you and your ass," I said shocked at what I blurted out. We both laughed. "They can't wait to see your tight buns run down the field and score and then take off that helmet and show that lovely smile of yours."

"And here I am thinking it was because of the love of the game."

"Think again!" We laughed again and talked for a little while longer. He reminded me how much he liked me and I told him that he was alright also. Before hanging up he tried to make sure that I was going to call him next week. I gave him the same line I gave him the first night we met, "I'm not making any promises."

Talking to Juwaun on the phone made me feel good. Today was a good day, I hoped tomorrow would be even better.

As I drove up to my, soon to be, former residence, I reminisced on the times that Damien and I had before it turned bad. We had made plans to get married, buy a house, and have kids. Guess all those dreams are gone up in smoke now. I try to tell myself that I'm not mad or that it doesn't really affect me but the truth is I'm really pissed off at him for taking that dream away from me. He was supposed to be my savior.

I was anxious about my pre-arranged sex session so I had trouble getting to sleep that night. To make matters worse, when I did finally get to sleep I had another dream about Him.

In the dream, I was sleeping under my comforter when He came in from work and showered. I take it that we were living together or at least I knew him well enough for him to have a key. He stepped into the doorway naked and just stood there looking at me with his arms out as if he were Samson pressing against the two stone pillars.

He gently removed the comforter and looked at my plump ass as if he was about to fall on his knees and worship it. Now that would be a sight to see, a man actually worshiping a booty god.

He licked his lips and tilted his head, taking it all in. While wiping the corners of his mouth he gently grabbed both of my legs and spread them apart. He climbed between my limbs, scooting north until his face aligned with my onion. He then spread his fingers and softly palmed me. I jerked from the shock of his touch, but didn't need to look back or open my eyes for I knew my lover's grasp. He spread my ass cheeks apart, lowered his head and made his tongue do laps around my balloon knot. Flicking, fluttering, and licking every inch. I loved when he tossed my salad, probably just as much as getting ate out.

He replaced his tongue with his lips and began smacking and making slurping noises. He was driving me crazy. My man was so damn freaky, just the way I liked it. The spit from his mouth was dripping down my ass crack, splitting into two separate streams running alongside both of my now plumped and throbbing pussy lips. That, mixed with my own nectar was leaving a nice size wet spot on the sheets.

I wanted him to insert himself inside of me or at least lick my pussy. I needed him to do something, anything to take away from the unbelievable ecstasy I was receiving on my rectum. But he wasn't having it. His appetite was set and he came home with a taste for tossed salad. He looked like he was at an all you can eat salad bar, eating with his head down, face covered, both hands on the table and not coming up for air.

He normally had such good table manners when he ate out, but not tonight. Not at Big Momma Angie's All You Can Eat Buffet. Here we encouraged smacking, slurping, and bad table manners. And just like all of the restaurants in the hood, we usually ran out of something. Tonight, we were all out of breadsticks for his salad, so I took it upon myself and personally provided him with an endless supply of warm, soft buns instead.

My pussy was now pulsating and my asshole was doing the same. I could no longer hold it in. Both of my holes came at the same time. I shivered uncontrollably as he continued to suck. Damn! Orgasm was so strong. Looking at the expression on my man's face, he was full and satisfied. I returned the look of satisfaction because I truly was. I smiled even though I wasn't full from eating like he was but my heart was full from the love that he made me feel. I loved my man.

When I awoke Saturday morning, my legs were still spread apart resembling the first letter in my name, well now more like an upside down V for vanished, because the line that was supposed to lay in between to connect those two angled lines, were nowhere in sight.

I reached between my legs and immediately felt the cold wet spot on the sheets and stickiness in between my thighs. I closed my eyes tight and let out a long sigh. What the hell was wrong with me? I didn't understand all this daydreaming or night dreaming or all-the-damn-time-dreaming about this guy. My horny level was now through the roof. It increased every time I think about Him.

After about 10 minutes of trying to get my head right, I finally hopped out of bed and went through my normal Saturday morning routine of watching my cartoons, drinking a hot cup of tea, and showering. It took me a while but I had finally picked out something cute to wear. I decided on a form fitting, short sleeve terrycloth jogging suit. I didn't want to look too sophisticated since we were going to lunch before doing the do. In the back of my mind, I think the real reason for picking this outfit was that it was a lot easier to take off than a pair of jeans.

I had lost track of time until Tierra called.

"Hey, Tee."

"Hey, girl," she answered with enthusiasm pouring from her voice. "Happy Dick Day!"

"What!" I screamed while laughing. "You are too much." No matter what, Tierra always made me smile.

"It's Dick Day girl! Whatever, don't be trying to act like you're not excited to be getting some. You probably didn't sleep a wink last night. Like a kid waiting to go to Cedar Point the next morning."

I thought about the restless moments I had before actually falling asleep and the total bliss that followed. With a devilish grin on my face I replied, "Actually I slept pretty well."

"Mmm hmm, so are you excited?" Tierra asked.

"I think that I'm more nervous than excited. It's been a minute since I had sex and that person was my first and only. I just don't want it to be too awkward. When I was doing it with stupid ass, I thought that I was pretty damn good, but that's according to me. What if out in the real world I'm stale?" We both laughed, but it was actually the truth.

"Please Angel, don't even worry about it. I'm telling you, once the juices get to flowing that freak inside will get going. I'm not so much worried about you as I am him. I really hope that you don't hurt the damn guy."

"Yeah, I thought about that too," I said snickering. "I don't want to come off as too freaky. I'm not supposed to give him all of my tricks up front am I?"

Tierra busted out laughing at me. "What the hell? Is this Fucking 101? I think that you are thinking too much. Let him decide what you are going to do. If he's stale in bed, then you be stale right back, but if he's wonderful, then you wonderfully fuck his ass right back." I felt like I was a virgin getting taught about sex for the first time. "Oh yeah and make sure you bring condoms with you because guys will try to run game on you. You know they want to get that raw nookie."

"Glad you reminded me about that one," I said as I walked into my room and checked my bottom drawer for condoms. "I think I have a couple of Magnums left over from Damien."

"Well let's just hope that this guy is a Magnum brother, because all black guys aren't."

I was about to ask how did she know because all of the feedback that we received from her sexual sessions were always Magnum and Magnum XL quality. "Well he better be because I'm not stopping for condoms."

We chatted for a little while longer and I told her that I would fill her in later. I had to go get dressed. Darnell wanted to pick me up but I decided it would be better if I met him. That way if anything went wrong, I wasn't obligated to stay and I wouldn't have to kiss ass to make sure that I had a ride home.

We agreed to meet at Applebee's in Canton because he lived in Belleville. It was a nice median for the both of us. He had called to let me know that he was doing call-ahead seating for 4:00 because the restaurant was known for getting a little busy during lunchtime.

Before I left my apartment, I slowly looked myself over in the full-length mirror. I smiled, "Nice, real nice. Don't even know why I'm worried." As good as I looked, I shouldn't have to do anything but lie in bed. I ran both of my hands down to my waist and around both thighs then back up to my butt. "Thanks Ma," I said turning around now to get a better view of what I had inherited from my mother. I wish I loved my legs as much. To me, they looked so skinny and slender. Even though I have some meat on them now from working out, I think I will always see them as chicken legs.

I arrived about 15 minutes early and sat in my car for the first five. I figured that I would go in and maybe sit at the bar and order a drink to relax. When I walked in the waiting area Darnell's face was the first that I saw. His smile was wide and bright.

"Hey Angel!"

"Hey Darnell, I see you're early."

"Of course I am. You're not going to be dogging me."

"I would have too," I said.

"I know. So what's up, your day going good so far?" he

asked while briefly looking me over.

"Yeah, I can't complain. Think I might be getting a little hungry now." I placed my hand on my stomach as I felt it rumble. The aroma in this place was wonderful. It was driving me and my gut crazy.

"It shouldn't be too—" Before Darnell finished his sentence, the square light sensor that notified you when your table was ready flashed and vibrated in his hands. "Guess they heard you," he said smiling.

"Guess so." We were led to our table and the waiter asked us if we wanted drinks. I ordered a glass of Riesling and he ordered something called a Black and Blue.

"What is a Black and Blue? I've never heard of it."

"Yeah, it's not too popular. Well, not with us anyway." He pointed to the backside of his hand to let me know that the "us" that he was referring to was black people. It's two beers mixed, Guinness and Blue Moon."

"Sounds interesting," I replied.

"Wait until you see it," he said raising his brows.

Normally I wouldn't drink so early in the day but under the circumstances, I had to take the edge off. The waiter brought out our drinks and I looked on in amazement at Darnell's drink. It resembled some kind of chemistry project. The darker beer was actually floating on top of the lighter colored beer. Neat! I hope he's this creative when it comes to sex. We shared good conversation, it flowed a lot better than I thought it would. I also used the time to really study Darnell's face. He wasn't drop dead gorgeous or nothing. And even though he's a little overweight, he presented himself very well. He kept a nice line up and trimmed goatee. He dressed nice and crisp. Today he was wearing a cream short-sleeved Polo jogging suit and a crispy white pair of Air Force Ones.

He continued giving me compliments, telling me how pretty my face was, how good my body looked, and how I should take my jacket off and tie it around my waist before I stand back up to hide my booty. I laughed while thinking back to when I checked myself out in the mirror to make sure how good it looked.

As we both started on our second drink, our conversation moved from generally physical to semi-sexual.

"I hope us hooking up don't mess up our friendship," I said while sipping on my wine. I made sure I paid attention to his facial expression to get his reaction.

"I don't see why it would. Look, we are both grown adults. You don't have to worry about me blowing up your phone afterwards or following you around at work like a little puppy dog."

I laughed at his sarcasm. Sure, you say that now but that's because you haven't had a taste of this peach cobbler yet. You better hope that it doesn't turn you into a stalker.

Thanks to the alcohol and a little horniness, all the uncertainty from earlier was now gone and replaced by confidence. Darnell started looking better with each sip. I was feeling a little frisky now. I felt myself occasionally licking my lips and seductively placing my index finger in my mouth to bite my nail. Every time he spoke my eyes went directly to his lips. Mmm, can't wait to feel them on mine. Both sets!

Darnell was all in and staring intensely. I slid my shoe off and rubbed my foot against his calf. Good thing for him that I was sitting across from him instead of beside him or else I would've been sizing him up with my hands right now.

After finishing lunch and two and a half glasses of wine, I was full and ready for dessert. Not the edible kind either... well in his case maybe. Now, I officially wanted dick.

We looked at each other for about 10 seconds without saying a word, but our eyes were speaking clearly. His were saying, "Damn, I want you so bad right now."

"Come on big boy, show me what you got!" mine replied.

I finished my third glass of wine and ran my finger over the rim of my glass. I looked him directly in the eyes and said, "I'm ready to go."

"Me too. Your place or mine?" he asked.

"Yours!"

"Come on let's go." He paid for the meal and left a generous tip. Then he grabbed me by the hand and led me through the restaurant.

"Have a nice day and come again!" the door greeter said cheerfully. Man, I hope so, I thought to myself, hopefully I'll cum again and again. Lord knows I need too!

"I'm in the black F-150 parked at the end," he said walking me to my car. "When I pull out, just follow me." I smiled at a sexual comeback to his statement that popped up in my head but decided against saying it out loud.

About 10 minutes later, we turned onto his street. He lived in a nice cozy neighborhood of uniformed brick, ranch size houses with manicured lawns. I parked in front of his house and he waited on the porch for me. While walking towards him, I remembered that I had left my purse on the front seat and jogged back to get it. I figured that I would use this as chance to let him get a real good glimpse of my ass bouncing up and down.

He led me into his home. I looked around briefly. "Nice. Really nice."

"Thanks," he replied.

He left me in the kitchen while he went into the living room. A couple seconds later, I heard Robin Thicke's album, *The Evolution of Robin Thicke*, come on. I loved him and knew every song. I leaned back on the ceramic island in the kitchen and hung my snuggly fitted jacket on one of his barstools.

I looked down at my baby tee and blushed at my hard nipples as they wrestled through lace and cotton to reveal themselves.

"Glad to see that you're just as excited as I am," Darnell said now staring at my breast. He walked over toward me.

"I… enjoyed lunch," was the only words that I could get out before he attacked my mouth with his tongue. It felt good to taste a man. No imagination, no day dreaming. This was as real as it gets. I became a little light headed from the sudden rush of blood flowing away from my brain to my tits and clit.

Darnell wrapped his hands around my waist and let them fall to my ass. He gripped my butt as if he had been waiting to do so all day, well, more like all year. Next thing I knew, I was airborne. He had picked me up and lifted me up onto the kitchen island. Our kissing became more passionate. I awkwardly removed his jacket letting it fall to the floor.

I wanted skin, didn't want to feel him through clothing. I wrapped my arms and legs around him and pulled him in closer. He started licking my neck, hitting that spot that made me wetter. I looked down and caught a nice glimpse of his jogging pants that were stretched outward to capacity. Damn is that his dick? I reached down to find out. My hands were greeted by what felt like at least eight inches of thick beef.

Kitty was really dripping now. At least I didn't have to worry about size and from the look of things, I wasn't going to have a problem being satisfied.

Darnell grabbed my arm and led me out of the kitchen. I think he may have been leading me into the bedroom but I was so horny that I couldn't even wait. I stopped him in the living room and fed him my tongue again. This was also a good time to get a better look at his goods. Feeling through clothing was one thing. I wanted to see it with my own eyes. As he grabbed a handful of my ass and squeezed the Charmin, I slipped his joggers and boxers down enough for me to witness his manhood.

"Wow!" unrepentantly escaped my mouth.

"You like baby?" he asked smiling.

"Mmm, hell yeah," I replied as I licked my lips. He had more than enough to satisfy and now having a closer look, he may have been a little bigger than eight. I was ready now. I released his dick back into his boxers when I noticed the couch behind us. I gave him a slight nudge and watched him as he fell back onto the comfort of the love seat. His dick stood at attention.

Darnell scooted to the edge of the couch and pulled me on top, making me straddle him. He wanted me just as bad. He pulled my shirt over my head and unhooked my bra.

"Damn you have some pretty nipples," he said gazing at my once silver dollar sized discs that had tightened to the size of a quarter. They also had doubled in length and sensitivity. I wanted to tell him to shut the hell up and suck but instead I grabbed the back of his head and made him do both.

"Ouuu yeah." I leaned my head back as the warmth of his mouth and flicking of his tongue made my pussy release more juices.

In the background my favorite song off Robin Thicke's CD had just began to play. "Lost without you…can't help myself, how does it feel?" Robin crooned.

"Mmmm, it feels so good baby," I moaned answering Robin. By the way he intensified his sucking, I think that Darnell thought that I was talking to him, but no matter, it was feeling good. I scooted down far enough where I could feel his hard dick on my sweet spot, and even though I had on my jogging pants, they were thin enough for me to feel his shape and thickness. I wanted him inside of me bad but this was feeling so good that I couldn't stop grinding on him.

"Ooouuu Darnell…feels—"

"Oh shiiiit, baby." His eyes rolled into the back of his head.

"You got condoms?" I asked trying to catch my breath.

"Over there," he said pointing to the end table. I noticed that he had Magnums, my kind of man. I can't wait to tell Tee.

I stood up and saw the wet spot on his boxers. I touched between my legs and realized I was so wet that it had soaked through my jogging pants and onto him.

"Damn sweetie, you are ready for real huh?" he asked smiling.

I felt a little embarrassed as I slid down my joggers and panties but snapped back into normality when Darnell stood in front of me holding his long dick and rolled the large condom on it. I tried to mask the smile that I felt forming on the corners of my mouth. I can't wait to tell Tierra that she's not the only member in the fuck-a-big-dick club. Ouuu I can't wait.

"What are you smiling at?" Darnell asked while sitting down in his original position, dick pointing straight up in the air. It reminded me of a lighthouse guiding me in from afar.

Robin was still asking me how it feels. I'll tell you in just one second. I took a deep breath and straddled my partner. I felt his plumped head as it met and spread my pussy lips. The first three inches actually hurt a little but I kept going until I had at least five inches of him inside of me. I gasped as I pulled myself back up to the tip and dipped about seven inches this time on my next thrust.

"Damn, Darnell, baby this dick feels...so, so damn good."

"Your pussy is so tight," he replied squeezing his eyes shut. "Shit, you are so damn wet."

I rose up and this time took all of him in. "Mmmm yeah." I was ready after getting that initial stretch out the way. Now it was time to work this dick. I grabbed the back of Darnell's neck and pumped him deep and slow. His dick was filling me up perfectly.

"Lost without you," Robin sung.

I pulled the back of his neck again as I enjoyed my second full thrust. A hundred more of these and I'll be nice.

"Can't help myself," Robin continued.

I held on tighter and clinched my pussy muscles as I pulled his dick to the tip of my kitty and made it disappear for a third time.

"Ba... baby, I think, I... think... ooouuu shit," Darnell slurred but I wasn't really paying him any attention, this was feeling too good. I waited entirely too long to be concerned with words. I just wanted dick. We can talk later.

"How does it feel?" Robin asked me again. Darnell finally came alive and gave me a couple of quick, sporadic, and unorthodox short thrusts. I heard Robin question me again. Um well just a second ago it was feeling damn good, but now... I opened my eyes as the once fulfilling super dick had now deflated. The once eight inch plus dick was now too small and too soft to even stay in.

I stared at Darnell's face as beads of sweat raced down his forehead onto his nose. He was breathing heavily. It's been a while since I've actually had sex, but I haven't been out of the loop long enough that I didn't recognize that face.

"Lost without you, can't help myself," Robin continued.

The fuck you can't help yourself, I thought as I looked at the poor sight in front of me.

"How does it feel?" Robin asked one last time.

Robin, you better shut the fuck up right now because nothing feels good about this sorry motherfucker in front of me cumming this motherfucking quick! I mean literally three pumps. You have to be kidding me.

"Baby, shit, I'm sorry...let me," Darnell panted.

"No you didn't," I said cutting him off and shaking my head.

"Baby," he said grabbing my waist.

I slapped his hands off of me. "No you fucking didn't," I said now lowering and sharpening my voice. Stay calm Angel, calm down. I felt my face tighten and my pulse rise. I dismounted Darnell and watched his now limp dick plop to the side. He laid back on the sofa and relaxed his head.

"Give me," he barely could get his words out, "give me bout 15, 20 minutes Angel. I'll be ready."

I really can't believe this shit. I was standing in front of him naked with my hands on my hips. You selfish fat bastard! At first, I know I said that he was solid and slightly overweight but now I'm definitely changing my assumption to fat!

"Where is the restroom?" I flatly asked.

INEVITABLE

"First door...on the left," he said sounding halfway asleep. I briskly walked to the bathroom, shut the door, and locked it behind me. I looked at myself in the mirror. "Huhhhhhhhhhh," I sighed out loud and shook my head from side to side. There is nothing wrong with you. You are too good for this loser. I started to get more upset the more I thought about it. I didn't even get to bust one. He sure fucking did though. I deserved to get me one, I thought with a devilish grin. "I'm going to get me one," I quietly told myself. But, now his dick will never ever get into my sweet stuff again. Not after that lame ass performance. I'm a firm believer of good first impressions. Playboy, you fucked that up. Now, your mouth on the other hand is about to play makeup.

I turned around walked out the door and back into the living room. I don't care if I have to rape his face. I'm getting mine today.

When I entered the living room, Darnell was lying vertical on the couch, stretched out and his dick still limp. No matter, I had no need for that. I saw my newly purchased bra and panties on the floor. What a waste. I played with my clit to get the juices back to flowing. I guess Kitty was still turned on in spite of the mishap because when I slid my fingers in between my folds she was still hot and soaking wet. Mmm and still sensitive.

Okay, your turn fat boy. I climbed on the couch and all the way up to Darnell's face. I made sure that my pussy lips were aligned with the lips on his face before I pressed down. At first, it didn't even seem like he noticed. I think he had slightly dozed off. After a couple seconds of my moisture on his mouth, he quickly got the picture and lent me his tongue.

He darted it in and out, too fast and a little too hard. "Keep your tongue out." I demanded. "Don't move it." Shit, he had done enough already, didn't want him ruining my nut. I was now creaming all over his face, his goatee was coated with my pussy juices. I held on to the couch to get more leverage. I used the tip of his tongue to stimulate my clit.

"Ooouuu damn," I panted. Yeah, this is much better than earlier. I mean I still needed dick, just not his.

"Damn bah, you awh sooo wehhh," he mumbled, I could barely make out what he was saying while he was wearing my pussy muzzle.

I was almost to my destination. I felt it coming down. "Mmm, here it is, I'm... bout to... cum... mmmmmm." Ecstasy, ah yes. I grinded for a few more seconds then removed Kitty from his face. I laughed to myself as I looked down at Darnell. It looked like he was getting a facial and I threw in the coochie juice mask free of charge.

"Damn baby, I didn't know your shit was going to be this tasty," he said while licking his lips. I smiled while I walked around the couch for my panties. "Give me a few Angel. I have to go pee. I'll be right back. I'm going to tear that pussy up," he said, walking down the hallway.

Now was the time to make my great escape. I scurried along, getting dressed in the process. I wanted to hurry up and make my exit before he came back. I trotted to the kitchen put on my jacket and grabbed my purse from the chair.

As I headed to the door I heard Darnell. "Okay baby, I'm ready now. I hope you are because I'm—"

"Whatever," I said slamming the door behind me. I needed to hurry up and put this lame ass day behind me. I'm glad I didn't live far away because it didn't give me too much driving time to think about the situation and add fuel to the fire. But it did give me time nevertheless.

I felt my pussy jumping. It wasn't satisfied at all. Hell, we weren't satisfied. I didn't set up this date just to get ate out. Even though I do love mouth action, I would rather it to be an appetizer, not the main course.

I shook my head thinking that I was sounding like a hoe but it was the truth. I was still horny. I started squeezing my thighs together to take some of the pressure off but it just made matters worse. I was almost home and it's a wonder how I didn't get in an accident because everything that I saw while driving, the road, other cars, traffic lights, my windshield wipers, all were replaced, in my head, by giant penises, my vibrator Mr. Dependable to be exact, and I was racing home to him.

When I entered my apartment I tore my clothes off. My arms were caught in my jacket, I tripped over my jogging pants leg, and by the time I reached my bed, one of my arms was still in my bra.

I didn't even want to waste any energy sliding my panties off. They just had to come along for this ride. I reached for my dildo and caught a glimpse of my phone that was flung to the nightstand. "Damien? Shit!" I said I wouldn't speak his name again. My ex. My cheating, no-good, non-respecting, low down, guaranteed to fuck me good and make me cum at least twice, ex! "Auuugghhhh," I screamed out loud. I wanted to call him so bad. He was familiar, he knew me, knew my body, and definitely knew Kitty.

I looked at the phone a little longer then decided against making a fool out of myself. Well, not today anyways. Today it was just Mr. Dependable and I. I turned the black end cap clockwise as far as it would go and shivered as it strongly vibrated in my hand.

"Do what you do best baby, make momma cum!" I said as I laid back, opened up and received my only real lover for the evening. What a life!

CAROLINA

"Hey M.A. I got your message." I laughed to myself remembering from my younger years how I spelled out Ma instead of actually calling her that. It kind of stuck with me and I've been doing it ever since

"Hey baby, I was calling to let you know that I talked to Carolina today and she said she has another piece of investment property for us to look at."

I smiled thinking how far I had come. I can remember my younger days when I would almost cry because my parents would make me save my money. I would go out, bust my ass cutting grass or shoveling snow all day and I couldn't even spend it the way that I wanted. Guess you don't see the bigger picture until you get a little older.

My parents were grooming me at a young age not to fall victim to what plagues most Americans, especially African Americans, today, spending and not being able to afford it.

Now I'm able to buy things that I want and I owe it all to them. I see it clearly now, five investment properties later. Possibly six, depending on how this new one that Carolina wanted to talk about goes. The extra money brought in from the three houses we are renting out is lovely. A great addition to the already lovely pay I'm receiving from working at Ford and the nice investments that I have made in the stock market.

"So anyways," my mother said in a pleading voice, "since I have a couple of errands to run and your dad is acting like a little baby over his back aching I was wondering—"

"Yes M.A., I guess I can take up the slack for my less than enthusiastic business partners."

"What?" she asked, now raising her voice. "I know you're not getting smart with your mother boy, I'll—"

"Dang M.A. chill out. You know I'm just playing, dang. Of course I'll handle it," I said cutting her off before she became more irate. "You know I'm the President behind this organization anyways, so I'm used to it."

"Oh boy, hush. You wouldn't even be in this little organization as you call it, if it weren't for your dad and me."

"I know M.A., and I appreciate it, you know I do. Man, can't even joke anymore. I heard that came with old age though," I said, jokingly. The truth was I really liked handling the business. It was a nice contrast to working in an automotive factory. Plus, I always learned a lot from Carolina. I loved flirting with her too, even though I knew she would never cheat on her husband with me, it was nice to try my game on a nice looking woman close to 10 years my senior.

"So where's my daddy? I bet he'll be a little nicer to me."

My mother let out a quiet chuckle. "You know your dad. He's either in the room watching the news or some type of sports game." She knew her husband well and she should after being married for 30 years this year. "Do you want to speak to him?"

"Yeah, let me holla at the old man for a minute."

"You better not let him hear you say that. Baby! Your son is on the phone," my mom yelled.

I heard my dad in the background yelling then he picked up the phone. "Hey, hey, what up doe?" My dad always killed me trying to keep up with the latest sayings and slang. "What, what's so funny. I didn't say it right?"

"Yeah, you said it right." I was still laughing my ass off.

"Oh, I heard a couple of young boys walking up the block saying it. Figured I'd put it in my lingo."

"Seriously Dad, stop please."

"So what's up? You dropping by today?"

"Maybe a little later. I have a little running around to do."

"Oh okay, did your mom tell you about Carolina calling?"

"Yep, I'm about to call her as soon as I hang up with you." I replied.

"Good, good." My dad sounded satisfied. It made me feel really good to please him. Hands down, I think he's the best father and best man in existence. I can only hope that one day I can be half as good as he is. "You are getting pretty good at this real estate thing huh?"

"Yeah, I'm doing a little something. Pretty soon you and M.A. are going to be able to sit back and relax."

"Sounds good to me," he said chuckling. "About time we get a little VIP treatment. We took care of you all of these years, time for you to return the favor."

"Hey don't get too excited yet. I'm still in my learning phase, which means the three of us are still in this together for a while." My parents were already financially set. They've always saved and invested and both have a very nice retirement fund because of it. Even though they never said it, I knew it all was for me. They wanted me to be financially stable way before I became their age. I was truly blessed in the parent department.

"We'll see you when you get here. Oh wait your mom wants to speak back at you."

"Future?"

"Yes M.A.," I answered my mom unenthusiastically for I knew what was coming next.

"Are you coming to church Sunday?" Yep, I knew my mom. She loved church and at every moment tried to get me back into it.

"Huh, what did you say? Can't hear you."

"I said—"

"Crriiiiikkcraaakkkkchissss!" I tried my best to imitate static noises over the phone, "I...can't...crrrr...I can't hear you M.A., must be a bad connection."

"Yeah, Satan," she replied laughing, "he's the bad connection." Even though I wasn't near her, I could feel that she had her hand on her hip. "Don't try to play me for stupid, you heard what I said."

"Come on M.A. do you have to ask me that every time we talk?"

"Yes!" she answered.

I sighed, "Okay I'll try. I'm not saying yes, but I'll try."

"Wow, that's a big improvement from 'naw I don't think so'. In a couple of months, maybe I'll get a maybe."

"Ha ha ha, very funny. I'll try."

"Okay, call me later and let me know how the meeting with Carolina goes."

"Will do. I love you."

"Love you too." Then we hung up.

I found Carolina's name in my phone and dialed. Buddy did a little jerk to let me know that he was excited to hear from her also.

"Hello?" an elegant and pleasant voice answered.

"Hey, how is my favorite realtor slash financial advisor doing?"

"This has to be Future. No one gives me as many compliments when I answer the phone as you."

"Yeah it's me. Dang woman, where have you been? I missed you!" I knew Carolina was married and older than I was, but I could always tell that she loved my flirting.

"Whatever, I can't tell. My number hasn't changed," she joked.

"That's because I didn't want your hubby to catch wind of our little affair."

"Future, be honest with yourself. You know you couldn't handle me." Her laugh was surrounded by nervousness, probably from not knowing what I would say next. We always treaded dangerous waters. We never swam, never dived. But, if treading was all I could do, I was going to tread like I was in the middle of the ocean with no lifeboat in sight.

"With all due respect Mrs. Carolina Montgomery, I think you can't handle the fact that you know I can handle you, and very well at that." She confirmed my suspicions with brief silence. I think she was trying to decide if she wanted to continue treading or submerge herself.

"You are crazy. You know that?" she responded with a more subtle voice.

Guess the treading continues. "Like a fox," I answered.

"So I take it you talked to your mom."

"Yes, just got off of the phone with her."

"I love her, you know that. She is such a nice woman. I mean she really helped my sisters and I through some tough times after my mother died." My mother and Carolina's mom were best friends. She died when Carolina was young and my mom stepped in and took over that mother role even though her and her sisters went to live with their aunt. To this day, Carolina and her sisters call my mom their mother.

"Yeah, she good peoples. Guess that's where I get my charm from, huh?"

"Charm? And who told you that you were charming?" she asked laughing.

"All of my women tell me all the time."

"I almost forgot that you were a player. But I wouldn't call them women. You must've forgotten last year when I saw you downtown at the African Festival with that hoochie."

"Hoochie?" I chuckled at her old school word.

"Yes, hoochie. What would you call a woman wearing shorts up to her booty cheeks and all of her chest hanging out?"

"A good time?"

She laughed and I loved hearing it. It was proper, upscale, and casual with a hint of class. "So where are you right now? We really need to discuss this property. It is not going to be around for long."

"When do you want to meet?"

"Today, if possible."

"Okay, I was on my way to the barber shop, how about an hour from now?"

"That's good, wait…let's make it an hour and a half. So 6:30 p.m., is that cool?"

"Perfect! Are we meeting at the office?" I asked.

"Actually, I was thinking Double Olive," she responded.

"The martini bar?" I had to make sure I was hearing her right.

"Yes, is that a problem?"

"You mean the martini bar that sells alcohol?"

She laughed. "Yes, what other kind of martini bar is there? If you don't think you can handle that then we can meet at the office."

"No, no, I'll be a good boy, I promise." I admit that I was a little excited. This was the first time that she suggested meeting at a bar. I wasn't thinking that she would get drunk and sleep with me. It was more like it'll be fun just seeing her in a different element and a little looser. This should be interesting.

"Well you better be. Oh and it's the one in Dearborn not Canton."

"Cool, see ya there." And with that, we ended our call.

I pulled up to Kutz Barbershop owned by the barber that I have been going to for over 10 years. As I walked up to the door, I heard the boisterous voices coming from inside. Two men waiting on an open chair were arguing.

"Nigga please, both of them don't have anything on Tami!"

"Tami? Who is Tami?"

"The one chick that was in that Jeezy video," another patron that was getting his hair cut chimed in.

"Yeah, I think he got y'all on that one. Ole girl ass is huge and she got the tits to match."

"Thank you. Good to see that there is one smart person in here besides me," the loud mouth guy said. "And she has a pretty face. Buffie the Body almost looks like a dude." All the fellas in the shop started laughing.

After I gave my barber, Keith, a pound and sat in his chair, I did what I usually do, joined the conversation.

"Aye, I have to agree with my man over there," I said nodding to the loudest guy in the shop.

Keith wrapped the barbers' apron around my neck and interjected. "Now if anyone in here knows about ass, it's this guy. He is a booty connoisseur for real," Keith informed the young customers.

"Sho' ya right," I said in my old school voice. "I like ass as much as the next man, probably more but we gotta stop saying that these chicks are tight just because of the ass."

"Amen, preach brother preach." Loud mouth was super amped now that he had backing.

"That's why I say Beyoncé is the best of any woman out there."

"Ooouuuweee!" a gray haired old head yelled out. "I'm liable to catch a heart attack when I see her shaking her jelly on TV." Everyone laughed at the old man.

"See, now that's settling down material right there. We have to start giving our dicks more credit and stop doing it to anything and everything."

"Aye for real," loudmouth spoke up again, "that's real talk.

"Y'all know he learned all his game from me," Keith proudly stated.

"Some of it, not all," I teased. Keith was three years older than I was. Back in high school when I was a freshman, he and his boys were seniors. They took me up under their wings and showed me the ropes.

The other guys continued talking about their big booty idols while Keith and I kicked it for a little while longer. He has been married now for seven or eight years and they have two kids and a dog and he's only 30. I remember about five years ago when he used to tell us man whatever you do don't ever get married; please wait. Now it's an entire 180-degree turn around. Maybe his wife transformed him or something. Whatever it was I admit it really did seem genuine.

I have seen them out, even at the club and they really seem to click. I can't believe that he would bring sand to the beach. Yeah, she must've brain washed him.

"So what happened to you in the last couple of years Keith? Because I remember not too long ago you were singing a different tune."

He looked at me and laughed. "Future, that's because I didn't know how good I had it. I really didn't realize how much of a blessing it is to have a good woman, a good wife. That's when we were having most of our problems, when I was worried about what was out there and what I thought I was missing out on. It's unfortunate that it took so long to realize that I've had the best thing with me all along."

This was the first time ever and I mean ever that someone married actually made me feel that being single was not as good. I used to look at young married guys with their wives and just shake my head. Keith was making me feel like I was missing out on life because I wasn't married.

I paid my barber his usual 25 dollars and watched as he wrapped it around a large money roll and placed it back in his pocket.

Keith looked over at one of the older barbers in the shop. "Jerry, I'm going to walk outside for a second."

As we walked out of the door, he put his arm around my shoulder and continued to school me.

"I don't mean to preach, but you know I have a daughter now and when I look her in her eyes I can't imagine having another guy playing her and hurting her feelings. That really opened up my eyes because all the women out here are someone else's daughter."

"I feel you," I said walking to my car. "Well partner that was a pretty good speech," I tried to act as if I wasn't affected at all by it, "but I gotta get out of here."

"Alright. I'll holla at you," he said waving me off before walking back into the shop.

While driving down Michigan Avenue I stopped at a red light and felt my jaws clench because the color immediately reminded me of Kandi. I can't believe that bitch almost had me jacking off.

When I looked over at the car next to me my mood instantly lightened. I raised my eyebrows as the woman in the passenger seat leaned over to give the driver three kisses. It didn't seem like any tongue was used, but the kisses, although brief, seemed to have meaning, purpose. The woman ran her finger across his chest as she returned to her original position in the passenger seat.

You can tell that the kisses weren't sexual or had a hidden agenda. She only wanted to show her love for him. Their energy made you want what they had. Their energy made me want...Her, the mystery woman from the club. Okay, have to get Her out of my head. Carolina, here I come!

PERSONAL TRAINER

"OH my God, please tell me that you are lying," Tierra said, trying to catch her breath from laughing.

"I wish that I was. I mean he could've at least made it to the end of the damn song."

"Stop please, stop!"

"Shut up tramp. It's not that funny." I had to laugh over the situation. Darnell was a sad case. In hindsight, him cumming that fast was funny.

"That shit is hilarious," Tierra continued. "That's like something that only happens in the movies or in black fiction novels. Okay, okay, I'll try to get it together. Hold on." The way she was sniffling, I knew that she had tears streaming down her face. "It's just that the first piece of dick that you get since being a free, unattached, single woman, couldn't even stay hard long enough for you to really get it." She continued her laughing session. "What did he say to you when you saw him at work?"

"Girl, I haven't even had a chance to say anything. Every time he sees me he damn near breaks his neck to duck and head in the opposite direction."

"Well that's what he needs to do. If I were you, I would put him on blast. Post his picture and a brief…and I do mean brief, description of what he's capable of because I definitely wouldn't want to come anywhere near him. You'll be okay though. Just be patient, you'll be fucking a big fat dick in no time."

"Shut up girl, it's not even that serious. You're talking like I'm fiend out or something." I tried hard to mask the fact that I really was. What I wouldn't give right now for a stiff one.

"Mmm hmm, if you say so. So are you going out tonight?"

"Yeah, I might," I said with a play attitude.

"Have you talked to Bri?"

"Earlier in the week."

"I talked to her earlier. She said that she was going to call you today."

"I'm sure she will," I said still thinking about my bum date.

"Oh I forgot to tell you earlier, probably because of all the laughing that I was doing, guess who's back in town."

I tried to think of anyone that I knew that had left out of town and drew a blank. "I give up, who?"

"Pierre," Tierra said low and direct like I definitely knew who she was talking about.

"For real, Pierre? Are you serious?" I responded with excitement.

Tierra laughed. "You don't have any idea who I'm talking about do you?"

"Not a damn clue." We both laughed.

"Girl, Pierre! Pierre, our first personal trainer. Remember I dated his cousin with the big dick. The Pierre that always tried to get with you. Tall, dark, and chocolate Pierre."

"Damn, are you serious?" My memory was definitely jogged now. "Where did you see him?"

"I was at GNC today getting me some fiber pills, because you know I've been a little constipated lately, when I saw him at the checkout counter. When I say he looks good, giirrrrlll! I gave him my number to give to his cousin and you know he asked about you."

"Did he? And what did you tell him?"

"Well, he asked me if you were still with Damien and I told him that he would have to ask you about any of your personal business. So he gave me his number to give to you and said to tell you to call him ASAP!"

"Wow, okay." I was a little geeked that someone would want to get at me like that.

She waited for a couple of seconds. "So, do you want it?"

"Um, sure, I guess."

"Stop acting like you're not geeked."

"Naw for real, Pierre was hot three years ago when he moved to Vegas to compete for body building. I can only imagine how he looks now. It was so hard for me to pretend like I didn't want to do him when I was with Damien."

"So, do you want the number or not?"

"Of course I want it," I yelled.

"That's my girl. I bet you don't have to worry about his stamina. Nigga probably will fuck you all night."

"Shut up crazy." My heart actually sped up a little at the thought. Mmmm, an all-night session is just what I needed. Tierra gave me the number and I locked it in my phone. "Okay Tee, I'll call you later when I get home from the gym."

"Don't work out so hard that you can't stay up tonight…or

rather tell him too!" She started laughing again.

"Bye!" I started thinking that I had made a mistake by telling her what had happened. I returned my car stereo to its normal volume and listened in as Michael Baisden graced my radio with his high-energy voice.

"Today ladies, the show is for you! Today you get to air it all out. Yeah that's right! Today you get to put the fellas on blast. Today's show is about the men who are horrible in the bedroom. Call me up ladies. Somebody is going to get in trouuuble today! We'll be right back after Missy Elliot takes us back and tell y'all how she don't want no... one minute man."

"Break me off, show me what you got... 'cause I don't want no one minute man." Missy's words blared through my speakers letting the world in on exactly how I was feeling.

"You tell 'em girl," I said, thinking back on last weekend. I should put Darnell's sorry ass on blast. I'm not that type of woman to put someone's business out in the street. Well, I might not be that type of woman, but Halo certainly is. I entered the number to Michael's show and pressed send.

"Michael Baisden show!" the receptionist answered.

"Yes, I was calling to comment on the topic," I shyly said.

"Okay, and your age?"

"Twenty-five."

"Name?"

A smiled formed across my face as I called out my alias, "Halo."

"Halo, I remember you. Girl you kicked ass the last time you were on," the receptionist said.

I laughed at how hyped she sounded. I could tell she was a youngster. "Thanks, I think."

"Mr. Baisden told me to put you right on the next time you called in."

"Wow, okay, are you sure?" I was shocked.

"Yeah, seems like you and Baby Boy get the VIP hookup. Mr. Baisden doesn't do that for a lot of people."

"Wait, did you say Baby Boy?" Even though he got on my last nerve, I couldn't deny the intrigue that he created for me.

"Yep, the one and only," she answered.

"Mr. Asshole would be more like it," I said, thinking back on our last battle of the sexes.

"Call him what you want," the young receptionist said in an exhilarating tone, "just don't call him ugly. I was introduced to him at the latest function we had in Detroit and girrrl he is foine!"

"Is that so?"

"Definitely. Tall, dark, chocolate, luscious lips, nice ass body. On top of that, he gets ratings. Actually, I think most of his personality on the air is a front. Women love to hate him. When he calls, our phones go crazy. Half the women call to curse him out while the other half call to try to date him." We both laughed. "The last time we had the both of you guys on was one of the best-rated shows this year. Let me put you on hold girl. You are going to end up getting me in trouble. You didn't hear this from me but Baby Boy already confirmed to be on today's show."

"Today? Um, okay." I felt myself getting nervous like I was about to go on a first date or something.

"Yep, so the next voice you will hear will be Michael Baisden's. Go get'em girl," she cheered.

"I'm going to try my best," I tried to reassure her and myself. "By the way, what is your name?"

"Jada."

"Jada, pretty name. Maybe we'll meet when you come back to Detroit."

"I'd like that." And with that, she placed me on hold. I turned my radio up a little to hear Michael and the current caller.

"Trina from Virginia, what up baby? How is everythang?"

"Everythang is everythang!"

"What you mad about girl? Tell daddy all about it."

"Y'all suck!" the caller yelled.

"Oh no you didn't, no she didn't say y'all."

"Oh yes I did, y'all… men… suck when it comes to pleasing women in bed. And unfortunately, y'all don't suck good enough when it comes to pleasing a woman in bed."

"Wait a minute! Wait just a doggone minute! Don't be putting me in a category with these busters! I put it down in the bedroom baby," Michael screamed.

The caller began to laugh at Michael pretending to be upset. "Okay Michael, maybe not you, but the rest of them are horrible. I never knew that there are so many grown men out there that can't—"

"Whoa watch your tongue now, this is a family show," Michael started laughing. "And how do you know that all men are horrible? Have you dated all of them?"

"I have had my share, but I have friends, co-workers sisters, cousins and they all say the same thing. Never expect too much from a guy sexually, because you'll get let down each and every time."

"Trina, you are too much. Let me get to my next caller. Wait a minute; is this who I think it is? The infamous Halo from Detroit? What up mama? How is everythang?"

"Everythang is everythang Mike," I said laughing. "The infamous Halo, huh?"

"A little too much?" he asked, much quieter now.

"Little bit." I responded while laughing.

"So what took you so long calling me back? You mad at me or something?"

I took the bait and played along with him, after all it's his show. "Of course not, you know that I could never be mad at you, but the other men, mm mmm mmmm!" I shook my head as if Michael could see me. "Michael it is really a shame."

"No, not you too! So you telling me that you agree with my last caller?"

"Absolutely, and Trina if you are still listening, high five girl! I feel what you are saying. Michael I am telling you, I think you need at least three men to halfway satisfy you. You want a man who's big enough to hit all your hidden spots and secret rooms, but chances are if he's that big, he's going to give you a hysterectomy or he's a two-minute brother. Now, if you get that guy with just enough length and thickness who can do it right, chances are he's not going to know how to perform oral to save his life. But if you get the oral specialist, nine times out of 10 he's going to be a Tiny Tim."

"Damn woman, breathe! Take a damn breath. I can't believe you're gonna play us like that huh?"

I laughed a little. Felt good to let that out. "I think y'all do a good job at that without our help."

"Girl, you have my call board lit up. Bet you it's all the women calling to agree with that nonsense."

"Whatever, you know I'm not lying. And normally I don't do this, but I'm going to put him on blast because I feel that's what he did to me." I felt myself getting into character now, felt kind of good bringing the drama.

"Put it out there then, you have the floor."

"Okay. I recently had an encounter."

"An encounter?" he asked sarcastically.

"Yes, an encounter… okay a scheduled booty call with a guy who normally wouldn't have received that kind of encounter with me. Not because I'm stuck up or something, but because honestly he wasn't exactly my type physically."

"What? Was he fat or something?"

I thought about saying the first thing that popped in my head but instead went with, "Um, no, not fat, just not what I normally like."

"Okay, I can give you that. Physical attraction is definitely important."

I continued, "Point two is that we work together, not close, but in the same building."

Michael cut in, "Okay these are two valid and good reasons not to give a guy some, so why did you girl?" he asked, raising his voice.

"Well Michael, I'm single now and this guy has been trying for a long time to get it. I thought who better to reward for their persistence?" Michael got a real kick out of that. I tried to keep it spicy for the listeners.

"Halo, you are too much girl!"

"But the main reason was," I hesitated to emphasize my point, "I might not have a man but I'm not dead. I was horny as hell Mike!" Michael Baisden started laughing and couldn't stop. "I mean, you want me to keep it real right?"

"That's what...awww man! That's what you are supposed to do baby. So what happened? What did he do or didn't do?"

"Michael, this guy was through before we even really started."

"What do you mean?" he asked laughing.

"I mean three minutes."

"Three minutes?"

"Three quick, nonproductive minutes. Oh and that's including the kissing and touching."

"Wow, are you sure that you mean three minutes, as in 180 seconds." Michael kept questioning me as if it wasn't possible.

"Let me put it to you in another way... four pumps."

"Are you serious?"

"Yep!" I responded laughing at the situation now myself.

"Dayum, dayum, dayum!" he said doing his Florida Evans imitation. Please say it ain't so."

"It's definitely so," I said now starting to regret even letting Darnell get close to Kitty. "So you see that's why I think you guys suck sexually. He was talking all this crap about what he was going to do to me, had me all hyped up. Now don't get me wrong, I love my black men. But let's face it there are a lot of you out there, and you know who you are, that are terrible in bed.

"Well Ms. Halo, I have a caller on the other line that totally disagrees with you," Mike said calmly.

"Must be a man. Hope it's not the three minute guy from my job," I joked. I tried to act as if I was clueless to the surprise guest. My girl Jada had already hooked me up with the inside scoop.

"Nope, not unless you made out with Baby Boy. What up

dawg! How is everythang?" Michael said hyped up now that his boy was on the phone.

"Come on Mike, you know everythang is everythang."

"Have you been listening to this woman? Come help the men out. I know you remember Halo." Michael said sarcastically.

"Of course I do. How could I forget a voice as lovely as hers? How are you doing Halo?" Baby Boy asked.

God he sounded good. He had the kind of voice that you would love hearing talk to you before, during, and after sex. "I'm doing fine, how about you?"

"A lot better now," he shot back.

I thought it should be me to break up this romantic mood. "Okay, now that we've gotten all of the formalities out of the way, you ready to do battle?"

Baby Boy knew that I meant every word. "Let's!" he answered frank and sincere. My opponent was definitely ready.

"That's what I'm talking about," Michael Baisden said ready for the drama and controversy, but mostly the ratings. "Let's get ready to rummmmmble!"

"So Baby Boy, I'm taking it that you don't agree with my comments or the views of the other women on the show today. And I'm guessing that you have no complaints in the bedroom about you, am I right?" I asked, rolling my eyes while driving.

Baby Boy cleared his throat. "Well, answering your questions in reverse order, no I don't get complaints; I get standing ovations and applause. And to your first question... hell naw I don't agree."

"Get her Baby Boy, get her," Coach Michael exclaimed.

"Halo, the problem is not how bad a man performs in the bedroom or how much he sucks... or don't suck, depending on the situation." I couldn't help but to smile on that one. "The problem is the lack of communication that some women have sexually."

He really threw me a curveball on that one. I didn't even see it coming. "Wait a minute," I gripped my steering wheel tighter and adjusted my Bluetooth earpiece, "are you saying that your subpar performance in the bedroom is our fault? Wow, I can't wait for you to explain this one to me."

"Me neither," Mike said laughing, "explain it to me too so I can use it for an excuse when I perform badly." All three of us laughed. I know his entire audience did too.

Baby Boy continued, "Most of the time women don't tell men what they like or dislike. If he's banging you too fast and—"

I cut him off and figured I would play with him for a while. After all this wasn't me, it was Halo. "Fast in which position?"

"Uh oh, watch out now," Michael warned.

I could hear the smile forming on Baby Boy's face. "From the back of course, does that work for you?" he asked seductively.

"Yeah, real good," I continued to tease.

"And let's just say that you didn't particularly like it that way or didn't want it that way that night. Instead, you wanted slow and sensual. Most women would be so turned off from him just trying to break your back off that you would fake like it feels good just so that he'll hurry up and get finished and get off of you."

I slightly giggled, remembering how many similar stories I have heard women tell me like that. I was actually guilty of that with Damien a couple of times myself.

"There is absolutely no reason for a woman to fake pleasure or an orgasm. No reason at all. Just tell me what I have to do to get that real one out and I'll do it. You feel me Mike?"

"Uh oh Halo, you okay over there? You are a little quiet."

"I'm just taking it all in, that's all." I answered.

"That's because she knows I'm telling the truth. You see what women don't realize is that most men, not all, kiss and have sex like they did with their last partner. They are used to doing what their last partner liked. So, when he comes to you, he's giving you what the type of woman he's used to dealing with liked. That's not to say that he sucks or doesn't know how to please women Halo, he just hasn't been taught how to particularly please you."

Wow. He was good and it was true. I never thought of it like that.

"I'm telling you Mike, these women will have you thinking that you are not worth anything if you let them. And have men thinking that they have to be 10 inches or longer to satisfy."

Michael was cracking up now. "Baby Boy you a mess man!" he managed to get out in between laughing.

"I'm serious man. If a woman knows what she likes and what satisfies her, she would be able to teach that guy with five inches to achieve her goal as well. And let me tell you, every woman who thinks that they want 10 inches… can't even handle it, trust me." My Kitty did three quick twitches at that one. Sounded like he was insinuating that was his size or damn near close.

"People need to be freakier with their mates. You know what I'm saying Mike? Have more freaky talking going on during sex." Baby Boy continued, "That's why freaks get satisfied, because I know when I'm up in it I'm like," he lowered that already mesmerizing voice of his, "you like that baby? Mmmmmm, tell me how you want it. Tell me what you need me to do. Now if she can't speak up, I'm going to hit it like I want to hit it so don't go dogging me to your girls after it's over and done."

"You tell'em dawg. I think you got your girl over here stunned. It might be a TKO Baby Boy."

"No, I'm here," I answered, "I had just kind of zoned out when he was doing that bedroom voice." I cleared my throat and laughed along with the guys. "I was listening, and I must admit, he does bring up some valid points. Even I'm guilty of doing some of them sometimes."

"Wow, I think I'm going to have to give this one to Baby Boy. Maybe you should think about retirement." He and Baby Boy laughed.

"What? Retirement? Don't count me out that fast now," I said. "I do agree with some of the things he said, but I think all of the women will agree with me when I say that it's not that easy to tell a man what to do, especially during sex."

"Uh oh, she's getting up off of the canvas," Michael joked.

"Sometimes, Baby Boy, we have to take one for the team and not say anything because we don't want to bruise your little ego. You might not take it too well, might get a little limp or even get mad at us. Most men think that they already know what we like. They think that they already know how to pleasure every woman. Then, if we do tell you what we like or God forbid, what we do not like, the next time around, you still don't do it!"

"She's pulling herself up by the ropes, Baby Boy." The two men continued to laugh.

"So Mr. Baby Boy, instead of telling you what we don't like during sex, we sometimes don't say anything and yes, fake it, because if we did tell you what we didn't like during sex chances are the list would be so damn long that we wouldn't be able to finish anyways."

"She swings and down goes Baby Boy!" Michael was all the way live now. "Man, my phone lines are off the chain right now. I am going to have to call this one a draw ladies and gents."

"Come on Mike, if you weren't counting so damn slow she wouldn't have even stood up when I knocked her down. I think I was robbed," Baby Boy playfully said.

I giggled, "Aw come on now, don't be a sore loser."

"You know what? I'll lose to you any day Halo. If you really want bedroom satisfaction, just let me know. I can definitely help you out with that."

"Is that so?" I inquired.

"Yes, it is!"

"Humph, I'll make sure I keep that in mind. But for now I have a little something that's getting me through and I don't even have to give him instructions… just batteries."

"And on that note we have to take a break. We'll be back in a few, so stay tuned," Michael instructed his loyal listeners. A couple of seconds later he called my name.

"Yeah, I'm here," I answered.

"Baby Boy?" Michael called out to my opponent.

"What up doe?" he answered in Detroit's greeting of choice.

"You guys did great today. The ratings go through the roof when you two are on. You are like fire and ice. Man, I would love to see a sex scene involving you two."

"What?" I asked shocked.

"Me too," Baby Boy said.

"Look, here's the deal. I need to find a way for you two to call in on the same day, preferably days that we do the battle of the sexes. In return for now, whenever there is a concert event or get-together in the D that the station is sponsoring, I'll make sure that you guys get the VIP hookup. Now if this thing keeps going the way it is now, I might be able to get y'all on the payroll or something. Give me a chance to try and work something out. So how does that sound?"

Baby Boy spoke up first, "What are you asking for, one day a week?"

"If that, but at least once every two weeks," Michael answered.

"Well, I'm down if Halo's down." Baby Boy said and waited on my response.

I thought about the chance of getting to spar with sexy voice regularly and couldn't pass, but I didn't want to make it seem obvious. "I'm down. I can't make any promises that I'll be available every week." I cleared my throat, "Especially without a contract and all," Michael laughed at me, "but I'll try my best."

"Cool, I'll connect you with my receptionist. Baby Boy, I think she has all of your info, that way I can get you guys through directly. Okay guys, I have a show to finish. Till next time."

"Hey Halo," Baby boy called frantically probably thinking the same as me, that we would soon be disconnected from each other. "So you're living in Detroit huh?"

"Really close to it," I answered not wanting to give him too much information about me, at least not yet.

"So maybe we could meet up somewhere or something like that."

"Yeah, maybe," I said reeling him in.

"Cool, so how—" I heard a click and with that Baby Boy was disconnected from me by Jada. She logged in my contact information before we said our goodbyes.

I thought about how Baby Boy would look in person. I wondered if he really was packing and if he could really please me the way that he insinuated he could. My phone rang and brought my attention back to the road, where it should've been anyways.

"Hello."

"Hey Angel, what are you doing?" Brianna asked.

"Nothing much, just pulling up to the gym."

"See how you do. Now you know that I told you to tell me the next time you went because I wanted to go with you."

I rolled my eyes knowing that every time I asked her or Tee to go to the gym they always came with some lame excuse. "Sorry, I forgot," I answered in a monotone voice. "Plus if you start going to the gym, there is a chance you might lose that badunkadunk."

"More like, big fat ass. I want it to be more perky and firm like yours. It's starting to bounce around too much."

"Well, I want mine to be juicy like yours," I shot back.

"Well then, let's trade," Brianna said laughing. "Oh I almost forgot the reason I called you. Are you listening to 92.3 FM?"

My eyes widened and my breathing became nonexistent. "Uh, yeah, why?"

"Girl, Michael Baisden's show is off the hook today," she screamed.

I instantly became nervous. Guess I never thought about the fact that someone might notice my voice on the radio, even though I changed my name. "Yeah, I guess it was."

"That cumming too quick thing must be contagious or something girl, because a caller on there today had a story similar to the one that you just had."

"Crazy huh?" I wanted to switch the subject so bad but didn't want to seem too obvious. I just stuck with saying as little as possible.

"I think her name is Halo. She called the show a couple weeks ago too. I really like her, she tells it like it is, no holds barred." The more Bri talked, the more I realized that she didn't have a clue that Halo and I were, in fact, one and the same.

"I wonder if she and Baby Boy are ever going to hookup, because the way they go at it, you can tell that they definitely want each other."

"Really? Why? Just because they disagree?" I asked trying to defend myself on the sly.

"Naw, it's the way they argue. You can tell there is definitely some sexual tension between the two."

"I don't think so. I think that they are just two different people trying to make their arguments from two different points of view." I didn't notice how loud my voice had risen until it was too late.

There was a couple seconds of uncomfortable silence, and then Brianna spoke up. "Ooookayyyy, are they like personal friends of yours or something? Damn, why are you on the defense?"

I thought about whether I should tell my friend my little secret and how she would look at me afterwards if I did. What the hell!

"All I was saying is that—"

I cut Brianna off, "It's me okay! It's me! Please don't think I'm stupid." I sat in the parking lot of the gym with my car turned off, gripping the steering wheel tight with my eyes closed. I refused to open them, embarrassed of what she was going to think and say.

"Uh, who's you? What are you talking about Angel?" she asked, still clueless to the situation.

I opened one of my eyes, slowly, as if one of my feet was already in a hot tub of water and I was just stepping the other one in. "I'm her," I whispered.

"What? I can't—"

"I'm her!" I shouted, "I'm Halo, she's me!"

More silence. "Are you, wait... Halo? Angel? Angels wear Ha... ohhhhh I get it. Hell naw, I can't believe my girl is a star. You sound so different over the radio." Brianna started laughing her ass off, which caught me off guard, but made me comfortable enough to open both eyes now. "Wow, I can't believe that she's you. Halo is so... so, bold and edgy and..."

"Different. I know, I know," I said completing her sentence.

"It's like she's your alter ego. Wow, I guess that means that you really put Darnell's ass on blast."

"Don't say that! I didn't air him out. It's not like I said his name."

"Mmm hmm, if you say so. Girl, do you know that you have a mini fan club?" she said raising her voice again.

"Shut up Bri." She was taking it too far now.

"No, Angel, I'm serious after that last time that you called my co-workers and I talked about that for the entire week. You really say what a lot of women think, but are not able or just too scared to say. How many times have you called in anyways?"

I giggled. "This was only my second time, I swear. But he did offer for me to be on the show at least every other week." My mind swiftly switched to Baby Boy and back. "Me and what's-his-name."

"Like you don't remember his name," Brianna said sarcastically bringing a smile to my face. "So y'all on the payroll now? Did you get the digits yet? Have y'all been talking off the air at all?" Brianna rambled her questions off without taking a breath.

"Damn Brianna, slow down. We are not getting paid as of yet. He offered the VIP hookup at concert and events though."

"Shit, that's good enough, as long as you get three tickets. Please tell me you're accepting?" Brianna pleaded. She sounded more excited than me.

"I went into diva mode. I told him that I'd try my best and that I had to check my schedule. You know how busy I am."

"Please, you don't even have a schedule."

"We know that, but he doesn't." We both laughed.

"Okay, now for the million dollar question," she paused for a few seconds, "what's up with Baby Boy? Did you get the scoop?"

"Actually Bri, I only know what you know."

"I heard he was a cutie pie. Not a pretty boy, but put together well indeed. One of my co-workers said that she saw him at a record release party talking to Michael Baisden a couple months back and knew it was him when she heard Michael call out his name. Wonder what his real name is?"

"Really?" This was beginning to make my curiosity grow even more.

"Yes really. So if you are not interested when you meet him, pass him on down to me."

"Bri? Can I ask you a personal question?"

"Angel, you know that you can ask me anything. What's up?"

"I was a little hesitant about asking Brianna anything about her preference in lovers. I never wanted to offend her or cross the line. "Are you all the way talking to guys now or are you still feeling women?"

She laughed before answering me. "Honestly, right now I'm feeling guys. I started off liking guys. I didn't have my first bisexual experience until my first year in college. But even then, I don't think it was something that I thought I was going to do forever. I guess I don't put any limitations on myself. I like who I like. When I'm with a woman, it's like more of a risk, it's fun, it's something that makes me feel good for the moment, but deep in my heart I will always want a man."

"So you're only like 40 percent bi?"

"Um, more like 38 and a half."

"Girl, you are crazy. Okay, I'll call you when I get out of here. Gotta go get my sweat on," I said finally stepping out of my car.

"You need to be getting your sweat on with Baby Boy."

"Whatever." I was trying to get him out of my head and here Brianna was putting him right back in.

"Okay Angel, I'll talk to you later."

I walked to the gym entrance still thinking of Baby Boy putting me in that doggy style position that he spoke of earlier. Something is definitely wrong with me, I thought while shaking my head. I have to remember to make an appointment with my doctor.

"Hi beautiful," a short stocky guy spoke, breaking my train of thought.

"Hey," I shot back trying not to be rude.

He looked me up and down. "Now you know you don't even need to be working out at all."

"It can always be a little better right?" I felt his eyes burning a hole in my butt as I passed him up and headed for the door.

I felt sorry for short men. I know for a fact that none of my girls would date them and I think a lot of women share the same sentiment.

I sighed as I returned back to my original train of thought. I was fantasizing over a man who I've spoken to but never seen and over another who I've seen but have never spoken to. Yep, Angel you have finally flipped your lid. I felt a sudden twitch in Kitty as I imagined the two mystery men running a train on me. Baby Boy eating me out from the back as I sucked my mystery man from the club. Damn! I needed some dick… bad.

After changing in the locker room, I did my usual routine, stretched and did 15 minutes on the elliptical machine to warm up. Today was leg day, my least favorite body part a couple of years ago. As I stood in front of the mirror and stretched my quads, I noticed just how far I have come. Still lean, but nowhere near those skinny chicken legs. My limbs were now long, shapely, and sculpted providing a nice curvy pathway to my favorite part on my body, my onion.

It was time to get to work. I placed the padded Smith Machine bar behind my neck and with 10 pounds on each side, I started my three sets of 12. After completing my third set, I turned around to go to the leg extension machine and bumped into what felt to be a brick wall.

"You know if you ever become famous or anything, I'm taking credit for that nice ass body of yours." Now this was a man, I thought to myself as my eyes fixated on his chest. By the time they made their way to his face, I couldn't believe who was standing directly in front of me.

"Pierre, is that you?" I said giving him a hug. "What up baby?" Ain't this a blimp, Tierra spoke his ass up. It was my first real trainer who taught me a lot about fitness, nutrition, and not to mention how a man's body is supposed to look.

"Hey mama! Damn, where is your waist?" He took a couple steps back and took in all of me. "What's it been about three years?"

"Feels a lot longer, wow!" And I did mean wow!

"This is crazy. I was just talking about you earlier. I ran into your girl Tierra at GNC today."

"Did you?" I asked trying to sound surprised.

"Guess you haven't talked to her yet," Pierre said sounding a little disappointed.

"Naw, not today," I answered, lying through my teeth.

"Oh, okay then."

"Look at you. You're competing in bodybuilding now right?"

"Yeah, I've done a few, won a few," he said bragging on himself. "I also train a few celebrities here and there." He talked a little more but I swear I didn't hear a word. Tierra wasn't lying at all about Pierre, he had to be about 30 pounds heavier from the last time that I saw him and it was all muscle. He had on a pair of Jordan basketball shorts with a matching beater. Every time he moved, pointed or turned, a different muscle would pop out. I remember him always asking me out but I was with Stupid Ass at the time and blind as hell.

"So what do you think?" Pierre asked and stared at me with raised eyebrows.

"What do I think?" I asked obviously missing something that he had said while staring at him.

"Yeah, about me working out with you today?"

"Oh, um sure. Wait, you're not trying to charge me are you because a sista is broke right now. Plus, you're big time, I couldn't even afford you anyway."

"You know I wouldn't charge you. I just noticed you were doing legs and since that's what I'm working on today, I thought maybe I could show you a couple of exercises to add to your regimen. He licked his lips and looked down at my legs as if they were dipped in batter and deep fried. "Dang Angel, you really look good." A faint moan escaped from his mouth. "Really good."

"Thanks Pierre," I said with my hands on my hips. "And just because you haven't seen me in a while, you don't have to try to be nice to me." I smiled and enjoyed the way he hungrily looked at me.

"Naw, I'm serious. Come on let's go over to these dumbbells." I grabbed my towel and followed him. He was bald headed with broad shoulders, wide back, small waist, nice ass, and thick muscular legs. From head to toe he was good. Now I was the one who was licking my lips.

For the next 45 minutes, he taxed my legs like they have never been taxed before. I'm talking they were burning so bad that I almost told him that I had enough a couple of times. But every time I looked at him, or when he would touch my leg to explain what muscle was working, I totally forgot about the pain.

"So...what do you think? Did you like the workout?"

I wiped the sweat from my face. "Yeah, I liked it. Didn't enjoy it, but I liked it." I still was trying to catch my breath.

He laughed, mouth wide open, showing his supple pink tongue. "No pain, no gain and plus you would only have to do that workout once every two weeks."

"Oh, trust me you didn't even have to tell me that."

Pierre bent down and grabbed his water bottle behind the bench where I stood. I watched him in the mirror as he casually stared at my ass. He stood back up and took a few gulps. "I see you've been hitting the squats pretty good." He smiled.

"Something like that," I said while laughing.

"Looks good. You still with the same guy?"

"Thankfully not."

"Wow!" His eyebrows raised and created three deep lines. "I remember how in love you were back then. Humph, shot down all of my advances." He placed his bottle and towel in his gym bag and threw it around his shoulders.

I took a sip from my water bottle and looked him in the eyes. "I wouldn't shoot them down now." Our eyes stayed connected for a few but we were quickly distracted by each other's body. I felt my nipples getting hard and his eyes let me know that they noticed. It was clear what we both wanted. This wasn't a yearning for conversation or catch up. Our bodies wanted each other in the worst way.

"How long are you in town for?" I asked breaking the silence.

"Till tomorrow. Flight leaves at 4 p.m." His eyes traveled back to my nipples, mine back to his chest. More silence. "I think you should give me your number." He said directly.

I quickly answered, "I think that's a good idea." We flipped our phones open at the same time. I noticed that I had two missed calls, but they could wait. First things first. I gave him my number and then I entered his and pretended to save it. I didn't want him to know that I had already gotten it from Tierra. We grabbed our bags and headed for the door.

"Well Angel, it was definitely good to see you again." He did one last look over. "All of you!"

"Same here," I said, feeling myself blush.

"Well, I better get out of here. Gotta couple errands to run. I'll hit you up."

"Okay." He waved back before opening the doors of his triple black Infiniti truck. Guess the competition thing is doing him good. "Don't have me waiting for too long," I yelled loud enough to make up for the distance between us. Can't believe I just said that, now I probably seem desperate.

"Couldn't even if I tried." He smiled and stepped in his truck. I sat in my car and closed the door.

"Damn he's fine," I said aloud before turning the ignition. Before heading home, I figured I would go and visit my parents. My phone vibrated and reminded me about my missed calls from earlier. One was from T-Mobile reminding me that my bill was overdue. I scrolled down the call log and my heart skipped a beat when I saw that the other call was from Juwaun. I couldn't believe that he still was interested enough to call me. I noticed that I had a new voicemail, too.

After deleting the first six messages, I finally came to the only one that mattered. "Hi Angel, this is Juwaun. Ummmmm, I'm just really not good with leaving messages, so whenever you get a chance, no matter what time it is, hit me up." I looked at the time of the call, I didn't want to return it too fast and seem desperate. It was almost an hour ago. That's long enough, I said to myself as I dialed his number.

He answered on the first ring. "Hello?"

"Juwaun?"

"Yeah, this is me. How are you doing Angel?"

"I can't complain," I answered, trying to suppress the big grin on my face, but couldn't seem to do so. "What's up with you?"

"Oh nothing, you know I just figured that I would follow

the normal routine of me calling you because you never call me, that's all."

"Ha, ha, ha, very funny." I gave the first excuse that popped into my mind, "I've just been a little busy that's all.

"Mmm hmm just too busy for me. But it's all good because I'm starting to get used to you dissing me and I think it's starting to turn me on," he joked.

I laughed out loud. I loved a man who could make me laugh. "You are so silly."

"I am glad that you took the time out of your busy schedule to call me back. I just wanted to inform you of how it's going down."

I was a little confused. Maybe I had missed something. "How it's going down?" I repeated.

"On our lunch date tomorrow," he confidently said.

I laughed as my eyes widened from shock. "Wait, what did you say? Our lunch date? Tomorrow?"

"That's exactly what I said." I was trying to find the humor in his voice and couldn't find any. "Actually, I would love nothing more for you to go out on the town with me tonight, but I thought on such short notice you would make excuses like you don't have your hair or nails done or something to wear. So I decided on lunch because if push comes to shove you can wrap your head up with a scarf and throw on something you already have at the crib."

I think that I was starting to be turned on by his perseverance. "Wow, you really put a lot of thought into this, huh?"

"Sure did," he responded, "so go ahead and have fun with the girls tonight but don't have too much fun because I'm going to need you rested up for tomorrow. I'll be in front of your place at 1 p.m. sharp!"

How does he know where I live? God please don't let him be a stalker. "In front of my place?" I reluctantly asked, "And how do you know where that is?"

"I don't. You're about to tell me." He was so serious. I liked his new demanding role. There was a brief silence followed by numbers and directions from me. I think I would've given him my social security number too, if he had asked for it.. "See how easy that was?" he said, humor returning to his voice. "Look for a dark blue Range Rover. You're not going to need a wakeup call are you?"

"No, I think I can handle that much."

"Cool. Now that we have that out of the way, how did this week go for you?"

"Overall, it has been okay. What's all the noise in the background?" I asked, hearing a lot of different voices.

"I was just walking out of a business meeting when you called."

"Okay, so how did that go?"

"It's okay, Angel. You don't have to pretend like you care."

"What do you mean pretend? If I didn't I wouldn't have asked."

"So are you saying that you do care about me?" It sounded like he was holding his breath for my answer.

"Actually, that would be caring about what you were doing not necessarily about you," I said smiling.

"You play so hard to get, you know that?"

"Now you know that you wouldn't want me if I was easy. Then you would treat me like you treat your other groupies."

"Actually, I treat them pretty damn good. Just kidding!" he quickly interjected.

"Whatever, you know that you are telling the truth."

"I don't want to take up too much of your time, so I'll talk to you tomorrow beautiful."

I smiled, not really wanting to get off the phone with him even though I knew since he was a superstar athlete he had to have a lot on his plate. "Bye bye Juwaun." I held the phone until I heard the dial tone. Damn, Angel in a couple months' time you have gone from bums to ballplayers. I have to be dreaming right now.

TO SWIM OR NOT TO SWIM

WHEN I pulled up to Double Olive, Sally drew her usual attention. Mouths opened and fingers pointed. The atmosphere in Dearborn was great. It had very trendy stores, plenty of places to eat, and there were a lot of new hot spots like Cigar Lounge and Double Olive. Another reason I loved it here was that it didn't play host to the immature crowd.

Walking towards the entrance, I removed my phone and dialed Carolina. "Hey you!" a bright cheery voice greeted me on the first ring.

"Hey you!" I tried not to sound surprised at the excitement in her voice. I didn't know if it was for me or if she had an early start on her spirits.

"Where are you?"

I looked at my watch it was 6:24. "I'm here. Don't be acting like I'm late, I still have six minutes."

"A gentleman never keeps a woman waiting till the last minute," she instructed in a conjured up Old English accent. "Plus a wise man once told me that when opportunity knocks, you run to the door to answer it, not walk."

"Wow, I never heard of that one."
"I know that's because I just made it up."
"Thought so," I said chuckling.
"Future?"
"Yes?"
"I'm knocking, knock… knock… knock!"
"Now is that you… or the opportunity?" I asked hoping that the early jump on spirits idea would give me a little opening.

She giggled like a schoolgirl and lowered her voice to a whisper, "Both."

"Then I'm running to the door darling." And that I did. Upon entering, I noticed a generous crowd, not packed yet but well on its way. People were enjoying what was left of the happy hour specials. I caught a couple of eyes while walking deeper into the trendy, swank bar; one woman who was with two of her girls and another who was sitting with who appeared to be a less than exciting date.

Then I spotted Carolina. She had selected a table in a corner in the back of the bar. The brightness from the lights had reached as far as they could. In this part of the bar, lamps and candles took over the job.

Even though it was dim, I couldn't mistake her for anyone else. Her hair made her stand apart from any other woman I had ever seen. It was radiant and silver and didn't add one day or a second of time to her lovely face. She looked not a day over 25. I found out a few years back that the silver hair was passed down to her from her great-great-grandmother. On first sight you might be caught off guard. But the more you gander the more intrigued you become. In her younger years, she could've easily been a model with her strong facial features and streamlined body. Hell, she looks better than a lot of younger women I know.

She finally caught eyes with me and stood to wave me over giving me a chance to glance at her form fitting business suit that in no way hid her curves.

"Future." She let my name slowly slip out of her mouth as she stepped to the side of the table.

"Carolina," I replied while wrapping my right arm around her giving her a hug that signified we were a little bit more than associates. This was my friend.

She kissed me on the cheek, right where the corner of my mouth began. I wrapped my other hand briefly around her, now showing that we were in fact, good friends. "Love your scent," she said then inhaled deeply again.

"Thanks, I was thinking about coming up in here sweaty and stinking."

"You better not have. I don't hold my tongue too often, I would've told you." She smiled. I loved her smile. I wanted her to laugh. I wanted to see the inside of her mouth, the wetness of her tongue.

"So what's been up with you? Haven't seen you in a minute," I said taking a seat.

"I've been so busy lately trying to finalize the papers on the Wind Crest Condos."

"Yeah, I rode past them a couple weeks ago. I've never seen condos that looked that good and that big to start in the 110's. That's a really good price for that area."

"It's an excellent price," she replied. "I'm so excited that I did this one on my own. This is my baby. Hopefully there will be more to come." Carolina sported a smile that illuminated the entire room. She probably was thinking of all that revenue that her project would bring in.

"I'm sure it will. I'm glad everything is going well for you."

She looked at me, tilting her head to the side. "Well, aren't you going to tell me?"

I looked at her confused. "Um, tell you what?"

"How much you just love my hair. I even took it out of the ponytail, just for you." She squinted, focusing her eyes on mine.

I tried to hold in my smile but couldn't. "Excuse me? I don't...what are you talking about?" I placed my hand on my chest and tried to look as innocent as I could, but I was obviously busted.

"Hello, can I get you guys something to drink?" The waitress momentarily saved me. I pointed to Carolina so she could place her order first. I saw that my earlier thought of her starting without me was correct when the waitress removed an empty martini glass from the table.

"I'll have another cherry apple martini."

"And I'll have a Guinness."

"I'll be right back with your drinks." The waitress then disappeared into the more lit portion of the bar.

"Future!" Carolina called out.

"Huh?" I knew she was about to go right back to where we left off.

"My hair, you're not off the hook." She was smiling hard now. Obviously, she liked when I complimented her hair. Hell, all women did. "You've been staring at my head ever since you sat down."

"That's because it's so big. I have to stare at it."

"Uh!" She now had her mouth wide open. "Shut up, no it is not." She smoothed the back of her hair down while sizing up her dome. "It's not, is it?"

I couldn't stop laughing. "No, no not at all. Your head and everything south of it is absolutely beautiful."

Her smile returned along with a blush. She tried to hide it by looking away. I loved how I affected her. "I almost forgot the reason that we were here." She reached into her leather briefcase to retrieve some papers and to regain her equanimity. She placed the manila folder on the table and slid it towards me.

"Let's see what you have here," I said, opening the folder.

"I'm telling you Future, it is a real gem."

I looked at the pictures Carolina had taken of the house and checked the dimensions of the rooms. "Looks nice." I kept glancing at all of the additional pictures. "Really nice." Someone had really put some TLC into the house. The landscaping was immaculate. There were designer shrubs, lights, lava rocks, privacy fence, and a huge outside patio.

Carolina added additional points that she wanted me to focus on. "New roof, new furnace, and central air. The kitchen was redone two years ago, as well as the three bathrooms. Um, let's see... the basement was also recently finished. I'm telling you the list goes on."

"Damn Carolina, is there anything at all wrong with the house?"

She took a sip of her martini, "Nothing."

I closed the folder, took a couple of sips of my drink and looked at her. She looked back and smiled. "Okay," I said preparing for the worst, "let's hear it."

She continued to smile. "Wow, this martini is good." She

licked the remainder from her lips. "But the price of the house tastes much better."

"So are you going to tell me today?"

"Seventy," she said flatly.

"Excuse me what was that?" That had to be a mistake. I think the alcohol was starting to take its affects.

"I said 70."

I opened the folder back up and reread the location at the top of the first page again. Dearborn Heights. I ran my fingers over it and read it again slowly. It didn't change. "Foreclosed?"

"Nope," she answered calmly.

"Short sale?"

"Nope, the house has been paid off for some time now."

"Is the economy that bad," I asked.

She laughed. "Not for them, they just hit the Mega Millions. It's a friend of Jessie's."

I was confused for a second until I remembered that Jessie was her older sister. "Are you serious? They're letting it go for seventy?"

"Yep! Told me they just wanted to sell it super quick, didn't care about a profit and was going to sell it to me for that."

"Seventy?" I asked again to make sure.

"Yep."

"You know the houses over there go for 200K easy."

"No dear, try 230, 240."

"They are basically—"

"Giving it away," she finished for me. I downed what was left of my drink and flagged down the bartender so that I could get another. Carolina said that the two martinis that she had were just fine.

"So I don't get why you didn't take this deal for yourself."

"Honestly, I thought about it, but right now I just have too much going on. So I thought, who better to reap the benefits of this deal than my little family of investors."

"Wow, that's so nice Carolina. For real, how can I ever thank you?"

She put her finger to her mouth, appearing to be in deep thought when the bartender brought my drink. I gave her two twenties and told her to keep the change. "Everything major that could go wrong on this house has already been replaced."

"So when can I see this place and tell them that I'm definitely interested in buying?"

"You can do both tomorrow morning. I already asked her to hold the house until Monday for me. So actually, if you could be ready at 10 in the morning, that'll be good." She began to play with the straw in her martini glass.

"I would do it today, now if I could."

We finished our drinks and let our eyes dance off each other. "You know Future, I am really proud of you. Not many young men your age could even take advantage of a deal like this. Either their credit is messed up or they just wouldn't have the capital."

She was stroking my ego nicely, had me almost blushing. "Thanks, but I can't take the credit for that. The honors all go to my parents."

"I disagree. Parents can't make us do anything we don't want to do. Even though they teach us the right things to do, all of us don't do it."

Carolina was attractive while laughing and smiling, but even more so when she was serious and intense. She continued talking and I kept admiring. Her silver hair moved freely as if it were a waterfall flowing on both sides of her face. The more I drank, the more she reminded me of Storm, the super heroine played by Halle Berry in the X-Men movies.

"Future! You're staring at my hair again," she said right before taking another sip.

"Damn it! I'm sorry. You know I can't help it. Anyways, how is the hubby?"

In an instant, her otherwise natural smile became forced. "Like you really care."

Our mood became solemn. "I do, well not really about him, but I care about you which in turn means—"

She sighed, "He's fine, works a lot, the usual."

"That's understandable. I mean the guy is rich. You have to work to become rich."

"That's true, but when you get there you shouldn't have to work as hard, at least not as much." Frustration arose in her voice.

I sipped, let my beer linger in my mouth and briefly thought about if I should ask my next question. "Are you happy? I mean knowing that you are absolutely financially free, doesn't that make you feel good?"

She shook her head. "Men are all the same." This time there was no sipping. She gulped down what was left of her martini. She seemed more relaxed now. I think it was time to vent. "Future, I'm going to give you some good advice. All women love to be spoiled, and yes we love money, but if a man who doesn't have that much money spent time with me and loved me unconditionally, that is worth more than any riches. Always make time for your woman Future. Make her feel like she's the most important thing in the world. Not your job or your money."

She looked vulnerable. She looked like she needed to feel... needed. I was buzzing and could tell that she was too, so, why not? "I want you. There, I said it."

"Excuse me?" The way she responded made me question if I should even repeat what I had just said. Did she not understand me?

I moved around a little uncomfortably in my chair and cleared my throat. "I said that I want you." I was now sitting up erect.

She snickered. "Where did that come from?"

"Always been there, you know that."

"Yeah," she said looking down at the table. I was staring directly at her. "I just didn't think that you would ever say it." She looked up at me and met my stare. "So, now that you finally got that out, how exactly do you want me?"

Damn, I guess I never thought that would be her response. "I want you..." Think Future, think. "...right here, right now." Good boy.

"So, in other words, you want me for the moment?"

Damn. She hit me with one of those damned if you do, damned if you don't questions. So the only way to combat that was, "I plead the fifth."

"Yeah, you better."

Now that I had taken the conversation to new unchartered territories, I noticed more intimate things about Carolina. Like the silhouette of her sizable areola when she took off her jacket, her long smooth neckline, and every single line and crease of her moist plump lips. "Honestly Carolina, I would say yes, I do want you for the moment. I know, and wouldn't expect you to leave your husband for me. Hell, I know you wouldn't cheat on him anyways."

"And how do you know all that?" she asked while rolling her neck.

"Because, I know that you are in love with him."

She shook her head. "Because that's what I want you to believe."

"You're not?" My eyebrows rose.

"Yes!" She looked towards the table again. "I do love him."

"That wasn't my question."

"I know that, but that's my answer." She stared. There was silence. Her stare went from my face to my chest, to my now folded arms then back up to my face. "How often do you work out?" she asked obviously changing the subject.

"I try to go at least five days per week."

She followed a straight line from my neck to my shoulders then back to my eyes again. "So, what would you do?" Her gaze was very serious now.

"On a typical day, I usually exercise one body part, do about five sets—"

She cut me off by outstretching her arm over the table. "What would you do if I gave you me… right here, right now?" She had taken my line and was now using it against me.

"Excuse me?" I said, borrowing one of her lines from earlier.

"Tell me." She was now leaning back in her chair. Tenderness was now replaced with curiosity. No more looking down, Carolina was looking directly at my mouth. I smiled knowing that she was now in my arena, playing my game. She probably figured that I would fumble or stutter. She must not have known who she was fucking with. If sex was a weapon, there was no question I had my CCW.

"I would start by ordering you another cherry apple martini and have you take a couple of sips right before I slid across the table and took that juicy bottom lip of yours in my mouth."

"Mmmmm," escaped from her mouth and she tried to mask it by clearing her throat.

"Then I would rip off that satin top that's doing a horrible job hiding those firm dark nipples of yours and tease them with my tongue." Carolina was all in now. The look in her eyes told me that she was imagining everything with me play by play.

"I'm behind you now. We are standing up, my hand is up under your skirt, and I'm gripping that pretty little thong that you are wearing, tighter, tighter making you gasp." Her breathing had become heavy and uneven. Her gaze was deep and her eyes narrowed. Her nipples were making themselves more visible through the thinness of her bra and blouse.

"I'm reaching my hand around your right leg." I saw her leg start to bounce under the table. "Feeling that wet slit, mmm, covering my two fingers with your juices. Do you feel me playing with your clit?"

She stopped biting her bottom lip long enough to mouth... Yes. I leaned in a little on the table. "I'm whispering in your ear...do you want me?" Carolina nodded her head up and down, slowly. "Do you want me baby?"

"Mmmmm hmmmm." This time her reply was audible.

"Tell me that you want me," I demanded in a faint whisper.

"I want you," she responded in the same manner.

"I wrap my left hand around that hair that I love so much and make a ponytail around my fist. I tell you to bend over. You bend, grab the edge of the table, and spread your lovely long legs.

I take this dick and slide it in you, deep, slow, long. I stroke you, softly knocking at the bottom door of that juicy pussy until your legs and arms can no longer hold you up. Mmmmmm, I stroke you until you cream all over me, collapsing on the table that we are now sitting at, the same table that I'm staring across, admiring one of the most beautiful women that I have ever, ever laid eyes on… the end." I smiled. She opened her eyes and turned red. I don't think she realized that she had her eyes closed. "You okay?" I asked knowing that she wasn't. I knew that pussy of hers had to be sticky now.

"Of course I am okay. Why wouldn't I be?"

"No reason. Sorry, I had to give you the short version. I didn't want to keep you past your curfew."

"Whatever silly, I do have to get out of here though. I have a lot of paper work to complete you know."

"Mmm hmmm." She was rattled. She stood and ran her fingers through that river of silver waves like she was checking to see if we had messed it up during our escapade. Then, she smoothed over her clothes. I stood stretched and made sure Buddy was situated.

"I appreciate you coming," she said, shaking her head and turning her gaze back towards the floor, "to the bar that is, on such short notice."

"Oh, it was my pleasure. We should do it…" I paused for emphasis, "come…to the bar, again, hopefully real soon."

"We'll see," she said grabbing her briefcase, "is it hot in here?" She still was looking a little flushed.

"Not at all. Actually," I said, looking at her still bulging nipples, "I was going to ask you if you were cold." We both busted out laughing. She grabbed her suit jacket from her chair and covered the twins.

"Would you stop? I'm trying to get myself together."

"Well hurry up and button that jacket, cover those things up."

"Stop it!" she whispered.

We walked out of Double Olive to a tangerine colored sky. Almost two hours had passed. My Movado read 8:10. Carolina and I joked a little more as I made sure that she made it to her car safely. She pushed a button on her keypad when we reached her silver BMW seven series that matched her hair color perfectly and her car softly chirped like a sparrow. I opened the driver's side door.

"Such a gentleman!"

"You know I try."

She started her car and rolled the windows down. I shut the driver's door and smiled.

She looked up at me and reciprocated the gesture. "You are really going to make someone very happy one day Future."

"Oh no, not me. I'm not looking for love at all."

"It doesn't matter if you are looking or not, love has a funny way of finding you."

"Okay, you're starting to scare me. You sound so sure," I said playfully backing away from the car.

She looked at me seriously. "I am, and do me a favor, not if, but when it finds you, don't reject it. You know you can be a little stubborn sometimes."

"Yeah I hear you," I said, even though I wasn't trying to.

"But are you listening?"

"Of course I am."

"Mmm hmm." She started laughing for no apparent reason. "What's wrong with you woman?"

"I was just thinking that if this little meeting of ours would have occurred before I was married, I would've taken your young ass home and wore you out." She looked so pretty with the sunset reflecting off of her face.

I laughed at her newfound cockiness. "There is nothing stopping that from happening now."

She looked down at the rock that graced her ring finger that had to at least be five carats. "Unfortunately there is. Even though he doesn't take our vows seriously...I do."

I leaned in close to the car. "Well if you ever need me, call me, for anything, anytime."

"It's good to know that offer is valid. What would your mom say if she knew we were carrying on like this?"

"I don't know and I don't want to find out," I said shaking my head.

"Me neither," she said laughing. "Call me first thing in the morning so we can get that property squared away."

"I will," I said watching her drive into the sunset.

PUSHING THE ENVELOPE

BEEP! Beep! Beep! What the…? I sat up in my bed and wiped the slob from the corners of my mouth. As I reached to cut off the alarm clock, I heard my phone vibrating on the nightstand. "What now?" I grabbed my phone and flipped it open. "Mm hello?" I groggily answered.

"Damn bastard! What took you so long to answer your phone? We've been trying to call you now for about an hour," Tierra screamed. "What are you doing over there? Getting some dick or something?"

"Shut up crazy!" I looked at my recently quieted clock and 9:40 illuminated on the display. Damn, is my clock right?"

"Yes 9:40, what's up, are you still going out?"

"Yeah, I'm going. Who's driving?" I said, looking at the clock again. I already knew what I was wearing tonight, so it wasn't going to take me that long to get dressed.

"I am. Brianna is driving over to my place and we're leaving out of here as soon as she arrives. Are you still sleeping girl?" She raised her voice even higher, hearing the silence on my end of the phone.

"No, and stop yelling. I'm getting my clothes out of the closet now."

"Oh yeah, before you do that…" I could tell that there was about to be a change in plans. "You might want to put that outfit back in the closet."

"What? Why? What's wrong with my outfit?" I asked as if she was here with me to see it.

"I'm sure nothing, it's just that Bri and I decided that we were going to dress slutty tonight."

I laughed out loud. "Slutty? And when did y'all decide this?" I asked.

"When you were sleeping bitch! If you would've answered your phone you could've given your input." Tierra's cursing always made me laugh. She calls Brianna and I bitch so often that I'm starting to think that's really our nickname.

"Whatever. So describe slutty, what does that word even mean, how does it look…I'm sure you know."

"Angel…bitch…now why are you trying to act all brand new? You know that you were just a slut two years ago so stop playing." She had me laughing so hard that I was holding my stomach. She obviously had a nice buzz going on. "We are both wearing minis so that's what you have to wear. A short mini."

"Now you know…"

She cut me off, "So…so what, I don't even want to hear it. You are wearing it. You have better looking legs than the both of us, so if we can do it, you definitely can. Oh and put on something to show off the twins too."

"Wow, we are really going to look like some hoochies, huh?"

"Yep, gonna drive them niggas crazy tonight. We should start doing this at least once a month."

"Girl, you are stupid. Okay let me get off of the phone so I can hurry up and get ready."

"Okay, Bri just pulled up so we'll be there at about 10:00."

"Bye."

I walked to the mini skirt section of my closet, which only included three. I pulled out the newest one; it was distressed, ripped, faded and really short. I matched it with a blouse that hung off the shoulders. After slipping on the skirt, I stared in the mirror.

"Damn, where is the rest of it?" I asked while tugging on the bottom as if it had extra material hidden somewhere. It came to the middle of my thighs, showing every inch of my long legs. This was by far the shortest skirt I have ever worn. Oh well, no turning back now. I walked into the kitchen and poured me a glass of wine. Time to finish getting ready.

While sprucing up my hair I heard my phone buzz again. Gotta take you off vibrate, I said to myself before answering. "Hello."

"Hey Angel."

"Hey Bri, where are you guys?"

"On Ford Road, I take it you received the slut-o-gram," she said laughing.

"Yeah, I got it. I'm getting into costume as we speak."

"You get enough rest?"

"Yeah, I'm good," I answered, still fiddling with my do.

"You know your girl is off the hook tonight. And for the record this was all her idea."

"Sell out!" I heard Tierra yelling in the background.

"Okay girl, we'll be at your place in a few."

I finished getting ready, sipped some more of my wine and

set out three pairs of shoes, because I could not decide what pair to wear. "Guess that's my girls," I said walking to the door that someone was banging away crazy on. "Yes, may I help you?" I asked, cracking the door a little.

"Um yes, actually you can," Tierra responded in a proper voice matching mine. "We're here with the Fuck You Company, and we were handing out free dicks and free fucks tonight. We were notified that someone at this address was in dire need of both." We all laughed as I let them in.

"Hey!" We all greeted each other at the same time.

"Damn Angel, where is the rest of your skirt?" Brianna asked walking around me.

"What? Do you think it's too short?" I grabbed at my skirt again trying to stretch the denim to a more comfortable length.

"I'm just playing girl, that skirt is hot!"

"Girl, I can't even front, you look good as hell. You should dress like this more often," Tierra said looking me over.

A smile crept over my face as I brushed my hands over my skimpy outfit and for the first time since my girls stepped in I noticed what they had on. "Look at y'all! Dang, looking all yummy. Brianna I know you're not saying anything about me. How in the hell did you slip that short ass skirt over that booty of yours." I walked up and smacked her on her luscious rump.

"Mmmm, I like being spanked. Do it again," she said looking at me with a kinky smile.

"I told her the same thing. I thought that I had an ass until I met Brianna. She makes mine look small." Tierra rubbed on her booty, checking her size compared to Brianna.

I looked at my two friends who were laughing at themselves in the mirrored wall in my living room. Tierra was right, she had junk in her trunk, but Brianna, she had luggage in hers. I'm talking the entire Louis Vuitton collection, not just the duffle bag. Even though it was big, it didn't look fat at all, just round and juicy. I laughed at how her booty had me staring at it like the guys when we are out.

 I loved my girls. They both decided on a silver pair of heels for me to wear. As I strapped them on, I asked them to give me the rundown on tonight's festivities.

 "Centaur Lounge first for a minute, after that, I know people throwing something at Privé and if that's wack we'll head over to Elysium." Tierra started playing with her ponytail. Something she did often when she talked. She was our personal party tour guide. She always knew what was going down, when and where. It was definitely good to have a girl like her on your team. To top it off, most of the places we went she got us in free. She knew some of everybody. I think mostly sexual but yet and still she knew them. She continued playing with her ponytail until we left the apartment.

 On our way to the club, one of Tierra's friends called her phone, leaving Brianna and I to entertain each other for the rest of the ride.

 "Sounds like someone is trying to set up a booty call," Brianna said leaning up from the back seat trying to whisper to me but Tierra obviously heard her and responded by giving us both the middle finger.

 "Actually, that don't sound too bad," I said looking outside at the downtown skyline. "I wish I…hmmmm."

 "Ooouuu, sounds like somebody's looking for trouble. I'm letting y'all know right now, I'm not going to be the only one going home alone tonight," Brianna said hitting on the seat.

I pulled my phone out from my purse. "I wonder what my personal trainer is doing tonight." I scrolled down to Pierre's name and was startled by Tierra abruptly closing her phone and yelling at me.

"Personal trainer? Don't tell me you are about to hook up with Pierre. Wait until you see him though, just wait."

"Um," I cleared my throat, "guess I forgot to tell you that I saw him today." I purposely avoided eye contact with Tierra.

"You what? When? I just talked to you earlier about him."

"I know and can you believe that when I got to the gym he was there and we worked out together."

"Wait," Brianna screamed from the back seat, "who the hell is Pierre?"

I turned around in my seat and explained. "I think this was before we even knew each other baby, but he was our personal trainer when we first started working out."

Tierra turned around briefly taking her eyes off of the road. "And he is foine. His cousin is too, mmm mm mmmmm. Angel you are going to have to get his cousin's number for me. Might have to get broke off again."

Brianna started laughing. "So, he's all that huh?"

"Yes! His body is crazy." I looked over at Tierra. "Body looks like...like that cute buffed up man in *Why Did I Get Married* and *Spawn*."

"Oh you're talking about Michael Jai White. Damn Angel, think you can handle all of that?" Brianna asked tapping on the back of my seat.

"Don't know, but I'm going to have fun trying," I answered.

"Are you about call him?"

"Naw, I'm texting. Going to thank him for the personal

lessons earlier. Want to see if he can talk first, he might be hooked up with some chick. You know how guys do."

Less than a minute later, my phone chimed, alerting me to my incoming text.

"Man, that was quick," I said while reading his response. **My pleasure, anytime you need a personal ANYTHING, you let me know!**

A big ass smile spread across my face.

"What did he say girl, let us see," Brianna asked, sounding like a little kid. I handed my phone to her and after she read it, she handed it to Tierra.

"Damn, looks like Pierre is ready!" Tierra yelled, handing my phone back to me.

"So what should I text back?" I asked, looking in the backseat at Brianna then to the front seat at Tierra.

"Ooouuu, I know." Brianna was anxious to play. "How about: I don't know, you worked me kind of hard today… ummmm," she thought of more as I began texting, "might be in need of a massage…and a deep stretch."

"That's a good one," I said, continuing to text while my two best friends gave each other high fives.

One minute later, my phone chimed again. My girls were all in, ready to hear Pierre's response. I opened the message and read it aloud. "Okay, let's see what he has to say." I read his response aloud to my girls. "Deep stretch huh? Good, cause that's my specialty, the only kind I know how to give."

"Girl, you know what that means." Brianna was now unbuckled and sitting up looking over my shoulder. "Personal trainer is packing."

Tierra looked over at me. "I was going to say the same thing. What are you going to say back?"

"Girl, you keep your eyes on the road and find us a close parking spot. I don't want to have to walk too far and have people thinking that we are hookers for real." Tierra sat back up smiling and darted for a spot that a car had just pulled out of. I texted: **Are you out? What if I need this personal training a little later tonight?**

Shortly after sending my message he texted back. **Yep, out with the fellas…later would be perfect. Are you out?**

I texted Pierre back. **Yes, out with the girls. What's your curfew, don't wanna get you in trouble.**

He immediately responded. **Lol hit me up, whatever time you get in…just don't party too hard. Ur gonna need your energy!**

You do the same

Will do, was his last response.

My girls looked at each other between freshening up their lip-gloss and hair. "Looks like somebody is getting some good loving tonight," Tierra said, while stepping out of the car. We were at our first destination, the Centaur Lounge.

I stepped out of the car and tried to stretch my short skirt again. "If there is one thing that I've learned it's never to give a man too much credit before he's earned it."

We walked into the trendy, dimly lit bar and immediately noticed how packed it was. A good way to describe this place is to say that it is like the perfect Long Island Iced Tea. The perfect mix of gender, class, race and swagger all mingling, interlocking and networking. It was very chic.

When the sun went down, Tierra turned into the queen of

nightlife, manipulating any guy within her grasp. As we climbed the stairs to the third level, she introduced us to everyone from men in business suits to dudes in Timberlands.

I leaned over to Brianna while we walked to the other side of the bar. "It's like she's a different person at night time," I whispered just loud enough for her to hear.

"I know, like a late night social vampire or something." We both laughed.

"Ladies," Tierra motioned for us to come closer, "I want to introduce y'all to Javier. Javier, these are my two best friends, Angel and Brianna. Javier is the owner of that new club opening up next month on Woodward, X Site."

The tall, lanky black man who appeared to be in his early 40's gently grabbed us both by the hand. "Ladies, it is my pleasure to meet you." Brianna and I looked at each other like *how does she meet these people?*

"Same here," I said, trying to mask the look that was on my face.

He looked around at each one of us. "You ladies are absolutely beautiful, just the type of women that I want in my club, so when we open I'll personally make sure that you are taken care of. Friends of Tierra's are friends of mine." While Javier continued to talk to Brianna and I, Tierra discretely rubbed her fingers together to tell us that Mr. Javier was indeed paid. "Please, have a drink. There are bottles of Ace over at my tables. Please help yourselves." He then gave Tierra another hug. "Call me later."

"Okay," Tierra said looking like it was no big deal. "Y'all heard the man, let's drink up. We're not staying here for too long."

We walked over to one of the reserved tables and filled our

champagne flutes with Ace of Spades. After two glasses, we were feeling quite bubbly.

"Hey, where is Tee?" Brianna asked, looking around for our fast moving friend.

"Now you know we never can keep tabs on her." We looked around and noticed that we had many eyes staring at us. All of a sudden, I felt naked again. "I feel like a piece of meat." I felt my body stiffen.

"Loosen up girl! It's just legs. Let'em look. Aye, there she is, way on the other side of the room." I followed her finger and saw Tierra and her long ponytail moving around on the other side of the club.

Brianna grabbed me by the hand and led us through the dense crowd. I felt my skirt creep up and inch below my ass cheeks I fought the urge to pull it down. Tonight, I'm going to relax. The effect from the Ace aided in me doing so. As I walked behind Brianna, I saw why all the men went crazy over her ass. With each step, it bounced left, right, left, right. Her legs were thick, smooth and even toned. For a brief moment, I imagined myself as her girlfriend. I giggled at myself having these crazy thoughts. I know I'm buzzing now.

"You alright girl?" Brianna asked me while pausing on our journey to recover our best friend.

I was starting to feel better by the second. I smiled at her. "Yeah! Yeah, I'm good!"

"I see," she said while laughing, and then she continued maneuvering through the crowd. She briefly released her grasp on my hand and then grabbed it again but this time she interlocked her fingers in between mine. Thoughts raced and I tried to stop them. Let loose, I reminded myself, just going to have fun tonight. I tightened the lock of our fingers. Brianna looked back searching my eyes. They told her that tonight, I was feeling exactly the way I was looking...

Naughty!

Frisky!

We finally saw our destination in sight. Tierra was hugged up in the corner with some dude. But before we got there...

"Aye mami! I know y'all not leaving already?" an iced out cutie screamed with outstretched arms.

"Unfortunately yes, we have another party to go too." Guess we all were letting loose tonight because thugs were typically not Brianna's type but by her stopping and cheesing the way that she was, I could tell that she was definitely all in.

"Oh it's like that, you're gonna just skip my party for someone else's?" He tried his best to pretend he was upset. "My birthday don't mean anything, huh?" He took off his fitted cap revealing a perfect pattern of 360-degree tsunami waves. He was a pretty thug indeed.

Brianna smiled even harder. "Well, if I would've known beforehand maybe I would have stayed." She was in full flirt mode now, but she still held my hand while putting the other one on her hip.

"That's what's up! My boy over there pointed you and your girl out from across the room shorty." He cocked his head to the side looking around Brianna. "Mmm mm mmmmm, damn, how you get all that ass in that little ass skirt?"

"What, you don't like it or something?" she asked, taking a brief look along with him.

"Are you crazy, I love it! Y'all the baddest muhfuckas up in here, for real. Damn, I'm sorry, being all rude and shit, y'all want some Ace of Spades?" the pretty thug asked, holding up his black and gold champagne bottle.

"Naw, think we had enough for now."

He looked at her thighs and then her tits. He was really undressing her with his eyes. "So what's your name shorty?" I couldn't tell if he was a rapper or if he owned a jewelry store but in any case, he was covered in ice.

"Brianna, but you can call me Bri."

"Shit, I would like it better if I could call you mine," he responded. She blushed.

One of his boys came over and put their hands on his shoulder. "Come on Gee, let's go take another shot." Gee wasn't trying to hear it. He wasn't about to let Brianna out of his sight.

"Give me a minute." Gee looked at me and then at our interlocking hands. A broad smile graced his face. "So what's up Bri? I'm taking it that this here must be your friend."

Brianna was about to answer when I cut her off. "Actually, what was your name again?" I asked him, knowing that he never gave it to us.

"Oh my bad, I'm Glen, call me Gee though."

"Okay Gee, I'm not just Bri's friend," I said releasing our grasp and moving close to her, "I'm her really...really," I opened my palms wide and palmed her voluptuous ass, "really good friend!" Brianna played it off perfectly. She didn't look at me strange or raise her eyebrows in shock. She just stared directly at Gee, which was what I was doing. He was speechless. The thug had disappeared for a moment, leaving behind just a man.

"Thaaaat's whatsuuup," he said, licking his lips again.

I squeezed her ass tighter, "And by the way…the name's Angel."

He looked at the both of us, back and forth. "You sure y'all have to go?"

We both suppressed our laughter at how soft his voice had become. "Unfortunately," Brianna answered. "How about you give me your number and I'll call you later." She pulled out her phone and he quickly ran out his number. "Okay Gee, nice meeting you and happy birthday." Brianna grabbed my hand and started walking again. We headed to the corner that we previously saw our friend in. Upon reaching her, we both instinctively dropped hands, which actually felt stranger than walking around with them interlocked.

"Hey Tee," I said, breaking up the sweet nothings that the guy was whispering in her ear.

"Hey girls. Where were y'all? I was looking all over for you guys."

Brianna and I looked at each other then back at Tierra with our lips twisted to the side. I looked down at my Seiko charm bracelet watch pretending to check the time. "We're ready when you are."

She whispered something in the guy's ear that made him smile from cheek to cheek, definitely something sexual. She stood and walked closer to us. "Come on ladies, let's go. Damn it's crazy in here. Okay Brianna, give me your hand and you grab Angel's, I'm going to lead us out of here." She looked around at us when we busted out laughing. "What's so funny?"

"Nothing, just an inside joke. Lead the way." With that, Brianna and I rejoined hands this time accompanied by Tierra forming our train of friendship. We attracted a crazy amount of attention the entire way out of the club.

"So how did you enjoy your first time here, Angel?" she asked on our way to the car. She and Brianna had come here numerous times and tried to get me to come, but that was when I was in my relationship phase.

"Um, busy, definitely busy, but I enjoyed it. It's a nice pre-party." I stumbled over a crack or what I thought to be a crack and my girls busted out laughing. "Shut up, don't laugh at me I'm drunk!" We loaded up in Tierra's car and headed toward Congress Street.

Tierra glanced over at the center console. "11:30, oh we are still in good time. So which is it going to be? Privé or Elysium?"

"Don't matter to me," Brianna slurred.

"Me neither," I added. "We're following your lead. You're the party expert."

Tierra popped her invisible collar. "That I am," she said, proud of her partying credentials. She was looking super cute though, kept it ghetto with the extra-long ponytail, but it went very well with her. She had the smallest ass out of all of us, but it wasn't small, by any means. She just had a lot of competition when it came to her girls. What she lacked in cushion she more than made up for with her juicy breasts. They bounced up and down every time she laughed.

"Tee, what size bra do you wear girl?" Brianna laughed at my question from the back seat.

Tierra took one of her hands from the steering wheel and began massaging her right breast. "H's baby and proud of it." she responded. "The thing I really don't like though are these big ass nipples, they stay hard."

I continued looking at her breasts from the passenger seat. "Big as in round or long?" I asked.

"Well, not so much long, even though they do poke out. I'm talking about the round dark part."

Brianna laughed. "Girl, you don't even know the name of your own body parts, it's an areola."

"Yeah, my areo…whatever, it takes up the entire front of my titty…look!" she said pulling her wrap around the neck top to the side and exposed her right tit.

"Wow! It is kind of large. Damn Tee Tee, you really do have some big ass titties."

"I know, I know, and the fellas love these babies," she said with a smile.

"I bet they do," I said, not able to take my eyes off of them.

Brianna sat in the back and couldn't stop laughing. "Y'all are crazy. This chick is really driving around with her boob out."

"I just wanted to show y'all. I mean, y'all are my niggas right? You see me naked all the time at my crib, robe flying open and shit. I've seen y'all in just panties and I'm comfortable with y'all seeing my titties out. Now, let's say one of y'all hoes hop over here and try to put my tit in ya mouth…Brianna…then there's going to be a problem."

"Aw fuck you bitch," Brianna laughed. I was laughing so hard I could barely catch my breath. "I tend to like my chicks with titties that won't suffocate me during sex."

"Ooouuu!" I howled instigating.

"Shut up, they ain't that big…are they?"

"Uh yeah!" Brianna and I both agreed.

"Well let me see y'all's, so I can see how abnormal my areo-whatever's are." She glanced over at me while she was driving.

"What? Right now?"

"Naw, when we go in the club," Tierra sarcastically answered, throwing her arm in the air. "Of course right now."

I reminded myself again that this was Let-Loose-Day and with no further hesitation, I uncovered my left breast.

"You're right…my nipples are big, well compared to yours. Brianna lemme see…" Tierra glanced towards the back seat but obviously, Brianna was thinking ahead.

"Damn Bri!" Tierra screamed, scaring me to put my breast back in my shirt. I quickly turned around to both of Brianna's bright yellow titties staring right at us. Tierra and I were cracking up.

"What?" Brianna asked serious as hell. "Y'all hoes always leaving me out of stuff, flashing tits and shit! Damn it, I'm the bisexual one." She pounded her hands on the seat like a young girl throwing a tantrum.

Beep! Beep! A guy in an all-white Charger honked his horn while his eyes zoomed in on Brianna's tits. He gave her two thumbs up and smiled hard. She thanked him by sticking out her long slithery tongue and licked her nipple. The poor guy almost crashed into the car in front of him.

"Let me put these things away before someone gets hurt," she said covering her melons.

"Please do," I pleaded shaking my head. "It's crazy that at the slightest sight of skin, guys absolutely lose their minds."

Brianna finished buttoning up her shirt. "Well sis, normally I would agree with you about the guys, but seeing all these titties flashed in front of me, I know exactly how they feel. Gotta bitch back here having bisexual relapses." She joined in with Tierra and I laughing but still had a look on her face that suggested that she meant every word.

Driving west on Congress, Privé Lounge came up first. Tierra called one of her coworkers who was already inside for the scoop. "Hey, what's up girl? I can't...can't hear you. No not yet...about a block away. Is it popping? Whaaaaa, no niggas? What do you mean...naw, I'm not even gonna waste my time, we're gonna head over to Elysium. Are you coming through? Mmm hmmm, yeah, okay, well call or text me and I'll come out and get you in. Okay, bye." She finally ended her call and closed her phone. "Well ladies, looks like Privé's out. My coworker said that it's nothing but ladies in there. So if you want me to drop you off, Brianna, and pick you up later, now is the time to speak up."

"Here's my answer right here bitch!" Brianna said flipping Tee the bird.

"I'm just saying."

"Saying what? For your information, I happen to be digging dick for the moment." Brianna said, laughing at herself.

"Well you are going to have to start sending us email alerts or newsletters or something. Shit! It's getting hard keeping up with your sexuality."

I looked back at Brianna laughing. "You know I don't think I like you," she said looking in my direction while rolling her eyes.

"Why, what I do?" I said, trying to stop my laughter.

"Not you," she responded, now looking at Tierra, "I'm talking about your big breasted friend over there."

"Shut up, they are not that big!"

"You know what y'all," I said, breaking up the back and forth banter, "I love you guys."

"Awwww." Brianna reached up and around the front seat grabbing my shoulders.

"Yep! It's official, Angie's drunk," Tierra said pulling up to valet.

"No I'm not. Well I don't think I am, and who in the hell is Angie? But seriously, I really do mean it. Y'all have always been there for me, even though I practically shut you out of my life when I was with Asshole. You're really my best friends and I love you guys for that."

Tierra became serious for a moment. "Well, I don't think that it's wrong for you to spend less time with your friends when you have a man. You have to work on your relationship. Lord knows that when I get an official man, you hoes are cut off!"

"Same here," Brianna said, giving Tierra a high five.

"Forget y'all."

"Naw seriously, we love you too Angel. You know we'll always be BFF's. Now let's go holla at these niggas!"

We hopped out of Tierra's car, received the valet ticket, and walked to the front of the line. If eyes could talk, we would be all kinds of bitches from the girls that were waiting in the long line to enter the club.

"Hey, handsome." It was time for Tierra to work her magic.

"Hey Tee, what's up baby girl!" the tall thick muscled bouncer responded.

"Looks like it's pretty hype in there tonight huh?"

"Come on now, you know it's not a party in there until you get in," he said smiling.

"True dat! Cortney, I'd like you to meet my two bestest, most favoritest friends in the whole wide world, Angel and Brianna." Tierra was the master when it came to making up words.

Cortney looked us up and down. "Good Lawd! Y'all know y'all wrong for coming up in here looking this good."

Tierra looked over at us and smiled. "I went to school with Cortney. He's the owner and president of Black Bird Security." She placed her hands on her hips. "So what are you doing out here working?"

"I was a little short staffed tonight, so I had to come in and work."

All three of us looked around at what had to be at least eight bouncers outside. "Short staffed?" Tee asked, "Damn, how many bouncers does one club need?"

Cortney laughed aloud, and so did we. "Okay, you got me. Truth is, I broke up with my girl about a month ago and a brother is getting a little lonely. Shit, I'm trying to find me a breezy." He released the clamp to the red velvet rope, letting us step through.

"You should've called me," she said leading us toward the door. "I could've hooked you up with one of my girls."

"That's what's up!" Cortney said, obviously interested in that thought by the grin that he displayed.

"Where was he last week?" I whispered as we walked to the door, "we wouldn't have had to wait in that long ass line then."

"He just got the contract for here last week," Tierra informed me. After entering the club, we went straight to the bar. It's a good thing too because my buzz was starting to wear down a little. It seemed like an eternity before we actually reached the bar. It was a little shocking that so many people still came out to party even though the economy was not that great. They probably came out to take their minds off how bad things really were.

Brianna continued to try to flag down a bartender and began to get frustrated, as usual. "You know, I am really going to try not to get mad tonight. I am really, really going to try."

I looked over at Tierra who was looking at her phone. "This chick needs to get in good with one of these bartenders."

Without looking at me Tierra responded, "I'm working on it."

Finally a bartender. "Ladies," the busty blond greeted us as she sat what appeared to be three Cosmo's in front of us.

"Dang Tierra! That was fast," Brianna said looking shocked.

"Oh I'm good, but not that good."

"The drinks are compliments of the handsome gentleman across the bar," the bartender informed us nodding in the direction that we were already facing. We simultaneously focused our eyes until they locked on...

"Wow, knight in shining armor. He rescues us again. What was his name?" Brianna tapped her fingers on the bar trying to jog her memory.

Tierra stared without blinking. "He would only have to tell me his name one time and I bet you any amount of money that I would remember it...forever. You didn't get his number?"

"Nope, didn't get a chance too. Looking at him now though, I think I might be regretting it."

"Well looks like you get another chance."

"I don't know, don't want to seem like I'm all on him," Brianna responded.

"Well if you don't want to be all on him, I will. What do you think, Angel? Angel?"

"Huh, what?" I felt like I had missed something very important from the way my two friends were honing their eyes on me.

"Wow, somebody is all in!" Tierra said

"Who, me?" I tried to act nonchalant.

"Yeah you," Brianna teased. "What do you think about us hooking you up?"

"With?"

"Uh duh, with the guy that you're practically drooling over." Brianna got me on that one.

"I'm not drooling, he's not even all of that," I said with a big grin on my face, trying to convince myself.

Brianna had her lips all twisted up. "Girl you need to stop, you know that man is fine as hell and your type 100 percent. At least go over and thank him for our drinks."

"Why me, he's your friend. He was sending them to you."

"No, he sent them to us. Oh and what happened to Ms. Easygoing from earlier?" Brianna asked.

Looking at him made my easygoing spirit and everything else in my head fly right out of the window. "Yeah, you're right, the least I could do is to go over and thank him." At that moment, he looked right into my mouth, as if he had heard me. His stare had me paralyzed, but I managed to mouth a thank you. I then raised my glass to him. He nodded his head, slowly raised his glass and mouthed back, 'My pleasure.' Damn his lips are so... kissable!

"You chicken! You were supposed to go over and thank him," Brianna teased.

"Be right back, girls," Tierra said closing her phone. "My coworkers are at the door. I'm about to get Cortney to let them in." She hurriedly walked through the crowd toward the entrance, leaving Brianna and I alone as usual.

"Angel, you know you're feeling him, so stop fronting."

"What do you mean? Me? You were the one lounging with him last week." I felt my pulse rising thinking about her and Him together.

"I wasn't lounging with him, I just didn't want to leave him hanging because he sped up the process of us getting our drinks," she said.

"Mmmm hmmmm, that's all huh?"

"Yes, that's all!"

"Now are you sure about that, Miss I'ma jack off to him when I get home?"

Bri's mouth opened wide and her face turned fire engine red. "I uh…guess I did say that huh?"

"Yep!"

"Look at him though."

"I know," escaped my mouth before I knew it. We both looked at him. He glanced back. Brianna waved, not so much with her hand but with each individual finger. He nodded again, this time reversed, head started down and then he brought it up. I smiled at how cool he was. I could definitely tell that he was a patient lover, just by the way he sipped his drink. It seemed that he savored the taste in his mouth before swallowing. He made me tingle. My smile went from conservative to showing teeth.

I patted Brianna on the shoulder while still admiring Him. "You know what, I think you're right. I should go over and properly thank him." I waited for her to back me up and she said nothing. Just as I started to repeat myself, I turned and saw my girl grinding all up on some yellow dude. I took another sip from the drink that my boo just bought for me and noticed my buzz returning. I have to credit that to the bartender. Damn, this Cosmo is strong! Okay, one more sip.

I tapped Brianna on the shoulder again. "Aye, I'll be right back." She nodded and I began my journey to the other side of the bar.

For a moment, I lost sight of my target. Where is he? I asked myself while taking a couple more slow meticulous steps. And then, there he was. He stood about 20 feet in front of me. I immediately started itching under my arms, my pulse started to rise, and I felt a sudden hot flash. Either I was starting menopause or this nigga had a strong ass effect on me.

Come on feet. Please don't stop! I fought the urge to turn around. Tonight, I was going to claim my prize. I closed the distance between us even more. All of the thoughts, all of the dreams and visions that I've been having lately all flashed in front of me. Fifteen feet, ten… Here goes nothing. The start of my new life… with my new… What the? Who is this all up on my man?

I had to save face. Had to get out of sight before he saw me. Shit! I made a sharp right turn and walked until I knew for sure that I was out of his sight. I turned around to see if I could spot him and the hooker in the red dress that was all up in his face. I couldn't at first, but then, I saw Him. Standing in the same spot with the same chick.

I crept closer and used unsuspecting club goers as shield and cover. I swallowed what was left of this stupid ass, nasty Cosmo that some stupid ass man just bought me and sat the empty glass down on a nearby table.

Mr. Cool had his back to the bar, reclining, arms stretched wide. The lady in red was looking up at his face while she placed her hands on his chest and slithered it slowly down to his abs. And you're just going to stand there? I can't believe that you are just going to stand there and let her do that to you.

I think that I've had enough. Plus, I already have something lined up for later, who just happens to look better than you. I was really trying to convince myself now. As I began to take my first steps to elude the scene, my eyes caught the bitch in red moving her hand down until she cupped his crotch. The only move he made was to take a sip from his drink. Other than that, he just stood there enjoying, in plain sight.

"Damn, baby is getting her some when she leaves!" a female said as she looked at the free peep show when she walked by me with her girls. They all gave each other fives.

Yep, in plain view for me and everyone else to see. She moved her hand around slightly, now massaging him. I felt the inside of my womb warm. I tried to see more but she kept on moving her body to block the two of them.

"Hey, sexy! Would you...?"

"No thanks," I said to the guy who came into my view to try and spit game.

"But you don't know what I was going to ask," he said, hands up in the air in surrender like he had been getting turned down all night. Oh well, it wasn't my concern.

"Whatever it is, I'm not interested." Usually I wasn't this sharp, but this was different. I looked around to relock on my target. The poor guy that I had just turned down walked away with his head down.

The tramp in the red dress was still playing pool with my cue stick. At first, he seemed unfazed and professional, but after his body moved a little to the left and her hand went back to his chest, it revealed that he was human after all. If you weren't looking directly at him, you wouldn't have noticed, but I was and I did. I noticed his bulge. He had to be wearing boxer briefs. It looked like his length went down instead of out and I couldn't take my eyes off of it.

My mind instantly started to imagine how it would look uncovered. I stood there in the crowd, unknown to anyone, squeezing my pussy muscles, trying my best to put out this fire that had been ignited.

The effect that this guy had over me was crazy. The things that he made me want to do were more insane. I wanted so bad to put my hand under my skirt and cool the heat that was coming from inside of me. I imagined myself standing with my legs spread wide and two fingers deep inside my slippery wet slit.

"What's up Angel?" Tierra's voice brought me out of my trance.

I tried my best to play it off like everything was normal. The way Kitty was twitching let me know that everything wasn't. "Hey girl! I thought that you were lost."

"Whatever, these are my co-workers," Tierra responded and started running down names, but I tuned them out as soon as I saw Him and bitch in red head to the dance floor. "Y'all, this is my best friend, Angel. Where is Bri?"

"Last time I saw her, she was hip rolling on some guy on the other side of the bar."

"Look, there she is right there," Tierra said pointing, "trying to get her dick on." We all looked across the bar at Brianna dancing like a stripper.

"You are crazy girl!"

"And what are you doing over here by yourself? You trying to holla at that guy we saw earlier?" she asked, smiling.

"What girl, naw." I think I might have answered a little too quick to be believable.

"Mmm hmm, anyways, we all need to be following Bri's lead and go get us a guy to hip roll on."

"My sentiments exactly." That way I could keep a closer eye on Mr. Cool and his hoochie and perhaps cut in on their private party. Right before we reached the dance floor, Cortney, the big bouncer who let us in front of the line earlier, stopped us dead in our tracks.

"So ladies, we meet again!" He said looking directly at Tierra's melons. She loved getting that attention from men, so to show her appreciation she straightened up her back and poked her chest out even further exposing more of that deep cleavage.

"Looks like it, big daddy." She now had one of her hands around Cortney's big folded arms.

"Even though I wouldn't mind spending time with you ladies, it looks like someone wants you a little more than me." He managed to separate his eyes from Tierra's twins and looked at me. "You're Angel, right?"

"Uh, yeah, I think so," I answered while squinting my eyes.

"Well, your presence has been requested upstairs in the VIP area, along with your girls, of course." Cortney's eyes were dancing off all of us like he was a kid at a candy store.

Tierra and I looked at each other. She looked just as shocked as I was. "VIP? But we don't have any wristbands," I said looking at my bare wrists.

He gently grabbed my arm. "That's been taken care of."

"For all of us?" I questioned, to be sure of what I was hearing.

"Yep!" He responded taking wristbands from his back pocket and placing one on all of our wrists. The reactions from Tierra's co-workers made me believe that this was their first time ever going to VIP. "There is one missing...where's the redbone with the fat ass?"

We laughed at his description of Brianna. "There she is over there," I said, pointing to her still getting her grind on.

"Okay y'all, wait right here. I'll be back." We watched as Cortney walked over to Brianna. He leaned down towards her ear, not fazed that she was dancing with someone. I guess that's what all that size does for you. Her dance partner wiggled from behind her and squealed away from the Michael Clark Duncan look-a-like. Brianna laughed at the sweet nothings that Cortney whispered in her ear. Then she grabbed a hold of his extended arm and he escorted her to us.

"So superstar," Tierra teased, "who do we owe the honors of getting upstairs?"

I hunched my shoulders. "Shit, your guess is as good as mine. I'll ask Cortney before going up."

"Hey ladies! Heard we are getting special treatment courtesy of my girl!" Brianna was talking extra loud. She definitely had hit her dance partner up for another drink.

"Speaking of that," I said, looking up towards Cortney. "Who's doing all of this?"

He smiled. "Told me not to say, now if you beautiful ladies would follow me."

My mind raced. Really couldn't think of anyone sending for me. I don't think that I was really thinking clearly anyway, especially when we walked right passed the horny couple. He and I caught eyes and held our stares until we reached the top of the stairs. Red Dress was working her ass all up on him, but the look in his eyes suggested that he would rather have his crotch all up on me.

When we reached the VIP section, it was as if we stepped into an entirely different club. The decor was elegant. The couches were plush and the men dressed more professionally. The women on the other hand made our short skirts look like nun outfits. They were barely clothed. See-through tops with no bra seemed to be the norm. This was the grown up section for real.

Cortney led us through the first section and I tried to see if I recognized anyone, but I didn't. We then entered another room through a set of heavy paisley drapes that reached from the ceiling to the floor.

"Ladies," Cortney said after completing his mission. He then pointed us to a herd of thick necked, big backed men and then...

"Hi beautiful." Juwaun stood in front of me sporting a smile as bright as the sun.

"Hey you, I should've known," I said unable to mask my smile.

All of Tierra's friends were totally star struck. Two of them had their mouths wide open and the other one asked, "Is that Juwaun Jones, oh my God is that him?" I introduced him to the newbies and reintroduced him to my girls.

"Yes, how could I forget your beautiful friends? Let me introduce you to a couple of mine. This here is one of the linemen, J.T."

Tierra butted in. "Hi J.T."

Then he turned slightly to his right, "This is my quarterback, without him there wouldn't have been any broken records for me. Ladies, Joe Powers."

"Hi Joe!" all the ladies harmonized like they were the new En Vogue. Joe was a very handsome white man and not your typical bland white. He was white with swag, edge, and soul. Joe was Robin Thicke white.

"What's up ladies," Joe responded. Mmmm and he was a white man with a deep ass voice. The girls had turned into putty.

"Joe, get the ladies something to drink. I have to talk to Angel alone for a second.

"My pleasure! Ladies, let's go over to the bar." Joe escorted my friends to one of the four bars that were located on each corner of the VIP section. Brianna looked back at me on her alcoholic voyage and gave me the thumbs up. I laughed at her. She had gone from switching genders to now, potentially switching races.

"So Angel, did you honor my request to take it light on the partying tonight?"

I smiled slightly. "Nope, been partying all night like it's 1999. How did you know I was here anyways?"

"I just happened to be looking over the balcony when you and your girls came in."

I turned my back to him pretending to look over the railing when in reality I wondered how long he was watching me. I hope he didn't see me in stalker mode.

"I would've come down and got you myself, but it probably would've taken me an hour how crowded it is in here."

I turned back to him and was greeted with a shot of Patron and two limes. "Well the important thing is that you have me right now," I said. His eyebrows shot to the top of his head. "That is, have me up here."

"It's okay, keep playing hard to get."

"I will," I said before throwing the shot back and placing a lime in between my lips. Patron was a dangerous thing. So smooth that you really had to watch how many shots you take.

I turned back to the railing and glanced at the now enormous crowd. Juwaun came up from behind and placed his hands on my shoulders. I felt his strength in his fingertips. He closed in on the couple inches of personal space that was between us, making my back touch his front. Even though I wanted to, I had to dismiss the thoughts of me going home with him tonight.

I looked towards the dance floor and saw the guy that I would be a groupie for in a heartbeat. Then, I brought my thoughts back to the man who was presently in reach. No reason why I can't have fun with him. I backed into his embrace to let him know that it was indeed welcomed.

"Come on," I said, grabbing his hand.

"Where are we going?"

"Downstairs." We walked past my girls who were schmoozing on the couch with more players from the Lions.

"Bri," I called out to no avail. She was too busy flirting to even hear me. "Brianna!"

"Yeah, what's up?"

"Be right back, I'm going downstairs."

"Alright! You better take care of my girl mister," she instructed Juwaun.

"Don't worry, I will. She's in good hands." He flashed that camera ready smile and winked at me. He was so damn handsome.

I continued walking downstairs to the main floor where all of the women looked at me like they wanted to take my prize at the first chance. Juwaun must have sensed it because he grabbed my hand tighter and switched positions with me. He was now the leader directing me to the dance floor.

"I take it this is where you wanted to come?" he asked. I acknowledged him by smiling. He was definitely getting cool points for treating me as if I was the only woman who mattered.

He was one of the most eligible bachelors in Michigan and here he is still all up on me despite me giving him a little attitude. The way he held my hand and kept smiling at me was letting every guy in here tonight know that if they were thinking about hollering at this one, think again.

Once we stepped on the dance floor, the music switched from a fast-paced Lil Jon to a slower Tre Songz, "I Need a Girl." He walked me into the middle of the dance floor. "Excuse me," he sternly said, almost bumping my future baby daddy out of the way. I pretended like I didn't see Him and stayed focused on Juwaun. My heart started pumping with adrenaline. I definitely wanted to get closer to the action, but this just might be a little too close for comfort. Juwaun stood behind me as we two-stepped. "Do you ballroom?"

"Um a little." I was a little reluctant to answer.

He laughed. "A little huh? Either you can or you can't."

I started to feel myself tense up a little. "If you make me." I shrugged my shoulders, not able to think of another answer.

"Just follow me baby," was all he said before grabbing my right hand and spinning me out in front of him. All the moves that I learned two years ago in ballroom class flashed in front of my face. Get it together, Angel. Get it together. Juwaun spun me around caught me with his left hand and double spun me back.

Whew, got through that one. In between twirling and twisting, I saw that people had stopped dancing and had started watching us. Juwaun was good. No, scratch that, he was really good. He was leading me so smoothly that I didn't even notice what I was doing until I did it. Over half of the moves he had me doing, I've neither attempted nor seen. He brought me back to him, went under my arm, brought me back the other way and switched positions with me behind his back.

Now, I was really impressed. I spun back to him and he held me close and tight. His hand felt good holding mine. My breast felt even better pressed up against him. He dipped me once, twice, and then a third time. I'm sure that everyone saw my panties on that last one. He ended by spinning me countless amounts of times, like a spinning top. Shit, didn't even know that I could do that.

The song ended and so did we. Some people applauded as we walked off. I felt like I was on Dancing with the Stars. I took my hand and placed it on his bicep. I looked at the jealous chicks that stared at me on our way back to VIP and fought the urge to poke out my tongue like a four year old.

"Damn Angel, I've been your girl all this time and I didn't even know that you could dance like that."

I put my hands on my hips. "Tierra, don't even front. I practically begged you to go with me to ballroom class."

"Well, I don't remember," she said taking a sip from a drink that had to have been recently refreshed.

"Mmm hmm, I'm sure you don't." I looked at Juwaun who was staring at me. "What's wrong?"

"Nothing, it's just," he paused, struggling with his words.

"What? Spit it out!" I had my arms outstretched.

"It's just that you're so beautiful to me. I'm really digging you Angel."

My heart melted right then and there. Who said dark-skinned people couldn't blush? "Awww, Juwaun. That is so sweet."

"It's the truth."

"Okay, stop." I put my head down ashamed at how hard he had me smiling. "What are you trying to do to me?"

He poured another shot of Patron from his personal liter; guess you can do things like that when you're the man. "Get you drunk, of course." He smiled.

"Too late."

"Drunk enough to spend the night with me?" he questioned.

"See, now you're pushing it."

"Damn," he said snapping his fingers, "one question too many." We both laughed. "I can't wait for tomorrow. Can't wait to spend more time with you."

"Same here," I said still blushing.

"Last call for alcohol!" the DJ screamed over the loud speakers.

"Guess that's your cue for you to go home and get your beauty sleep."

"Oh now you're trying to get rid of me, huh? Probably have some hoochies about to come up here and take my spot," I said, playfully punching him in the arm.

"Now you know that nobody can take your place." He looked sincere when he spoke. He swallowed his Patron. I followed his lead knowing this was the last thing that was going down my throat tonight, well, as far as liquor was concerned. I'm standing here looking at this guy and it's taking everything in me not to wrap my arms around him and taste his tongue. I was trying my best to play it cool.

He started laughing unexpectedly. "You should see the look on your face right now."

I leaned back with both forearms resting on the banister.

"Well, since I can't see myself, why don't you tell me how I'm looking?" We intensely stared at each other for a few seconds.

He walked over towards me and stood in between my legs. "You look...horny." The low, deep, slow vibrations from his voice in my ear sent vibrations down my spine and made my toes tingle. He was close enough to me that the scent of his cologne crept in my nose and teased every single hair.

I held my eye contact. "That's probably because I am horny." I spoke slow, seductive. Could tell that stunned him a little bit.

He kept his composure quite nicely though. "So what are you going to do about that?" he asked eagerly waiting for me to answer.

I leaned a little closer, the top of my lip now touching the bottom of his lobe. "Go home...and handle it."

"And while you are," he cleared his throat, "handling it, are you going to be thinking of me?"

"Should I?" I ask with a sinful smile.

"Of course."

"And why would I do something like that?" I turned away from him and towards the railing to mask how much fun I was having flirting and teasing.

He startled me when I felt him pressing up against my backside. His hands traced my arms until they both rested on top of my hands. "Because, you know how bad I want to handle that for you."

I turned my neck to the side as far as I could without separating my body from his. It felt too good to move right now. "How bad?" I whispered.

"This bad." One of my hands that he was holding was now on his crotch. Wow, he definitely has a handful. I gently squeezed him and there was no give. His dick was thick and hard as a rock. I'm so glad that I wore a panty liner or this would be a very interesting situation. "I think I better get you over to your girls."

I let out a quiet squeal, don't think he heard it, but I was starting to enjoy myself. "Yeah, I think you better before you get yourself in trouble." We stayed connected for a little while. I gave him a moment to calm down his friend, and then he escorted me back to the couches to where my girls were. "Y'all ready?"

Brianna looked at me with questionable eyes. "Man, we were over here waiting for you to get finished." The other girls started laughing.

"Okay, now I'm finished," I responded trying to shorten the outburst of laughter.

"I bet you are," Tierra responded, "do you need a cigarette?" I smiled and held my head down. I guess they saw our little session.

Juwaun sensed my nervousness so he jumped in and rescued me. "Well ladies, it was nice seeing you again and it was nice meeting y'all for the first time," he said looking from my girls to Tierra's. They all said their goodbyes to the other players. "Do you want me to walk you to your car?"

"No, thank you. You've done enough tonight." I looked at him and smiled. He caught our little inside joke and smiled back. "Plus we parked in valet, we should be cool."

"Alright then Angel, I guess I'll see you tomorrow morning. Twelve sharp."

"We'll see."

"We'll see? What do…?"

"Just kidding, I'll be ready," I said cutting him off to cool him down. I looked at my watch; it was 1:50a.m. I had just over 10 hours to get home, get some sleep, and be ready for Juwaun. Minus the time that Pierre would spend fucking my horniness away.

I pulled my phone out of my purse and looked at the missed message that I had from Pierre. He texted, **On my way home, can't wait to give you that stretch...hit me up when you're ready!**

I texted back, **Just leaving...can't wait either, I'll hit u up when I'm near home.** It's funny when you look at some of the things that women do. We would have sex with a man that is attractive to us, who we don't really care about or have deep feelings for with no hesitation. However, when it comes to a guy that we like or want to have a relationship with, we will play hard to get and make him jump through hoops. It's a damn shame. Almost seems backwards. Oh well, something that I'll definitely give more thought to tomorrow. Tonight, I'm going to fuck the attractive guy who I really don't care about!

The ride home felt like forever. Tierra and I were in a good mood because of the dick that we had lined up. Brianna, on the other hand, talked about another night alone with her dildo.

"So, why don't you call the guy that you were grinding all up on at the bar downstairs?" I asked Brianna.

"Are you serious, Angel? I'm saying, I know I'm not the prettiest bitch in the world, but I would like to think that I'm pretty hot. That guy was not take home, one night stand material. I mean I don't usually do one night stands, but when I do, you best believe when I wake up in the morning, I'm not going to have any regrets."

"I feel you girl. I mean, I know I'm not the prettiest either, but I am, well we are some pretty ass women with good ass jobs and nice asses."

Tierra cleared her throat and poked out her chest. "And titties!" I continued while laughing. "Now remind me again, why are we single?"

"I'll tell you why," Tierra interjected, "it's because it is so many of us women and so few of them. You see how the club is, it's like…like 10 to one. Why should a guy sweat one woman when he can have his cake, pie, cobbler, ice cream, doughnut with whip cream on top and eat it too?"

We all laughed. I reclined my head back and closed my eyes. Big mistake! It felt like I was on a roller coaster ride. "Damn y'all, I am fucked up. Juwaun kept giving me Patron shots like it was water."

"Aye on the real, you need to get with ole boy for your sake and ours," Tierra said.

Brianna giggled from the back seat. "Now you know I don't usually agree with…um," Brianna snapped her fingers trying to jog her memory, "Tierra, yeah, but in this case I think she may be right."

"Oh it's like that bitch? You can't remember my name. I should put your drunk ass out and let you walk home."

"For real though," Brianna continued, "the guys that were up in VIP know how to treat a lady."

"Amen!" Tierra threw up her right hand like she was agreeing with a pastor at church.

"Whatever, you two would say anything right now because you're drunk. I am going to lunch with him tomorrow," I said speaking a little softer.

"Are you?" They both asked in unison.

Tierra looked over at me and hit me on the leg. "Why didn't you tell us earlier?"

"Guess I forgot."

"You forgot?" Brianna repeated.

"Yeah, forgot."

"You forgot?" Tierra re-repeated, staring at me.

"Yes, I forgot." I looked down at my phone and read the response from Pierre.

"Well, I guess I can see how you forgot that you were going on a date with the best player on the entire Detroit Lions team." Tierra raised her hand to the sky. "Yeah, I can see how you can do that."

"Whatever hater." We pulled in front of my apartment building and my heart started beating a little faster from the anticipation of my late night company. As I prepared to exit the car, Brianna prepared to take my place in the front seat.

"So is he still coming?" Brianna asked.

"Yeah, said he just got on the freeway. I'm about to hop in the shower real quick."

"Damn Bri, our girl is about to get some. Can you believe that?" Both of my girls gave each other fives as Brianna sat in the front.

"Shut up Tee, making me seem all desperate."

"Um newsflash, you are!"

"Oh my God!" Brianna screamed looking at her vibrating phone.

"Girl, tone it down before you wake up my neighbors," I whispered waving my hands.

"Guess who this is calling?"

"Who?" Tierra and I asked.

"It's Joe, the sexy ass white boy from the Lions." She started hopping up and down in her seat.

"So, are you gonna answer it?" I had to be nosey before going into my apartment.

"Hello? Heyyyyy, I was just talking about you…what…yes I was." She had a big ass cheese on her face. Don't think she'll be getting off of the phone anytime soon.

"Bye y'all," I whispered.

"Bye baby," Tierra said smiling.

Brianna blew me a kiss as Tierra pulled off.

I stumbled a little walking to my door. Think I'm going to have to cut back a little. One thing drinking is good for though is great sex.

I showered using my mango Bath and Body Works shower gel. Had to make sure I smelled edible. While drying off in front of the mirror I inspected my body from head to toe. "Pretty good," I said to myself as I twisted and turned.

Damn, I was so excited. This was the first time since my ex that a man has come into my place. The only reason that he is getting this privilege is because I know him a little, I'm horny as hell, and because he's fine as fuck. Humph! I guess that's more than one reason.

I slipped on my robe thinking that there was no need for extra clothing. This was an official booty call. There was going to be no watching movies, popping popcorn, or catching up. I'm bringing his ass in my room to take care of business.

I surveyed my room. Candles were lit. Light jazz oozed from the stereo and the Patron still had its grips on me. Seeing the imprints of dicks and grabbing crotches earlier had a sista feeling pretty frisky right about now.

I heard the buzzer from the front door go off and immediately became nervous again. Shit, okay girl breathe, calm down. I'm dedicating this night to you, Darnell. Five feet from the door, I inhaled, exhaled, inhaled...

Knock! Knock! Knock!

I exhaled, then opened the door. "Hey," he said looking just as good fully clothed as he did earlier with shorts and a cut off.

"Hey, yourself," I said welcoming him in.

"Mmmmm, you smell..." he licked his lips, "...edible."

My pussy fluttered with excitement. "That's because I am," I responded calmly, falling back on the door.

"I'll be the judge of that." His sniffs turned into licks and soft kisses on my neck. My kitty turned into a fountain as I moaned and swooned to the music in my head.

"Mmmm, you weren't lying. You are delectable." He lassoed swirls around my neck and ran his fingers through my hair. Damn, I loved that!

"Kiss me!" I had to speed things up, had to taste him back. Liquor still lingered on his palate. His tongue was so thick and fat that it filled my mouth. If it was any indication of his width, this was going to be a good night.

Our slow kissing turned into an intense tongue lashing. I couldn't wait any longer. It was time to take this into the bedroom.

"Come on baby." I grabbed his hand. "Follow me." I led him into my sanctuary that glowed from the flickering candles. "If I'm not mistaken, you owe me something," I said seductively letting my robe fall to the floor. By the look on his face, he appeared to be very pleased at what stood before him.

Pierre licked his lips and walked closer to me placing his hands on my ass. "You have oil?"

"Of course." I have to admit, I was a little disappointed. I was kind of hoping that he would see me naked and say, "Fuck the massage." Then throw me on the bed and bang me to sleep. However, I did really need a good rub down.

By the time I retrieved the oil out of my top drawer he had already taken off his shirt. I reminded myself not to drool as he started to unzip his pants. This guy's body was amazing, reminded me of Terrell Owens. He had muscles on top of muscles, abs of steel. His pants dropped to the floor exposing his black Calvin Klein boxers. The darkness of the room and the dark color of his underwear did me a disservice. It hid the most important muscle on his body.

We both climbed on the bed and he instructed me to lie back and relax. After about five minutes into the massage, I was glad that he stuck to the plan. I didn't realize how tense I was until he kneaded me with his fingertips.

He now had me on my back, one leg flat on the bed, one leg on his shoulder. He massaged my foot, my calves, my hips, and my thighs. "Damn she's pretty," he said. I slightly lifted my head and saw that he was staring at my parted pussy lips.

"Is she?" I snickered. "You know she loves to be kissed."

"Mmm, French kissed I hope."

"Is there any other way?" He gently grabbed my leg and slid his tongue down until it rested in the crease that connected the inside of my leg to the outside of my kitty. His tongue was so warm. He teased me for a few more seconds before diving in.

"Mmm, baby, that's it. Suck this pussy." I tried to hold still but couldn't. I was squirming all over the bed. He darted his thick tongue in and out making me cream even more.

"Ooouuu yeah, that's it right there, just like that." Yeah he was good. Pierre found my spot with his tongue and tried to make it his permanent residence. "Oh, my God!" I would have to pray for forgiveness later for using God's name in vain.

He rose up for a gasp of air. "You like that baby?"

"Mmm yes, I love it."

"Tell me." he said, while flicking again. "Tell me that you love it."

"Ooouuu shit yes…I do, I do. Damn baby, I'm about to cum, yes…yes!" My orgasm was so strong that I couldn't even get the scream out. I just stopped breathing. I thought I was going to faint.

"Baby," I managed to get out in between gasps of air.

"What's up?"

"Ba…by." I had managed to start back breathing.

"Yes," he answered again.

I inhaled and then exhaled. "Fuck me! Fuck me right now!" Pierre started rubbing my clit, throwing kerosene on my already blazing fire. I was ready, ready for anything that he wanted to do. "Condom?" I asked in between pants.

"Yep." He reached over the side of the bed into his pants pocket. I laid my head back on my down pillow enjoying the one finger that he now had inside of me. "Mmmmm, your pussy is so hot." His voice was low and deep. "Can't wait to be inside of you."

"Please…don't…don't wait. Take me now." I was drunk and horny. Don't know exactly what I was saying, but I know if I was sober hearing it I probably would've cracked up. It made me wish that I had a tape recorder so that I could get a good laugh later.

I heard the condom wrapper rip and a couple of seconds later I felt Pierre kneel over me. With my eyes closed, I anticipated his dick. I let out a long sigh, finally real dick. Not rubber, not plastic, but a real dick. He continued to finger fuck me, faster, harder. Instead of his middle finger, which he was using before, now it felt like he switched to his pinky.

"Come on baby, fuck me! Fuck me!" My pussy was longing to be filled but he continued ramming me with his finger. At this point, I'm thinking maybe he's doing this because he couldn't get hard. If that was the case, don't go down on your digits to the pinky, shit, go up! Use your thumb or add more fingers if you have too, but the pinky? My walls needed stretching.

"Baby! Come on, fuck me."

"What?" Pierre sounded a little confused.

I was a little drunk so maybe I was slurring my words or something where he couldn't understand me. "Stop teasing me and put it in." I put more effort into my word pronunciation this time. I made sure that I spoke more clearly. I felt his pinky inside of me moving slower and I decided enough talk, time for some assistance. "You know what, let me help you out," I said, sitting up a little. I thought that if I jacked him off for a little while that he could get hard and break me off.

I reached down for his dick and thought, maybe I grabbed to hard because I pulled the condom right off. I felt my face tense up as I reached back between his legs and felt what had to be his navel.

"What the…" I sat all the way up and looked at what had to be a joke. I saw what had to be the smallest, skinniest dick on planet Earth. "You…you, you were actually fucking me?" I don't think that the situation had really registered in my brain yet.

He looked as if he had an attitude as he made his way off the bed. "What are you trying to say?" His voice wasn't low and sultry any more. It was high and squeaky.

"I mean..." I pointed at the small package between his legs. "What is...oh, my God!" I started chuckling. "You got to be fucking kidding me. God, you are obviously punishing me for something," I said looking toward the heavens. I hurried up and put on my robe.

He put on his boxers and fumbled with his pants. "You know, you fucking black women kill me!"

No he didn't. "Excuse me?" I asked putting both hands on my hips. I didn't see that coming at all.

"You heard me. Acting like every man has to have an 11 or a 12 inch dick."

I cut him off. "First of all I never said that I want an 11 or 12 inch dick, but damn, can you at least give me a four or five? I'm the first one to say that size doesn't really matter but when you are two inches...and it's skinny, what the fuck am I supposed to do with that?" I shook my head and laughed at the mental picture that was in my head of his tiny dick,

He fastened his pants and buttoned up his shirt. "That's why all y'all are lonely to this day. White women never complain."

"That's because they are used to small ass dicks."

He looked stunned. Like this was the first time he realized he had such a small penis. "A few minutes ago I had you catching the Holy Ghost, calling on Jesus, now you are up here tripping."

"I'm saying, that's true, but I'm not a woman who can be ate out all night baby. I like dick, inside of me, deep inside of me." I placed my finger on my temples and tried to prevent what felt to be the beginning of a stress headache. "Your tongue is longer than your dick for heaven's sake. And I really thought that you were fingering me," I said lowering my voice.

Pierre rushed out of my bedroom. I followed behind him. "If your pussy was a little tighter then…"

Oh, don't even go there. Don't you dare try to put you having a tiny dick on me. I haven't had sex in over five months. My kitty is tight." His eyes widened at the shock of my confession. Actually, hearing the months that I've went without dick shocked me a little as well. "The blown out coochie excuse ain't even going to work."

He rolled his eyes as he reached for the doorknob and opened it. "Fuck you!" I guess he ran out of excuses.

"That's what I wanted you to do daddy, but you're obviously," I held up my index and thumb approximately two inches apart, "not a big enough man to get the job done." He walked away and slammed the door.

Walking back to my bedroom, I yelled out loud, "Shit, shit, shiiiiiiiit!" What the fuck a bitch gotta do to get some good quality dick? I dived in the bed and stared at the ceiling trying to think of what to do next. I have to let my girls know about this one.

I reached over for the phone and noticed that being horny and disappointed could not mask the fact that I was indeed drunk. After a few grabs I managed to finally retrieve my phone from the nightstand. I was too frustrated to even spend the time looking through the phone log for Brianna's name and decided to enter the numbers from memory. Instead of calling, I decided to text a message just in case she was occupied with something or someone.

I texted, **Girrrlll you aint gonna believe this one…I think I'm done with men…can't even get a decent fuck nowadayz. I think muscle man had surgery to remove most of his dick…had 2 inches…no fucking lie, lol.** Then I pressed send.

After about a minute with no response I looked at the time and figured that she was probably sleep. I stood up from the bed, blew out the candles, and turned my stereo down. As soon as my head reconnected with the pillow, my phone alerted me to a new text message.

You can't find a good fuck because you are not looking in the right place!!!

Wow, that's weird. I was looking in the same places that she was. I texted back, **And where do you suggest I look… smart ass…lol.**

My phone chimed again and I read the response. **Well Gabrielle, I suggest that you look in my direction.**

Okay, now I was really confused. I sat up in the bed looking at my phone. Wonder why she's calling me by my user name? Even though Bri was the one who gave me the name Gabrielle, making a play off the angel Gabriel from the Bible, she has never called me by it and I only use it when I'm texting

I don't think I'm shocked that she would hit on me especially after the night that we had, but it just didn't sound like something that she would say. Maybe someone has her phone, I said to myself as I texted back. **Who is this…better not have my friend's phone.** Then I pressed send and waited.

Hold on baby girl, you texted me…check the number that you sent your message too.

I did just that and on further inspection noticed that for the last number instead of pressing eight I pressed seven. I had sent my message to the wrong person. I felt a wave of embarrassment engulf me. Shit! And I sent it to a guy. Shit, shit! How stupid do I look right now airing out all of my business? Maybe he will just forget the entire thing.

My phone vibrated in my hand. **Gabrielle, I was serious about helping you out with your LITTLE problem…lol.**

I laughed at the caps. I text back, **Ha haha, very funny.**

So…do u want help or not? Mystery man texted back.

Couldn't believe he was still texting, oh well, can't go to sleep anyways and I have nothing else to do, I began pecking on my phones keyboard. **And how do you plan on helping me out, wait, let me guess, you can fuck good and you have a big dick?** I pressed send.

New message! **Damn, you must know me huh?**

I laughed and texted back. **If I had a dollar for every guy who thinks what you think.**

No thinking baby, I know.

His cockiness was beginning to pique my interest. Time to make him choke. A sly smile crept across my face as I texted him back. **Okay Dirk Diggler, if you're all that…prove it!** That ought to slow him down. I immediately thought differently after reading his response.

Sure what do you have in mind?

Actually, I didn't have anything in mind because I didn't think he would even respond, well at least not that quick. Couldn't let him back me down though. I had an idea. **Show me.**

What? You want me to come over?

Come over? You're not worthy of that yet baby. Prove what you said is true. You have a camera phone right?

I'm following you now!

Put up or shut up, Big Boy!!! I pressed send. "Your move," I said as I stared at the clock. One minute went by then two then three. "Humph," I knew it. Must admit though I was actually a little disappointed, I was just starting to have fun.

My phone sounded and vibrated in my hand. I saw that I had picture mail and my heart rate sped up. I had three pictures sent to me. "Okay, let's see what you are working with," I said as I opened the first picture. "Whoa!" I slowly maneuvered my phone as I stared at a fat juicy dick and an even juicer head. I hurriedly opened the other two pictures and saw that this gorgeous ass dick from two more angles. It didn't look enormous, it just looked, well, perfect.

So...what do you think, do I qualify?

I texted back, **Mmmmmm definitely, if this is really you.**

Lol, wow! Guess I'm over here taking pictures of another guy's dick huh?

You never know these days.

Well before you even ask, no! I'm not gay or bi. I'm straight like Indian hair. So what do you want me to do to prove it's all me?

I thought for a second before texting him back. **You have shaving cream?**

Yep!

I want you to write a "G" for my name in shaving cream, right on that juicy dick and send me a pic of it. About four minutes later my request was fulfilled.

Anything else my queen? He texted back.

Hold up! I'm still admiring your dick.

Lol...well I'm glad you approve. I apologize for the night you had. If I was your man, I'm sure you would get mad at

me for some things, sometime or other, but I promise you it would never be for not satisfying you sexually.

Mmmmm. More wetness. I contracted Kitty as I continued to look at his pictures. After a couple of minutes of me not responding, he texted me again. **What's the matter…done playing?**

Naw I'm here, still playing…so what do we do now? I typed curious and eager for what was next.

Now it's your turn!!!

My eye's became wide and felt like they were going to pop out of my head. I texted back pretending that I didn't know what he had in mind. **What do you mean, my turn?**

Come on now, I know you're a smart woman…I showed you mine now show me yours.

That wasn't in the plan!

It's in the new and revised one lol.

I thought long and hard, and the more I thought about it the wetter I became. He didn't know me. Didn't know who I was or my real name. It's not like we were sending face pics. Oh what the hell. I said tonight that I was going to be more carefree and as far as I'm concerned, the night was not over yet. I slowly spread my legs.

My phone vibrated as I prepared to take a picture and startled me. I read the text. **I'm waiting…**

I texted him back. **Okay, okay give me a minute.**

I zoomed in and took the picture. I knew that I was still drunk because I was now getting wet looking at my own kitty. I decided to take another picture, this time I used my fingers to spread my lips and took the money shot. I grouped the pics and sent them together. I immediately became nervous. I liked the way Kitty looked but would he? What am I doing?

He texted back. **Oh my god!!!!!**

Oh my God? Why would he text that? Shit, he doesn't like them. I knew it. **What's wrong?**

No...what's right? Are you really that wet or did you pour something on you?

Whewwww. I exhaled deeply and responded to his message. **No additives...that's all me 100%.**

Baby, I would suck on you all fuckin night...you have a beautiful pussy!

Beautiful and pussy in the same sentence, that's a first. I laughed as I pressed send. **You're funny, I like that.**

The dick looks delicious, hopefully you know how to use it...but are you good at oral? I pressed send.

A couple seconds later, he responded. **That's my specialty.**

Lol, so what aren't you good at? I texted and waited for him to answer.

Commitment! His answer threw me off for a minute. I definitely wasn't expecting that. My phone vibrated again. **Haven't found anyone who makes me even want to give it a try.**

Wow! And you're honest.

That's the only way to be.

I had fun with you tonight...thanks for making me feel better.

You're leaving me???

I thought about my date tomorrow and even though I didn't want to go, I had to end the fun. As I texted him back I began to yawn. **Yep! Have to get some sleep.**

Do you have to get it right now?

I laughed at his obvious objection to me leaving him. Guess I'll leave him with something good, I thought to myself as I texted him back. **Actually I'm about to masturbate to your pic...then I'm going to sleep.** Send.

Are you ever going to text me again?

Do you think you deserve that? I texted back while smiling.

Definitely!!!!

Cocky huh?

Confident.

I like confident.

Then you'll like me.

Well I'll see how hard you make me cum...that'll decide if you deserve me texting you again lol.

I'll take it.

Lol okay, bye.

BYE!

I'D never sexted before. It was somewhat different but fun nonetheless. I think it was the anticipation of what the next text was going to be. Whatever it was, I liked it a lot. Kitty definitely did too. I slid my middle finger through my warm folds. Mmmm, Kitty definitely did!

Even though I was turned on my mood was quickly soured by other thoughts that were going through my head. I mean don't get me wrong, I was absolutely happy to finally be done with my ex, and I thought I was ready for the single life but thinking about my recent encounters had me thinking that maybe I should be a nun. It's really starting to feel like I'm being Punk'd. I can't even get fucked! The best things that I have going for me right now are a multi-millionaire that I'm not so sure I'm into, a mystery guy that I haven't said one word to, but constantly captures and completely takes over my thoughts; and a wrong-number-texter that's giving me more pleasure than my last two sex attempts, big dick that came too fast and a baby dick that I confused with a finger. God, if you want me to stay single just say so, but, if my one is out there, please let him be known!

Made in the USA
Charleston, SC
02 January 2014